AN UNFORESEEN MOMENT

Rory did not answer her in words. Instead he cupped a palm beneath her chin and lowered his head.

For one moment, Chloe stared in confusion and then incredulity, but the moment his lips brushed over hers she relaxed and allowed the unexpected to happen. With a soft sigh, she closed her eyes and permitted her lips to experience the moment. Around her, the lilacs applauded softly as though pleased with her decision.

Rory didn't invade her mouth, not even after she parted her lips. The kiss remained almost chaste. But for all its lightness and brevity, Chloe felt a strong magic all the way to her curling toes, and it was a moment after the kiss ended before she was able to refocus on the twilit garden.

"You Patrick men are dangerous," she said softly, shaking her head.

Rory's white teeth gleamed briefly.

"Not me, sugar, I'm absolutely harmless."

Harmless? How he lied!

Melanie Jackson

WRIT ON WATER

LOVE SPELL NEW YORK CITY

LOVE SPELL®

March 2007

Published by

Dorchester Publishing Co., Inc.
200 Madison Avenue
New York, NY 10016

ISBN 0-505-52704-9

Printed in the United States of America.

Visit us on the web at www.dorchesterpub.com.

WRIT ON WATER

THIS GRAVE CONTAINS
ALL THAT WAS MORTAL OF
A YOUNG ENGLISH POET WHO
ON HIS DEATH-BED
IN THE BITTERNESS OF HIS HEART
at the malicious power of his enemies
desired these words to be engraved
on his tombstone
"HERE LIES ONE WHOSE NAME
WAS WRIT IN WATER"
FEB 24, 1821

—A self-composed epitaph from the
tombstone of the poet John Keats, commissioned
by his friend Joseph Severn after his death

This book is for all of us who know
that our names are writ on water.

Dad,

Try this quiz. I scored 5—no, I won't tell you how I got 5 points!—but think I should get extra credit for being named Chloe and spending the summer working in Virginia. Also, I almost got arrested at a protest march in college and I have lots and lots of parking tickets. Doesn't that count?

I'll write as soon as I arrive at Riverview. Don't worry. I don't plan on seeing Gran.

Love, Chloe

Who Should Sing The Blues?

Part 1

For every "no" in this section, give yourself 1 point.
For every "yes," subtract 1 point.

Do you know how many pairs of shoes you own?
☐ Yes
☐ No
☐ Yes, but I had to think about it

Do you have a subscription to *Town & Country*, a credit card, or an Audubon Field Guide?
☐ Yes
☐ No

Do you own golf clubs, Thomas Kincaid prints, or The Bee Gees' Greatest Hits?
☐ Yes
☐ No

Does your state of residence have the death penalty?
☐ Yes
☐ No

Do you live in Salt Lake City, Bangor, Duluth, or anywhere in California or Hawaii?
☐ Yes
☐ No

Are you a member of PETA, a country club, or the Republican Party?
☐ Yes
☐ No

Part 2

For every "yes" in this section, give yourself 1 point. For every "no," subtract 1 point.

Do you play a musical instrument?
☐ Yes
☐ No
(If you play harpsichord, bagpipes, zither, cello, castanets or the glockenspiel, subtract 5 points)

Do you own a suit?
☐ Yes
☐ No
(You may give yourself 5 points if the suit is from two or more decades ago and stolen from the man you killed in Memphis. If it's Armani, you must subtract 5 points)

Do you have any physical infirmities that would lend themselves to a stage name (i.e. Two-Fingers or One-Eye)?
☐ Yes
☐ No
(A list of acceptable infirmity names would not include hypoglycemia, dyslexia, impacted bowels, rosacea or tennis elbow. If you thought any of these were appropriate, subtract 1 point)

Have you ever been in jail?
☐ Yes
☐ No
(If it was for embezzlement, breach of fiduciary duty, or income tax evasion you get 0 points. If it involved murder, robbery, adultery, or auto theft give yourself an extra 2 points for each one. If you had sexual relations while in jail, add 3 points. If they were involuntary, add 5 points)

Do you drink alcoholic beverages every day?

☐ Yes

☐ No

(If you prefer single-malt whiskies, brand-name bourbons, Napoleon brandy, Calvados, Drambuie, Amaretto or any liqueurs add 0 points. If you make your own in the backyard add 2 points)

Have you ever consumed squeeze?

☐ Yes

☐ No

(Give yourself an extra 5 points if you make your own)

Are you named after a president?

☐ Yes

☐ No

(If it's Bush or Reagan, add no points. If it's Zachary (Taylor), Rutherford (Hayes), Chester (Arthur), Grover (Cleveland), or Calvin (Coolidge), add 2 points. If you are female, add 5 points)

If your total points are:

  20 to 36 you should sing the blues

  11 to 19 you could sing the blues above the Mason-Dixon Line

  0 to 10 you shouldn't sing the blues anywhere except your shower

-17 to 0 singing the blues would be blasphemy

Note: If you were able to accurately tally your score on this test then you need to subtract another 2 points from your total.

Whatsoever thy hand findest to do, do it with thy might; for there is no work, no device, no knowledge, no wisdom in the grave whither thou goest.
—*Ecclesiastes*

Prologue

Summer, 1998

Gran was a real witch. She was also a bitch much of the time and liked to play with her granddaughter's head. That was why Chloe wasn't real sure about how to interpret her current dream.

This one was bad, though. Interpret it any way she could, it kept coming out nasty. Walking in a garden was usually relaxing, but not in this shadowy place where her mind had taken to wandering. Beds of bloodred Adonis flowers had become feral. The blooms lost all sense of their formerly neat borders until they overgrew most of the stony path that led to the rusted iron gates; their falling petals were like clots of gore coagulating on the stony ground—evil's secret garden.

Beyond the metal portal where Chloe stood,

there were more overgrown gravel walks that zig-zagged across the cemetery in random fashion, resembling nothing so much as a crazy floral quilt that had its various beds stitched to each other with thorny cane stocks and creeping vines. This was not so unusual in her line of work, but here was not some delightful, secret plot where children played. The odor wasn't verdant, not what one would expect of a flower patch; it was rank and musty, tinged with a nastier smell than mere rotting vegetation.

Her goal, the Patrick family monument—what people in her trade would call a real resurrection-defier, made of darkest, hardest granite—brooded at the heart of the boscage. It seemed very far away from the gate where she stood, but that was what she had come to photograph, so she would have to find a way past the carnivorous foliage.

She looked up once to see if there were some marker that might tell her that she was in the wrong place, that she needn't go on, but the old iron rose arrow-straight to its arched sign: PATRICK. Mental sirens went off, but only in the distance, and their tone was stale, muted. It wasn't that she thought her senses were crying wolf, but she had been living in a state of almost perpetual worry since accepting this assignment and her nerves were dull.

Unhappily, she put a hand on one of the gates. They were cold to the touch, frozen even, but unlike something made of ice, they opened easily.

Chloe looked for a moment at her chilled fingers. They were striped with rusty red and dusted over with gray lichen.

The oak and the ash and the bonnie ivy tree, a voice whispered. But that was wrong! This wasn't a pretty, romantic place. She had grown used to working in necropoles, but this cemetery was ... different. Primeval almost. Forgotten except for the ghost.

She wiped her hands on her dress, leaving streaks behind.

Cold blows the wind to my true love, said the voice in her head, *and gently drops the rain, I never had but one sweetheart, and in greenwood she lies slain ...* Yes, that was closer. This looked like the spot for an unquiet grave.

Chloe turned, raised her camera to photograph the wrought-iron gates that guarded the cemetery, this last resting place of the Patricks. She had a re-flected glimpse in the viewfinder of something white, something drained of life like the fleshless bone left by a sky burial—only not so innocently naked as a skeleton. These denuded sticks had been shrink-wrapped in a gray skin, and they were not part of the stone monument behind her. No, it seemed for an instant that something living was peering at her vulnerable back from behind a crumbling stone tomb. It moved toward her with the dry creak of old twigs stressed to the point of breaking.

Chloe let the camera fall, the sudden weight of

the narrow strap cutting her neck. With muscles so tight they nearly popped off their moorings to her bones, she forced herself to turn and look to the left where she had seen movement. She didn't know what she would do if she actually saw something. She was supposed to photograph the monument—it was very important. She wasn't supposed to run away, and she would be punished if she failed.

But nothing was there, of course. Just some inquisitive daddy longlegs spiders who had crawled out onto the scabrous tombstones to observe her coming. She wasn't afraid of daddy longlegs, though she did wonder why there were so many spiders in this place of the dead. There was no sustenance to be had from the lichen-encrusted tombs. Spiders needed live prey. Yet . . . She looked down. There was a sudden promenade of stinging ants marching from the path down into the maze. They were carrying bits of crumbled white things toward the mausoleum.

So, there was something alive in the cemetery for the large spiders to eat after all. That should reassure her quaking nerves, which were telling her to run away from this assignment before it was too late.

Reluctant, yet having no choice but to go on, she again laid a hand on the heavy gate and pulled it shut behind her. The heavily brambled track was the only way to get to the mausoleum, but if she stayed to the center of it, surely she would be safe from the thorns and spiders. She walked slowly, feeling the path before her with cautious feet. The trail was long and curving, forcing her to review the Patrick dead as she made the hike—or at least their occasional tombstones. There was no wind, but the occasional stray vine reached out onto the walk and tore at her skirt as she forced her way into the maze.

As she drew closer to the mausoleum, she could see that the family building was covered in cobwebs so dense with dust they looked like grimy cheesecloth. A particularly large curtain of filthy silk hung over the open door. It swayed in and out with the earth's respirations coming at intervals from the passage beyond. She knew it for what it was—the stone grave's mouth and esophagus, which took in the bodies that were offered up it. No one had come for a long time, and its belly felt empty with just the naked bones of the long dead rattling around inside.

Her ligaments were tight with tension, ungainly and slow. As though she were a puppet, controlled by some unseen hand, Chloe walked the serpentine way toward the shrouded monument; left foot, right foot, one reluctant jerking step after another, a puppet pulled along by its master. It seemed to her that there was rustling under the ground, as if her clumsy passage stirred up things that were unhappy with their homes in the earth, things that wanted to rise up and follow her back out to the world where they had once lived. She didn't want to wake the Patrick dead, but her feet were awkward and heavy as she staggered deeper and deeper into the maze, and she knew that her footsteps called the ghosts like a knock upon the mausoleum door.

Suddenly she could hear the choking gurgle of water. Little liquid tendrils began creeping over the earth, weaving their way toward her. They were an ugly rusty red, like the ground was bleeding; the low ground near this rising river would soon grow too soggy to walk upon. Chloe looked about quickly, dreading the water's approach. Conveniently, a mat of cypress roots and carnivorous green creepers grew along the surface of the soil, stopping right at her feet. She stepped up onto the thorny mat. If she stayed on top of the vines, stepping from hummock to hummock so that she didn't touch the naked, sucking ground with her feet or tattered skirt, she would be fine. She could go on.

Reluctantly, Chloe resumed her walk. Soon she arrived at the dead heart of the cemetery——the mausoleum—and she circled the monument slowly, ready to take the much-needed pictures with her new digital camera. This house of the elite dead was withdrawn from its stone neighbors, facing away from them either in shame or disdain. The way was open, and she was able to wander to the back where she was supposed to see *the statue*, the funerary monument she had been sent to photograph.

The thing hiding under the cobwebs was huge—more than life-sized. It had the mass of a nightmare monster. Still reluctant to get too close, Chloe forced herself to look up at the beast squatting on the corbelled roof whose peak was just above her head. Through the grimy curtain she could see that it had wings on its back, but with its filthy veil of floral detritus it seemed closer kin to a gargoyle than a guardian angel. Surely no thief would ever want such a nightmarish creature. Yet this was her job, her quest. She had to complete her work.

It was dismaying, but she would have to clear the dirty webs if she were to take a clear photograph. She looked about, but there was nothing she could use as a broom or dust rag. She would have to get closer . . . would have to touch the sticky silk with her bare hands.

Shuddering, she stepped forward onto the iron fence, careful of the sharp spikes. She swept the cobwebs away, wiping her clammy fingers on the long white dress she had been given to wear on this special trip to the Patrick boneyard. The beast was at last revealed. It had a lion's mane—though thick and ropey like a nest of snakes—and a baboon's face filled with vicious viper's fangs. Its paws were a grotesque evolution of articulate human fingers and raptor claws. Its unnaturally long tail curved around the jagged eaves of the roof like a striking serpent, and reminded Chloe of a bloody Mayan god. Hurriedly she stepped back, tearing her dress on the fence's iron spikes.

Chloe looked down and saw that she had brought her old thirty-five millimeter camera. That was wrong, but she couldn't go back now. She raised the device with trembling hands and tried to focus. Through the lens, she could see the yellow lichen that had grown over the beast's eyes in a thick cataract. Her fingers depressed the shutter, but as the aperture snapped open, the petrified eyes seemed to contract and then twitch under their parasitic bandage.

No! She rejected that notion firmly. It was just the shadows moving around her, old tree leaves passing between the statue and the summer sun; that was what had caused the beast to go from light to dark and back again. It was not blinking. Its waxy skin did not move. It did not breathe. It was *not* animate.

Yet, as she watched, the stone talons seemed to flex themselves and the broad chest stirred.

She dropped her camera from nerveless fingers and stared with dilating pupils. The beast's eyes blinked again, shearing the lichen from their stony surface. The lips curled back from the horrible teeth and a narrow, whip-like tongue slithered from its mouth to reach for her. It flicked over her face, stinging like a cold lash everywhere it touched.

Chloe tried to run, but she had stepped off her hummock and the wet ground had sucked up her feet; the subterranean cypress roots had knotted at her ankles, holding her in place. The cold, tentacle noose of the beast's tongue curved around her neck. She began to scream, but it was too late. The monster choked off her breath as it drew her into its stony maw and down to its empty belly. . . .

"Geez!" Chloe wheezed in the darkness. It was a dream! Just a dream from the stress, she reminded her scrambling heart, panicking at her efforts to recall what she'd seen. She had been having a lot of dreams lately. This one was bad—the worst yet—but she was awake now and it would stop scaring her. Because it wasn't real.

"I've gotta quit watching those old DVDs—I don't care how sexy vampires are," she said. But that was just rationalization. Her nightmares weren't from the movies. They were most likely from her grandmother. And her great-grandmother. And all the other great-greats back to the seventh generation. The sins of the mothers were being visited upon the children, except that Chloe's mother hadn't lived long enough to say if she had also had "the Sight."

After a moment, Chloe snapped on her bedside lamp and reached for a book with a hand that still trembled. She hesitated a moment and then skipped over the murder mystery, reaching instead for a romance.

Reading at one A.M. was not the wisest choice of activities when she wanted to get an early start in the morning, but she needed to relax for a bit and she found solace in the written word. Chloe promised herself that she would stop reading after the first love scene, but that was a lie. Once she started a book, she would read straight through to the end. Especially if the alternative was facing another of the nightmares that lurked in her subconscious.

Maybe, she thought, it would have been wiser to have taken the job in Florida, alligators, heat, leeches and all. The assignment to photograph large reptiles couldn't have upset her any more than this trip to Virginia—to Gran's infernal territory.

For the sword outwears its sheath,
and the soul outwears the breast.
—Lord Byron

Chapter One

Jarvis Perth was in his accustomed place on Old Mill Road, which was to say that he was dead center of both lanes and trundling along at a solid seven miles per hour—the greatest speed his aging tractor could manage on the slightly uphill stretch of pavement. Or on a downhill stretch, unless it was tumbling end over end, which from the collection of branches and mud in the roll cage above the driver's seat, it would seem to have done quite recently.

Chloe knew that it was Jarvis Perth who was slowing the parade of muddy pickups through town because a woman dressed in a loudly patterned housecoat and filthy pink mules had bellowed out a greeting to him in a voice shrill enough to frighten off every crow in the southern states. The lady was the only one who was hollering though, so Chloe assumed that Jarvis was a beloved local character whose foibles were tolerated because of his immense charm and goodness. Anyway, the folks in Riverview, Virginia, didn't seem to be real rigid about things like traffic lanes and speed limits. Since she had entered the county, no one in the snail parade seemed to take the 55 MPH signs posted along the tree-lined roadway as anything other than roadside decorations. Perhaps it was because they all seemed very busy eating pork rinds and rearranging their gun racks as they drove.

Chloe mentally smacked herself for that last thought. Just because her granny was a backwoods horror show, that didn't mean everyone around here was backwards.

Normally, the tortoise-like pace along a smelly tar road being slowly torn up by tractor treads that punched deep grooves in the melting macadam and left the surface with an unattractive rash would cause frustration sweats and hyperventilation, but since she was in no particular hurry to arrive at the Riverview Plantation, and had missed her morning infusion of double-strength caffeine, Chloe was able to meander along with her humor unimpaired, occasionally waving and smiling at total strangers who cheerfully smiled and waved back. The superficial contact helped her resist the heat-induced somnambulism that had been threatening to overpower her for the last hour and more.

" 'Woke up this morning,' " she began to croon, doing her best Stevie Ray Vaughan voice. Except, she hadn't woken up this morning. She'd never actually gone back to sleep after that damned dream. And she probably shouldn't be singing the blues about this. That quiz had said that sleep deprivation in middle-class white females didn't count unless it was on account of being in jail, or being stabbed in a back alley by a woman whose man you had stolen. The blues weren't about psychic grandmothers, job stress and not having air conditioning.

Also, she wasn't sure people from downtown Atlanta could have the blues. True, it was a city in the South, but it was also fairly high-tech. The blues didn't go well with ultra-modern lighting and computers. You could get the blues in some parts of Texas, anywhere in Alabama or Mississippi, and of course in the older sections of Chicago or Detroit—and certainly anywhere in New Orleans—but not in California or Hawaii. It might be some rule about proximity to beaches, or perhaps the need to live in a flood plain or where they had deep snow in winters that lasted for six months. That wouldn't rule out Duluth or Aspen, though, and you never heard of great blues classics coming from there. . . .

Chloe shook her head. Maybe that quiz had been right about her after all.

Geography aside, the blues could be about running away. And that was sort of what she was doing, though not chased by an angry lover with a shotgun or a switchblade, or the law.

" 'O, I ran away this morning—but my troubles are chasin' me. Yeah, I ran away this mornin'—' " Running away sounded childish, though, when your life wasn't in danger. And it might not help her escape her personal baggage, which had been piling up of late. Especially given the direction she was running, because the travel-trunk of emotional baggage lived in Virginia. But she wouldn't know until she gave running a try. And surely anything was better than huddling in her bed, doing her best to avoid both the phone and sleep in the long hours that belonged to the street sweeper, and the stray cats who prowled the Dumpsters in the parking lot.

Forget the blues. She needed a paradigm shift. She wasn't running away. Instead, independent Chloe Smith was headed for a new—and possibly diplomatically challenging—job at Riverview Plantation. Which was why she wasn't in any hurry to arrive. There was no need to rush at her fate now that the meeting was scheduled. Didn't everyone keep saying that life was a journey and not a destination?

Of course, most people—as her father would say—were so full of it their eyes were brown. And that went double for the advice they gave.

Chloe consulted her map again, though there was no need. The road was straight and had no forks.

Her new client was a good buddy of her boss and mentor, Roland Lachaise. She had been thoroughly briefed—and reassured—about the delicate but benign nature of her assignment, but she was still feeling bemused and uneasy. And having super-sized anxiety dreams at night.

Her granny, a fey old witch who'd loved terrorizing her grandchild with tales of the weird anytime Chloe's parents were absent, had assured Chloe of the child's inheritance of the matrilineal curse of second Sight. Up until the week just past, Chloe had never believed it. Her traditional Methodist father had always called his mother-in-law's vision rituals "bullshit necrophilia" and would have nothing to do with Gran after his wife died. The taxidermy and dining on roadkill thing hadn't helped. Dad was a complete urbanite, and his world was not accommodating to certain rural ideas.

Gran wasn't a necrophiliac—not in the strictest technical sense of the word. Was there such a thing as a necrophile? That sounded closer, but Chloe had always thought the old woman was morbid and probably delusional. However, now she was beginning to wonder if Granny Claire had been right in her malicious prognostication. Could Chloe be seeing visions, perhaps—please, God, only metaphorical ones warning of future danger?

"No way," Chloe muttered. "That is all just *bull*. All you need is about fifty years of psychotherapy to sort out your family problems."

These words failed to convince her, though finding a therapist was probably a good idea. Chloe was haunted by her past life, whose ghosts refused to fade away. She had few clear memories of her mother and grandmother together, but those that stayed with her were not pleasant and overshadowed a lot of her life. It was amazing how little time it took to damage a child. The first and maybe worst of their encounters had happened around her fourth birthday. Her mother had taken Chloe to visit her grandmother for the first time then; and it had caused the first and only fight her mother and father had ever had in her presence.

No one had promised Chloe a cake and presents, but a part of her had half expected that there would be one or the other waiting for her at her mysterious granny's house. After all, she watched TV and had friends with grandmas: It was obligatory, that's what grannies did.

The ride into the backwoods had been a long one, and no cake or gifts were in evidence when they arrived, not even a pink envelope that might hold a card. But Chloe hadn't fussed. In fact, Chloe had enjoyed herself, in spite of her initial disappointment about not having a second birthday party. Granny Claire lived in an old cabin with a sod roof where birds foraged for lunch and a dirt floor which would have been great for making mud pies—something she never got to do indoors at home. Of course, one didn't just blurt out such a request, and Chloe thought that if she was good all the way until lunchtime, perhaps she could bring the idea up then especially since her grandmother had forgotten her birthday and would probably be feeling bad when this was pointed out.

However, it didn't take long for Chloe to sense that all was not well between her mother and Granny Claire, and that the chance of mud pies in the kitchen was becoming rapidly more distant. There hadn't even been time for the tea kettle to boil on the fire's grate before her mother was beside her, leaning down and asking her if she was ready to go.

"Is Mommy's angel ready for another ride?"

Chloe wasn't ready, but she knew how to answer.

"Angel?" Granny Claire had loomed over both of them, not bothering to bend down to Chloe's eye level. "I have never seen a child so lacking in curiosity. I left all these things out for her but all she's done is stare at the floor. She must be feeble-minded."

"She's four, not feeble-minded."

Chloe wasn't sure what feeble-minded was, but it couldn't be a good thing, because it made her mother's mouth get tight. It had been an unfair accusation as well, she'd realized later when she asked her father about it. Chloe had noticed the many weird things her grandmother had left strewn on the room's one round table, but her mother had warned her not to touch anything of her grandmother's and so she had been *a good girl.*

And anyway, Gran's collection of the arcane had been pretty gross—bones and a crow's wing and some scary tarot cards laid out in the pattern of a cross. Mud pies and the big spider cleaning up its web in the corner were way more interesting.

"And I see that you left that stuff out—in spite of my asking you to put it away. You know how Aaron feels about this! And Chloe didn't touch any of it because I told her not to. And now we're leaving," Chloe's mom had said, her voice flat and for once unhappy.

Chloe shot the old lady a so-there look. This would teach her to forget her granddaughter's birthday. But Gran's eyes got narrow and hard.

"Look at her! I think you brought the wrong child home from the hospital. I don't know why you had to have a baby in the city anyway." The words were aimed at her mother, but the old lady's gaze never wavered from Chloe's face.

Chloe dropped her eyes, frightened by this old woman who suddenly looked about twenty feet tall and as unfriendly as any fairy-tale giant. Sensing that her daughter was paralyzed by the criticism she didn't understand, Chloe's mother had taken her daughter's hand and tugged her toward the door.

"Goodbye, Mother. We'll try this again after the millennium." She'd added under her breath, "Don't mind the venomous asp, sweetie. They can't help being the way they are."

"Go, then! I should wash my hands of both of

you!" Gran had shouted before slamming the cabin door behind them.

But of course she hadn't washed her hands of them. Feeble-minded or not, Chloe was her only grandchild, and Chloe's mother hadn't been un-kind enough to order her grandmother away for-ever, not when the old lady had claimed to be ill and contrite. They had tried meeting annually un-til Chloe's mother died, without any real success at forging a loving relationship. After that, the family meetings stopped.

It was too late, though; the venomous asp had injected enough poison to affect Chloe's mind, and her father's distant rationalism hadn't been enough of an antidote. And now it seemed like the old woman was really sick. Her last letter had been written in a hand so shaky that Chloe had barely been able to make it out.

Trying to distract herself from thoughts of her grandmother, Chloe turned on the radio and re-viewed once more what she knew about her client and destination. Reading between the lines, she gathered that Riverview was owned and lorded over by one MacGregor Patrick, an unrepentent sexist who was "maybe one day younger than dirt and just as ugly,"—this according to her boss, who was himself a slightly sexist sexagenarian and homely as a Mississippi mudhen.

Neither her boss's friendship with the man nor the plantation would have been of professional in-terest to Chloe except for the fact that MacGregor

Patrick was also the proud owner of one very strange cemetery, which he wanted inventoried— immediately—and added to the statewide database of funerary monuments that was being compiled by law enforcement in Virginia. The state's cemetery files would eventually be added to the secure databases in other states to make up a nationwide catalog of pre-twentieth-century funerary monuments.

This was the part of the assignment that had Chloe shaking her head. Many genealogists wanted pictures of family headstones and monuments, and she had done several shoots for various genealogical organizations that were putting their information onto Web sites—she had even been sent to Europe for six weeks by a wealthy consortium that marketed photos of the graves of famous musicians and poets. But it wasn't genealogists or taphophiles that were making work for her now and causing headaches for law enforcement; it was interior decorators. The latest fashion trend was for something called "funerary chic," and interior designers were getting thousands of dollars—yen, pounds and deutsch marks too—for bits of American antique wrought-iron fence, statues and urns. Modern copies apparently just wouldn't do. The true trendsetters had to possess the authentic grave goods. They had been in *People* magazine and on CNN.

Naturally, tomb-robbing entrepreneurs were happy to fill this market niche of authentic—and stolen—grave goods. In spite of the five-hundred-dollar punitive fee a and year's jail time that went with a conviction for grave robbing, the thieves had grown so blatant that they were denuding old cemeteries of everything except their shrubberies—and that would doubtless follow as the fashion spread into the world of funerary horticulture, which was growing now that these criminals had moved out of New Orleans's stone cemeteries and into the lush countrysides of states like Virginia.

More distressing than the thefts themselves had been several incidents of contact between thieves and grieving relatives. So far, no one had died or even been too badly hurt, but police figured that it was only a matter of time before there was a confrontation between a greedy tomb-robber and some outraged guard who was intent on defending Granny's headstone at any and all costs.

Savannah and New Orleans had been especially hard hit by these robbers, but there had been problems in Williamsburg and as far north as Boston, and all the way out in California. The cops were doing their best to intercept and retrieve these unusual stolen goods, and were having some success, but they were soon stuck with warehouses full of unidentifiable tombstones and monuments, and left with no way to return the confiscated boodle to the rightful owners.

That was why, in an effort to aid future efforts at property restoration, various cities' famous, historic cemeteries were being photographed and added to a government database. But time and money for the project were both in short supply, so concerned owners of private cemeteries were left to take care of their own graveyards. To do that, they hired firms like Digital Memories, who specialized in such pictorial databases.

At least, Digital Memories had done pictorial monument databases for genealogists and Civil War historians. This living and working for a private person in his own home—and a reputedly eccentric home at that—was new territory. Usually they worked for small companies or nonprofits who could not afford to invest in expensive equipment. But as the plum jobs were already taken by the company's old-timers, and D.M. wasn't presently larded with job opportunities for their newest hire—in fact, it had been this gig in a private cemetery in Virginia for Chloe or a university-funded plant spore study in the pest-infested Everglades—she had bowed before the force of nature that was Roland Lachaise and accepted the job. She figured that old bones and thieves were better than live alligators and malaria, and the weather might be marginally superior at the more northern latitude—something to think seriously about, given that it was near hurricane season.

Besides, the Virginia job had come with access to the latest in the company's digital cameras, with wide-angle lenses and other toys. And she would only be an hour's ride from a metropolis where they would have Slurpees, fast food, and even foreign films, if such an urge for culture should overtake her.

Chloe wiped the sweat from her brow and checked her mirror to be sure that her lipstick wasn't running. She would have to get her air-conditioning fixed before the late summer heat arrived! The high temperatures and humidity were bad for the PC and her darling cameras, and it didn't do much for her complexion either. She grimaced and looked away from her image.

It was heresy to admit it, but most of what she did in her job was not that hard. The equipment was expensive, but anyone with a computer, the ability to learn a few image manipulation programs, and a reasonable ability with a camera could handle the job, if one was only after technical competence, not art. But she had discovered along the way that many people had a dislike of the technology that could help them, and the timid were willing to pay fairly big bucks to stay away from something that frightened them. This left the way clear for her, allowing her the scope to practice her art and still earn a decent wage.

And, she reminded herself, her work was top drawer. She knew her funerary history, and the people she had worked for in the past were beginning to request her for repeat jobs. It was strange, but she was the top dog in the cemetery photography biz. Roland Lachaise had even admitted that she was the biggest fish in this small but growing pond, and had given her a raise! Sure; it was a small one, but it was still a raise, which was something very rare at Digital Memories.

The great stone gates to Riverview Plantation eventually crawled into view. A sleepy Chloe gave her fellow travelers a toot on the horn and a last wave before turning off onto the gravel road.

And, she fell down a rabbit hole into Wonderland. Her first inkling that she had entered a new world was the drawbridge suspended over a sluggish brown moat. In point of fact, it was merely a suspension bridge, but with its rusty chains strung from a buttress that looked a great deal like a giant cargo container of the type used on ocean liners—though, being overrun with honeysuckle vines, it was difficult to tell just what was lurking down below the emerald runners—the resemblance to an abandoned drawbridge was fairly strong. There were even thick wooden planks unevenly laid along the course, and evidence of horses scattered about.

Chloe braked before venturing out onto the swaying structure with her car. The automobile was expendable, but the cameras were not. Like the warriors of old, she knew that she had to return with her shield or on it—either was probably fine with Roland, so long as he got his cameras back unharmed.

Sighing, Chloe hung her head out the window and squinted into the sun-reflecting water. The bridge looked solid enough to her untrained eye, but she had never fancied herself as Alan Quartermain or Evel Knievel. However, it was clearly the only path to the house, and she could see traces of dusty tire tracks on the graying planks, so she knew that other vehicles had traversed the bridge and survived to tell the tale.

Unfortunately, it looked like she could carry on after all.

She proceeded cautiously onto the causeway and was rewarded with a smooth ride and a safe conveyance the other side of the turgid stream, though the feeling that she had left the twentieth century behind on the paved highway remained strong.

The drive to the house after the bridge was an increasingly odd one. The road was long and narrow, and lined with a plethora of plaster, blue-shirted, green-hatted gnomes that were only inches from a hit-and-run accident with the sides of her car. The driveway looked like the entrance to a cut-rate theme park, or one of those roadside attractions like the two-headed mummy or the world's biggest ball of yarn, and she thought at first that it was some sort of a landscaping joke pulled by the local hoodlums. But after passing fifty or so of the squat gnomes, she concluded that this was too expensive to be a prank. Some garden statue aficionado had actually bought out the garden centers for the entire state and used his haul as curbstones for the drive.

Chloe stopped counting gnomes and started

watching her odometer. The colorful plaster chorus line went on uninterrupted for a half mile. Eventually the formal gardens came into view, and she slowed to a halt so that she could take a long look beyond the gnomes at the peculiar mulch that had been laid under the ancient azaleas and hydrangeas. The color was an unattractive liver brown and sported a waffle pattern that was visible even in the crepuscular light that had filtered under the giant shrubs.

Chloe laughed once in disbelief.

"Carpet padding!" Well, it probably made quite an effective weed barrier. Maybe she'd try it at home—buried under some conventional shredded bark, of course.

Chloe put the car back in motion and the identical, pointy-headed gnomes smiled approvingly as she resumed her trip down their seemingly endless ranks. She sincerely hoped that she was on a one-way road, as there wasn't room for two cars to pass without exchanging paint and bodywork and killing a lot of little plaster people.

Around the next bend, the river again hove into view. It was broad and sparkling in the sun like a mile of shattered glass, but pretty as it was, the water wasn't what caught Chloe's attention. Standing on the bank was a young man wielding both a fishing gaff and a net. He was stripped to the waist and tanned to nut brown. Beside him was what appeared to be a mountain of sodden purple, red and yellow bowling shoes. He looked up at her and smiled engagingly. His teeth were crooked and badly gapped, but it was an infectious smile for all that. There was really nothing for it; Chloe had to grin back.

She had read about some of the strange things that washed up on the banks of the river. Shipping crates frequently went overboard during storms. One town had been blessed with some fifty thousand pairs of athletic shoes that had been in good enough condition to wear. Of course, the sizes were all mismatched and had to be sorted out at the town swap meet, but everyone in the environs had ended up with enough new pairs of sneakers to prevent the town's shoe store from ordering any athletic shoes for over a year. Chloe suspected that these shoes were headed for a like fate. It would be a boon—if the town had a bowling alley. She hadn't seen one on the drive in.

She looked over at a smirking gnome and shook her head. On the other hand, given the *joie de vivre* demonstrated by the locals, maybe the bowling alley wasn't necessary. Or maybe the shoes were for these barefoot gnomes—what did she know? Maybe everyone here was slightly mad.

It occurred to her that the pile of sodden footwear supplied a reasonable explanation for the plaster statuary along the drive. She wondered also if this same teen had been the one to fish out the hideous carpet padding which she was fairly certain was more recycled river wrack.

Chloe began to wonder seriously about how eccentric her new client was. Previously, she had only been concerned with running into tomb-robbers and being polite to her boss's chum while he reminisced about women he had known. But perhaps that wasn't the greatest danger facing her.

Roland had suggested that MacGregor Patrick, while a bit of an old-style patriarch and firm about maintaining his privacy, was entirely rational and pleasant—not at all like his father, Callum Patrick, who had been fanatical about keeping his distance from outsiders, even to the point of shooting at them. Chloe had gathered that MacGregor's view of the world was a monochromatic one, but the color was rosy since he saw himself at the top of the hierarchy, God's own top-kick, and she had been given to believe he would welcome Roland's protégé into his domain with open doors, and likely open arms.

Yet, nothing had been said about the garden gnomes and there certainly hadn't been any in the one old photograph of Riverview she'd seen on Roland's wall at the office. Maybe this client had gotten weird since the last time Roland came to visit. Old age took some people that way. Chloe's Granny Claire had certainly crossed the line from being eccentric to downright nuts.

Of course, all this oddity was a far cry from the dark things Chloe subconscious had been planting in her dreams. This was quirky, not dangerous. Quirky she could live with. So it was, all in all, a relief to have finally arrived, and to put an end to her fears of haunted mansions and ghoulish graveyards.

Chloe drove along slowly. She'd have answers to all her questions soon enough. The house couldn't be too far on. The river took another turn less than a mile away; unless there was another bridge, Riverview had to be nearby.

She kept a weathered eye out for more oddities along the trail, and soon spotted a clematis hedge that proved to be growing on a frame made up entirely of deer antlers stitched together with—what else?—Virginia creeper. It was a formidable structure, perhaps not as long as the Great Wall of China, but it would serve to keep out anything larger than a mouse unless it could fly. The gap for the gravel road was the only break Chloe could see.

Roland had mentioned that MacGregor, in addition to liking his privacy, always had an eye out for a bargain. But wasn't this taking thriftiness and privacy to ridiculous lengths? There weren't enough deer in the state to supply the antlers for the hedge—not in one man's lifetime! What had he done; gone scrounging out-of-state for cast-off horns in bankrupt steakhouses and hunters' cabins? Why would anyone want or need such a fortification around one's home anyway?

Feeling both an enlarging curiosity and a return of mild trepidation, Chloe advanced slowly through the narrow, prickly gap and found Riverview itself waiting beyond the hedge.

"Well, damn."

It was a pleasant house, if somewhat over-wrought for modern tastes. Ornate pilasters supported baroque architraves at every door and window, and the porch was overloaded with Doric columns and sculptures. It was also just slightly too tall for its width, even considering the porte cochere that had been added on to the south side of the building sometime in the twenties. The two wings met up awkwardly, reminiscent of the masks of comedy and tragedy. Taken all together, it gave the visual impression of existing on the other side of a giant wide-angle lens.

But Chloe was too pleased with the shady trees and perfumed air to quibble with the architectural oddities. Whatever else might have been done with outer gardens that lined the drive, those closest to the house were immaculate and conventional, and pre–Civil War in their manicured magnificence. She hated to think what Mac-Gregor Patrick paid for their upkeep.

The only anachronism she spotted, after turning off the radio and climbing out of the car, was an abandoned tractor-mower that someone had left sitting in the shade of an ancient pecan tree. It seemed plausible to her that the gardener had been turned into a garden gnome by some southern cousin of the Medusa who attacked all pedestrians and transformed them into plaster garden ornaments, but it was more likely that he was at lunch. Or perhaps taking a siesta while waiting for the heat of the day to pass. Or maybe the mower had been abandoned by the boy at the river while he went fishing for bowling shoes. She wouldn't blame him for choosing the watery shade over the sunny lawn. It would take a truly ambitious person to tackle the remainder of the acre-plus meadow that was still unshorn while the temperatures were in the nineties and the humidity just as high.

Chloe stepped out of the car and enjoyed the old-fashioned sound of oyster shells crunching underfoot as she turned around to get a full view of the premises. She breathed deeply of the warm air that smelled of green things like honeysuckle and mown grass. On cue, the pure notes of birdsong filled the air.

"Ashley Wilkes, I've come home."

"Yeah. It's a regular Twelve Oaks," said a deep voice behind her. "We're short a few slaves though."

Chloe jumped and turned around, confronting a tall, tanned chest of the male variety. It was also a very sweaty chest, and had bits of grass lodged in its red-gold curls. The man—alas—couldn't be MacGregor Patrick. He was at least three decades too young.

The missing gardener, she thought with relief, urging her heart to calm down even as she pulled her eyes up another foot to somewhere near the seventy-two inch mark where it was more polite to stare. It wasn't a complete hardship to give up on the chest, as the face was likewise very attractive, though also sheened with sweat and adorned with grass clippings.

She couldn't guess how he had managed to sneak up on her over the oyster shells.

"I'm Rory," he told her, head tipped to one side as he studied her face. His smile was polite, but not particularly inviting. He didn't offer his hand either, but stayed three feet back while he stared hard into her sunglasses-covered eyes.

Intuition told her that his gaze was more assessing than admiring, and the failure to offer a hand in greeting was from reserve rather than a concern with staining her clothes or offending her nostrils with his body odor. Given the level of friendliness she had encountered in town, this cool first reaction suggested that there wasn't much chance for an immediate friendship with the hired help. It also quite ruined her fantasy about southern gentleman being invariably hospitable to the gentler sex.

Of course, he wasn't a *gentleman;* he was a lower-class working stiff. MacGregor would be different. Her fantasy could remain intact.

Amused with herself and the gardener's almost rude stare, Chloe's lips twitched as she turned her body to face the man dead-on. She took off her sunglasses and returned his cool gaze. Granny Claire had taught her how to use *the eye* to good effect; the man's hazel gaze at once riveted on her own and stayed there unblinking, just as it should.

This man might be staring like a besotted idiot, but that didn't mean anything. He was just doing the same double-take everyone did when they saw her irises in daylight for the first time. She had her Granny Claire's eyes, and she knew how mesmerizing they could be when they focused, unblinking, on their target. If the gardener was normal, the next thing he would do was either make the sign of the cross, or else say was something fatuous about her gaze. It depended on whether he was more horny or superstitious.

And if he was the type who liked *Gone With the Wind*, it was likely to be a lulu of a comment.

Chloe waited a moment in ladylike silence for the gardener to speak, but as he only continued to stare, she decided to take a hand in their conversation.

"Hello. So, what do you think?" She gestured at her face.

Rory blinked. The woman's eyes were the color of blueberries with the bloom still on them. They were deep wells of southern twilight, a dark shade so near purple that he suspected they were the result of colored contacts. He peered intently, but even the bright light of day failed to show a telltale ring around the iris that would reassure him that their color was man-made.

Witch eyes.

The bright light did, however, show a great deal of amusement lurking in her gaze. The dark eyelashes that fringed those amazing irises fluttered down in broad parody of silent movie flirtation, covering her dark eyes and allowing him a momentary reprieve during which he was able to pull his own gaze away.

"Hello. So, what do you think?" she repeated conversationally. "Sparkling sapphires? Or maybe twilight in the arctic, lit by a million gleaming stars?"

"No." He shook his head, feeling both bemused and slightly embarrassed by the accuracy of her question, which suggested that people often uttered silly platitudes when confronted with the unusual color of her eyes. "Blueberries."

She snorted.

"Ripe blueberries," he amplified, knowing he sounded stupid. "Or perhaps Concord grapes."

Her lips, which he finally got around to noticing, twitched once but remained prim in spite of the laughter in her eyes.

"Well, at least that's in keeping with your profession. So, where would I find Mr. Patrick?"

"Senior, junior or collateral?"

"Uh . . . senior."

"And your name is?" he prompted, wanting to be certain that this was the woman his father had been expecting. Nothing MacGregor had said about Roland's protégé had led him to think that she was particularly bright or so spectacularly gorgeous.

But then, his father wouldn't consider her mind to be of primary importance when he was looking for an employee. Loyalty and references—and some degree of charm—were all that mattered to MacGregor. Her appearance would simply be a bonus, eye candy to sweeten his day.

"Chloe Smith," she answered, handing over her keys along with her confirmation of identity. She didn't shake his hand. "Like the perfume. The one in the pretty pink box you see in all the magazines."

"I don't wear cologne too often. Is it a nice perfume?" he asked, accepting the keys with a straight face. He decided not to mention that he wasn't the hired help or that he was familiar with both the perfume and the third century Greek story about the lovers Daphnis and Chloe.

"It's supposed to be very sweetening. You should really try it."

"Peachy?" he asked, clinging to his agricultural theme.

"Just the box."

"Too bad. I really like Georgia peaches," he said, still completely deadpan.

She turned away to fetch two cases from the backseat of the car, but not before he'd seen her smile. It was slow, a tooth by tooth revelation that was halted almost as soon as it had begun.

"Allow me—," he began, in a belated effort to show some manners.

"No, thanks." Her face was once again under control. She wasn't the type to laugh at the locals, at least not to their faces. "But you can get the suitcase in the trunk for me. Just leave it on the porch—no need to track all that grass inside. So, where will I find Mr. Patrick, *senior?*"

"In the library. Straight through the foyer and hang a right," Rory said.

He didn't offer to escort her, since she clearly didn't expect him to step inside the house. Covered in lawn clippings as he was, that wasn't an entirely off-base assumption on her part, he admitted, fighting off a sudden irritation at being summarily dismissed. Women usually had to make a slightly greater effort to walk away from him.

"Thanks." She smiled fleetingly and pressed something into his hand. By the time he looked up from the five-dollar bill in his fist, Chloe Smith's shapely silhouette was disappearing through the back door. It was a nice tip and a very nice smile—and a truly exquisite walk.

Rory Patrick's own smile was lopsided. Miss Smith wasn't at all what he'd expected, and she had knocked his half-made plans off-kilter. He didn't want to encourage his father's paranoia about the cemetery, but the old man could get stubborn when crossed, and out of sheer obstinacy would hold on to a notion until it fossilized into the hardest stone and one needed a jackhammer to chip it away from his brain. So Rory had decided that it wouldn't be wise to show anything other than tepid interest in MacGregor's plans, in case he unwittingly woke further stubbornness in the old man's breast by demonstrating even mild dissension with the preparations to stop the imaginary grave-robbers who were staking out Riverview.

Keeping silent while MacGregor carried on had irked him unbearably in the last few days. MacGregor had always been eccentric—but this was way past his former levels of looniness. It was all such a ridiculous idea. There were no thieves. No one even knew about their cemetery. At least, they shouldn't know.

Rory frowned. Of course, there was that weasel, Claude. His cousin was always short on funds and none too scrupulous about how he made his living. He had seen the graveyard when his mother died and was—against Rory's wishes—interred there. But surely even Claude would draw the line at grave robbing his own ancestors. After all, he'd been raised a Patrick from the time his father abandoned him.

Or perhaps not, a new voice whispered. Little though he cared to admit it, MacGregor was a perspicacious devil. Sometimes his hunches bordered on second Sight. If anyone could predict the approach of trouble it was his sire.

Rory swore tiredly and looked at the half-mowed lawn.

Hiring a photographer to document the collection was a sensible precaution, which he supposed that he couldn't deny his father, even though he wanted to. But MacGregor's other ideas were completely unacceptable. Their privacy had to be maintained until the new security system in the house was installed. Someone at the insurance company had been reviewing their records and the latest evaluation of the art collection in the gallery had the insurance company insisting upon stronger measures of protection—an unwanted expense since most of the family money was tied up in an expansion of Rory's business.

But MacGregor did not understand what the company meant by "sensible precautions." He'd taken that as a green light to do anything short of starting a nuclear war. And what he cared about most was this damned graveyard. He'd been talking about hiring mercenaries to police it. If he'd had had any idea of how to go about it, he might have done it, too, in spite of Rory's arguments.

"Stubborn mule," Rory muttered, feeling hot and put-upon, and questioning the wisdom of coming back home to live.

As a sop to refusing his father armed guards and ferocious attack dogs, Rory had been staying at home a lot more in the week just past. He was even arranging his schedule so that he would be able to be there full-time after this next weekend. He had hoped that it would be enough to stop MacGregor from doing anything goofy—or something really crazy, like going on nightly patrol with a shotgun and shooting some horny kids who were only looking for a little privacy in the woods of Riverview.

Unfortunately, he had been out-maneuvered,

and MacGregor hired this photographer without consulting him.

And now she was here. It was a vast pity that Chloe wasn't rock stupid and hag-ridden; Mac-Gregor might have gotten bored with her then and sent her away. Since the cemetery's best defense was the fact that it was completely unknown—not even marked on county maps or historic registers—all Rory could do was hope that this young woman was as discreet as she was pretty, and completely ignorant about art. Because she was probably going to learn a lot of fascinating things about the family from MacGregor.

Yes, the old man appreciated attractive women. Rory really liked Chloe's intelligent blueberry eyes and the fact that her sense of humor hadn't atrophied in spite of working for Roland, and he and his father were enough alike for him to know that MacGregor would appreciate these things as well, and would want her around him all the time. But unlike Rory, MacGregor would feel no need to keep quiet about his art collection or his certainty that thieves were coming to Riverview. MacGregor equated beauty with innocence, and this woman worked for his old friend. He would never believe Rory's warning that silence on the subject was critical, that talking about possible theft to the outside world was making it a self-fulfilling prophecy. MacGregor would take one look at Chloe Smith and wouldn't be able to resist showing off by bragging about all the great sculptors whose art was in his cemetery. He was apt to insist that she learn the history of every person buried at Riverview, and the value of every marble piece that covered them. And that would lead straight up to the picture gallery where the ancient Patrick rogues were immortalized. Yes, *some* talk about the paintings' value was bound to ensue if Rory left them alone. Which was a lot of temptation to place before a working girl. Who wouldn't want to talk about this strange place and its priceless paintings and sculptures to a few close friends?

Miss Smith's photos were supposed to guard against thieves being able to fence their loot if they came sneaking into Riverview with a flatbed truck and a crane—an event that Rory's father believed was imminent. And if he convinced her of the danger, she would want to tell Roland and maybe the police about it so they could be on guard. That would never do.

"Well, damn it to hell in a little red wagon." It was going to be hard to keep Roland Lachaise's pet photographer in the dark about MacGregor's grandiose paranoia if she stayed very long.

Could she be bribed into silence? Probably not. The young were so often crusaders. His best hope was that she wouldn't be able to take the enforced boredom that went with life on a plantation where the inhabitants didn't bother with luxuries like TVs and telephones in every room. And perhaps if he devoted his spare time to her, escorted her to the graveyard, maybe took her out evenings, he could keep her time with MacGregor to a minimum and interest her in other things. . . .

Of course, demonstrating an interest in Chloe Smith would leave him open to a whole other realm of parental craziness. MacGregor was a veteran matchmaker, and would likely start in again about wanting grandkids if his son showed any predilection for Miss Smith's company.

All things considered, Rory decided, MacGregor's annoying hobby of finding his son a wife was marginally less dangerous than his obsession with a recurring dream of tomb raiders disturbing their ancestors' bones. If all else failed, he would be willing to sacrifice himself on the altar of duty and distract his father with a blatant flirtation. It wasn't like it would be torture sitting somewhere, gazing by candlelight into Chloe Smith's magnificent eyes.

And maybe all MacGregor's blatant hints about marriage and grandchildren would scare her away.

Chloe walked through the foyer, past a refectory table of splendid proportions, and waded through a deep pile Bokhara rug thick enough for ground squirrels to burrow in. She couldn't help being impressed. The other plantations she had visited had their treasures roped off from the general public. Here she could actually touch the priceless antiques.

"Ostentatious," she murmured, "but I could call it home."

"And so you shall," enthused a large voice coming from her left. She sighed. It apparently was her morning to be overheard making silly remarks, and this time it wasn't just the gardener who was listening in; it was the three-tailed bashaw himself.

"Mr. Patrick?"

A large shadow filled the gap between the pocket doors. MacGregor Patrick stepped into the room. She recognized his face from Roland's photographs, but was surprised by his theatrical presence. In demeanor and build he was a good double for John Wayne—except for the smile, which was too effervescent to be vintage "*Duke*."

"MacGregor to my friends, which I know you shall be. Come inside, my dear."

MacGregor took her hand in his own massive paw and towed her into the library. He relieved her of her small cases by stripping them off her shoulder and dumping them on the floor. Chloe squeaked once in protest of the rough treatment of her cameras, but he spoke over her protest. "Have a seat while we get you something cool to drink. Summer's comin' early this year. Can't have you wiltin' into decline on our very expensive carpet, now can we?"

"Er—no."

Chloe was momentarily deceived into thinking that he was just a normal man playing host to a normal guest and using a royal *we* as a jest. But he maintained his imperial image by immediately going to a corded bell pull and tugging vigorously. He apparently didn't actually mean to fetch refreshments himself. That meant servants.

Feeling more lost than ever, Chloe shook her head.

"Set, child!" He rushed back over to her and pressed her into a chair.

Feeling slightly overwhelmed, Chloe obediently sat—her knees were buckling anyway—and leaned back to enjoy her surroundings. Everything, from her host to the books in massive cases made of quarter-sawn oak, was very large.

MacGregor Patrick, instead of taking a seat behind the enormous desk covered in heavy tomes, seated himself in the wingback chair beside her. He beamed.

"Thank you, I am thirsty," she answered politely, awed by the giant folios around them and the smooth leather beneath her fingers. It was soft enough to be satin.

"And how is Roland, the old devil?" The voice was far from quiet. MacGregor was obviously unaware of the hushed reverence demanded by the library decor. To him, books—even when rare and expensive, and in great numbers—were to be read, not venerated in silence. It was his home; obviously he would speak as he pleased. "It's been an age since he's come up for some fishing. I can't imagine why he doesn't retire."

"He's fine. Busy this time of year," she answered politely, and in a less quiet voice than she would normally use since it occurred to her that maybe MacGregor was hard of hearing. Anyway, *when in Rome* . . . "And I doubt he'll ever retire. He has far too much fun cracking the whip over the wage slaves who work for him."

MacGregor gave a snort of laughter and slapped his knee. Again, Chloe was struck by the theatricality of the gesture. It was as though her host knew of his reputation as being larger than life and had decided to live up to the role.

A small shadow entered through the pocket doors. It reached the wingback chairs only slightly ahead of its owner. The lady, dressed in the traditional garb of a housekeeper, was so humped at the shoulders that her stance was nearly forty-five degrees off of vertical. She looked ancient and weary, suggesting her stoop had come about a full four-score and seven years ago.

Chloe blinked, but, being polite, was careful to show no other expression. Of course, MacGregor Patrick would have an ancient hunchbacked servant. Anything else would be pedestrian and clash with the decor.

"Morag, would you fetch in some lemon ice for our guest? Chloe, this is Morag MacDonald."

"How do you do?" Chloe said, firmly resisting the urge to get up and offer the frail soul her chair. The stern face that went with the stooped body did not suggest that the housekeeper would be accepting of any show of sympathy.

Morag nodded, but didn't speak before shuffling out of the room.

"Fearful old dragon," MacGregor whispered in
a voice that still managed to fill the room all the
way to its ornate crown molding. "Distant cousin
by marriage. She won't retire, either. I've tried for
years to get rid of her, but she's up every morning
just like the sun. Sneakin' around and listenin' at
keyholes! What a nosy pest! She has no respect
for my privacy. None at all. And my son abets her.
It's downright humiliatin'."

Chloe didn't answer. Finding a safe reply would
have been like trying to thread a needle with a very
small eye and a bit of very thick yarn. Especially as
she suspected that Morag MacDonald might very
well be able to hear them discussing her, and she
didn't want to piss the women off. The housekeeper might look slow, but that didn't mean she
was powerless.

"Did you meet my son? He said he'd be about
this morning. Fine strapping lad he is."

In a sudden burst of embarrassing intuition,
Chloe asked: "Rory? Yes, we did bump into each
other. He was taking a break from mowing the
lawn."

MacGregor frowned. "Mowing the lawn, is he?
Well, my son is very efficient. Very *democratic*—
likes to do things for himself." Chloe had the
feeling MacGregor meant bourgeois. "He's also
very opinionated. Not that having an opinion is

a bad thing! Not if you're a man," he added hastily.

"Of course not." Chloe suppressed a smile. Obviously his son's opinions were a foreign—and possibly degenerate—neighborhood where Mac-Gregor didn't often venture. She wondered what, besides mowing the lawn for himself, the two men might not agree about. Roland hadn't said anything about MacGregor's son—*the two-tailed bashaw?* she thought, suppressing an inappropriate grin at her title for Rory's official place in his father's hierarchical structure.

The room began to shimmer. Feeling suddenly lighthearted, Chloe leaned back in her chair and got comfortable. Obviously, she wasn't going to be hurried into efficiency, and she was getting very interested in Riverview and its inhabitants. It was a far cry from what she had imagined in her dreams. So much for the curse of prophesy. This was about as scary as Disneyland.

"The fact is . . . well, Rory is damned particular about the gardens and won't let the boys near the house. Brings his own two special assistants to help with the work when he can't do it himself."

If *the boys* were responsible for the carpet padding and the gnomes, then Chloe could hardly blame Rory for keeping them at bay. Some things were mere bad taste; others were sacrilege. She wouldn't allow these gardens to be desecrated either.

"The gardens are beautiful," she said diplomatically. "I don't think I've ever seen any lovelier."

MacGregor beamed, his giant teeth slowly revealed until he looked like the Cheshire cat. *Oh, Grandma, what biiiig teeth you have!* His pleasure at her words seemed gargantuan in proportion to the mild praise. She wondered for a moment if it was real, and decided that it probably was. MacGregor Patrick wouldn't bother to simulate pleasant emotions for the hired help.

"They are all Rory's doing. The boy's a genius with the flowers. His hybrids are always winning prizes. Builds his own show ponds too. There's nothing effete about that!"

Effete? Rory Patrick? Chloe blinked at the notion.

"What does he hybridize? Roses?" she asked, tactfully ignoring MacGregor's last observation. He likely wouldn't like it if she actually agreed with the standard red-necked male opinion that from the first faltering step of growing flowers it was only a short hop to cross-dressing and then a second small jump to a sex-change operation.

"Iris. His specialty is water irises, but he messes about with all sorts of flowers and moss. You may have seen some in his gardening catalog. Or maybe on one of those gardening shows on TV."

"Patrick's Botanics?" Chloe knew she sounded impressed. Patrick's was a bellwether among gardening enthusiasts.

"That's Rory," MacGregor said proudly, his

son's democracy and effeteness apparently forgotten in this flash of fatherly pride. "You are a gardener then?"

"When I have the time and space. Right now, I am confined to a few containers on a small patio. There's no point in having more when I travel so much."

MacGregor *tsk*ed. "That's a darned shame. While you are here you can make use of the gardens. I have lots of roses that need picking, if that's what you fancy."

"Perhaps Rory would dislike it," she demurred, thinking of his hostility if she descended into his place of work with pruning shears in hand.

"Nonsense!" MacGregor waved a large hand. "The two of you are clearly *beaux-esprit*. Besides," he added ingenuously, "they are my gardens. Rory has his own hothouses down the road a spell. He won't care as long as you don't dig anything up."

Chloe doubted that Rory would share his father's opinion of their spiritual kinship, so she declined to commit herself to any definite project. There was also the fact that she was there to do a job—one that would likely include all the fresh air, plant life, and sunshine she could stand.

"We'll see. My job is likely to keep me very busy. Roland says that your cemetery is a large one."

"Indeed. But there are actually two of them. One for the family and one for the slaves. I'll need pictures of both. I am afraid that they are rather overgrown and it may take some time to clear the brambles away from the stones in the slave cemetery. You could be here for weeks." The words were apologetic, but the tone gleeful.

Chloe didn't know what to make of his attitude. Maybe he was planning to harass his son by making him clear the brambles. That would be childish, but it was fine with Chloe. She had no desire to do it, and she got paid a regular wage however long the project took to complete.

MacGregor added: "That will also give you time to visit your kin. Roland said you had family here."

Chloe damned Roland as an interfering fussbudget.

"I did have, but Mother and her only cousin passed on several years ago. My father's family is from Georgia." And no way was she going to see Gran, no matter how close they were geographically. Pigs would ice skate in hell before that happened.

"I'm so sorry, my dear." And MacGregor did look sorrowful.

"Don't be," she heard herself say. "The loss isn't recent. And anyway, she is always with me, at least in spirit."

MacGregor's eyes widened, but before he could speak Morag came shuffling back into the room, carrying a tray with a tall glass of frosted lemonade. Chloe realized how thirsty and tired she actually was. Perhaps dehydration and the lack of sleep were causing her to make up things.

"Thank you." Chloe shivered as she sipped her tart drink. It was delicious. "This is wonderful. It's very sultry today."

Morag permitted herself a slight softening of the lips before tottering back out again. Chloe wondered if MacGregor had had her vocal chords cut.

"Old trout," MacGregor muttered darkly, and then smiled again. Chloe felt like she was getting mental whiplash trying to keep up with her client's moods. "Well, drink up, my dear, and we'll show you to your room. I can tell you about your job after you have had a chance to rest. This is going to be quite an experience for you, I promise."

MacGregor sat back in a show of relaxation, but some barely contained excitement kept him twitching and tapping his heels on the rug. As she expected, he was completely unable to settle down, and he bounded to his feet a few seconds later. Granny Claire would say that he had ants in his pants.

"All done with that?" he asked. "Then we'll show you upstairs. You'll want to rest for half an hour, but then we will talk some more."

Chloe swallowed her drink quickly and rose with some difficulty from the depths of her own chair. She guessed that the *we* he referred to was actually poor old Morag, and she was proved absolutely right in that assumption when MacGregor tugged on the bell pull and the long suffering woman shuffled back into the room.

Chloe scooped up her camera bags before

Morag could get to them. MacGregor frowned at her, but mercifully didn't comment as they made their way back into the hall.

"You go with Morag and have a little rest. It will just be the two of us at dinner, so don't bother dressing. We'll eat early. In the meanwhile, you just make yourself at home." He smiled benignly and waved as she slowly ascended the broad stairs at the shuffling pace set by the housekeeper.

"Thank you, I will."

Chloe shook her head. MacGregor Patrick didn't fetch drinks or climb stairs, not even for the protégé of his oldest friend. But he had, as Roland predicted, welcomed her into his house, family affairs, and opinions with open arms.

It was going to be an interesting job. She had MacGregor Patrick's word on it, and around here, she was certain that his word was law.

In the interest of being prepared, she would spend the afternoon checking out all her equipment, and if MacGregor didn't mind, spending a little time in his library reading up on Patrick family history. She always enjoyed a play more when she had a program with a synopsis and a list of all the characters, and something told her that MacGregor would be only too happy to supply her with the family's illustrious if fictitious pedigree if she asked. This wasn't a man who kept his light under a bushel—or even a fine Tiffany lampshade.

Golden lads and girls all must,
Like chimney-sweepers, come to dust.
—*Shakespeare*

An atheist is a man who has
no invisible means of support.
—*John Bachan*

Chapter Two

Chloe was surprised when she came downstairs
in the morning and found a flannel-shirted Mac-
Gregor waiting in the breakfast parlor on the far
side of the groaning board. The expanse of golden
wood that was the place of pre-noon dining was
so wide as to resemble an African savannah and,
except for the bright shirt, MacGregor himself
looked rather like the king of beasts enjoying a
fresh kill. It was clear that he recalled his stated intention of showing her the ancestral manse himself. He had planned this ambitious scheme on
the previous evening while showing off the many
portraits in the Patrick gallery on the second mez-
zanine, but as he had been well into a post-
prandial bottle of scotch at the time, Chloe had
discounted the possibility that he would remem-

ber volunteering for what would most likely be an arduous task.

Recalling that bottle of scotch, she walked into the parlor on light feet and looked her host over with a concerned eye. The unfiltered sunlight in the breakfast room showed the deep and numerous crow's feet around MacGregor's eyes. Chloe strongly suspected that they came from an overabundance of laughter rather than long days toiling in the sun. Her host's hands were as smooth and beautiful as the Limoges china from which he was eating. Surprisingly, he looked none the worse for the previous evening's debauch.

However, the morning light showed two other things that, in their own way, were disturbing. One was that the young prince of the kingdom—as MacGregor no doubt saw his son—scrubbed up nicely. She hadn't had a chance to see Rory spruced up the evening before, as he had been away on business. This morning's apparel made it obvious that he was not intending to spend the day on the tractor, or hiking about Riverview's cemeteries. The fine imported linen suit clinging to his impressive form was of a sartorial grandeur appropriate for a visit to a capital city—or a date with a fashion editor at *Vogue*. His tidiness, far exceeding her own, was rather annoying. No man should be prettier or more put together than she was first thing in the morning. It was all she could do to resist checking her hair, which had a tendency to curl wildly in humid weather.

The other odd sight at the table was also an expensive import, but this one was from Germany. MacGregor was having beer for breakfast, and, probably to irritate his son, he was drinking it out of the bottle. It wasn't a sight that gladdened Chloe's heart. MacGregor wasn't an ugly drunk, but he was certainly an expansive one. It could make her working day an unnaturally long—and long-winded—one.

As much as she liked MacGregor, she was glad she wasn't his child and saddled with the job of looking after such a willful parent. The thought made her feel a little better about not being so close to her own father.

She was allowed to make her visual observations in silence; the Patricks were seemingly too busy glaring at one another to notice her arrival. Feeling both mildly put out by this slight and also apprehensive of what might happen to her if the lions started to roar, Chloe stepped over to the laden sideboard and poured herself some orange juice. This didn't look to be the kind of day that one rushed into without some liquid sunshine.

"Good morning, Miss Chloe. A great day for a shutterbug," Rory finally said. His voice was exceedingly pleasant, with only the slightest shading of a drawl. He didn't rise, in spite of putting "miss" in front of her name. He also stared at her, a tidy Virtue reproving wild-haired Wantonness.

Chloe's ear was growing attuned to Patrick voices and she noticed right away more drawl than he'd had yesterday. It actually sounded mocking, and she felt certain that Rory was annoyed with MacGregor for hiring her. For that reason—and the suit at the breakfast table—she decided to be only marginally pleasant to him. She was sure his father wouldn't mind.

"Good morning, Rory. Off to see the grand panjandrums?" she asked while eyeing the various dishes. Morag—or someone—had been busy. The selection would rival a buffet at a good hotel.

"No, just some dirt diggers."

MacGregor snorted and half rose from his chair in a belated display of manners.

"Mighty high-class dirt diggers. I don't see why you couldn't put them off—"

"When people fly halfway around the world to see you, you don't put them off. You'll simply have to make do with peasant labor today. Your serfs will be here by nine. They can fetch and carry for you as well as I can." The drawl disappeared again and the two lions were back to glaring at each other across the damask linens and gardenia blossoms floating gently in a Waterford bowl.

"Peasants? Peasants are poor! With the wages you pay those boys—," MacGregor began only to be interrupted.

"What I pay them is my affair. And I would gladly pay them double wages to not have to spend the day hacking brambles off those gothic horrors—"

"Those are your family's final resting places! You will show some respect—"

"Oh, for God's sake!" Rory stood abruptly and threw his napkin down on the chair. It was a very nice napkin and an even nicer chair. Chloe thought that they deserved better treatment, but didn't say so. "I'll be back around four. You should stop drinking that swill unless you want to have a coronary while you're hiking the snake-infested outback."

"—Swill?"

"—Snake-infested?" MacGregor and Chloe exclaimed at the same time.

"Exactly," Rory said meanly and marched away.

Chloe cleared her throat as his angry footsteps receded. For a man wearing soft-soled shoes and walking on the finest Aubusson carpets, he managed to make a whole lot of noise. It had to be deliberate. He had managed to be quiet as a mouse when he sneaked up on her yesterday.

MacGregor slammed his bottle on the table and beamed at her. As the suds started to overflow the neck, he quickly returned the bottle to his mouth and polished off the offensive potation. Either the argument or the alcohol left him looking refreshed and pink as a rose.

"One more for the road?" he suggested.

Chloe eyed MacGregor's flushed face and then glanced at the three empty bottles on the sideboard. Her boss hadn't mentioned that MacGregor had a heart condition—or a drinking

problem. But maybe, like the mania for ugly garden statues, this was a recent development.

"No thanks," she said firmly. "Actually there's
no need for you to put yourself out. I—"

"Now, girl!" Clearly, interrupting people was a
familial trait. "Don't get in a lather. Rory just
doesn't understand that when a man's as dry as
dust he needs a little somethin' besides coffee to
quench his thirst. Anyway, my heart is sound as a
bell. That quack doesn't know what he's talkin'
about. I'll live to see a hundred!"

Chloe was beginning to have some belated sympathy for Rory Patrick. Keeping his dad out of
trouble must be a nearly full-time job. Chloe
couldn't have managed it. She had an attachment
to her father, but it was a rather elastic one. Pushed
to admit the truth, she would have to say that she
was closer to her dad's younger brother, Ben-
jamin, who was irresponsible and unmannered,
but a great deal more fun to be around. He was
also more open to New Age ideas. Specifically, he
believed in witchcraft, reincarnation and alien ab-
duction. Her father didn't even believe in God.

"Fine with me," Chloe answered. The boys
would be there at nine to handle the hard work.
They would just do a little leisurely supervising
until it was time for the noon break. Surely by
then MacGregor would be ready for a nap.

"Shall we go?" MacGregor stood.

Chloe cast a longing eye at the basket of scones
and the numerous chafing dishes from which

wafted alluring smells. She had enjoyed the same odors many times before, but in Riverview they were especially evocative. In a private home, this mix was the smell of good taste and old money liberally applied to already luxurious possessions. She was willing to bet the bagels were fresh and the eggs came from hens raised in palatial coops and fed baby greens and fresh corn.

"But it's only eight," she objected. "The boys won't be here until—"

"We'll do the family graveyard first. It's more interesting anyway," he said impatiently. "Grab a bun and come along. The weather is just going to get hotter."

He had a point. Chloe stopped sniffing, grabbed a scone, and followed her host down the hall that led to the back of the house. They were both booted in hiking shoes, and it sounded like a regiment of soldiers clomping through the confined space of the uncarpeted hallway.

They exited through a Victorian parlor draped in a plethora of red velvet swags that somehow managed to stay on the right side of tastefulness, and out onto a small stoop that had been painted white and stenciled with some sort of flowering vine pattern. Chloe would have enjoyed a lengthy ogle of both parlor and porch, but the roused MacGregor was in a hurry.

Several paths crisscrossed under the Herculean oaks at the rear of the house, but MacGregor ignored them in favor of directness as he set a double-time pace across the groundcover and marched toward the antler hedge that encircled the manse. Chloe hesitated a moment as she stared at the half-familiar sight, then shrugged off the sensation of déjà vu and started after her host.

They were joined on the expedition by a large black and white cat who, though walking in the master's shadow, wisely kept well away from MacGregor's crashing footsteps.

"This is Roger," MacGregor said by way of introduction. "Jolly Roger."

The intelligent feline looked back politely. Seeing the triangular patch of black over his left eye and the rolling gait that suggested a sailor pacing over the deck of ship during high seas, Chloe didn't bother to ask how he'd gotten the name.

"Hi, kitty," she said around a mouthful of pastry. The cat blinked once at her bad manners and then ignored her. It seemed that even Riverview's pet was superior to her, and unlike his owner, not inclined to be indulgent.

It soon became apparent that there actually was a small break in the antler fortification as MacGregor dodged right and was suddenly swallowed up by the hedge. Roger immediately followed him into the shrubbery and likewise disappeared.

Chloe hurried after, grateful that she wasn't burdened with her camera equipment. Whenever possible, she liked to reconnoiter before bringing her babies out into the hostile world, and this world was certainly hostile to humans, however fecund the pretty flora around them. This hedge was more than a polite request for privacy. It was prettier than barbed wire and broken glass, but many times more fearsome. A careless fall could leave someone maimed for life or even gored to death.

The strange, claustrophobic path through the hedgerow was narrow and went on for some distance. It eventually exited into a shady grove where the oak ceiling grew thick enough to shut out the worst of the sun. It was eerily still and quiet until MacGregor spoke. His cheerful voice shattered the air of peaceful melancholia, and seemed to stir up the dust and leaf mold missed by their hiking boots.

"Slave cemetery is that way . . ." He jerked a thumb to the right. Chloe couldn't see anything beyond a six-foot-tall pile of wild brambleberries whose upper reaches were smothered in cobwebs furred with dust and studded with catkins from the lone maple growing overhead. "The family is over this way." MacGregor headed in the opposite direction, fallen oak leaves crunching underfoot as he moved.

"Well, what do you think?" he continued. "Nice and quiet, isn't it? You don't get this kind of peace in Metairie. *Tourists?* What locusts! And frankly, I've always thought New Orleans overrated. Their grave goods aren't *that* nice. And ours are every bit as old."

Chloe didn't comment on his disparaging reference to one of New Orleans's famous cemeteries. An old man had to be allowed some partiality for his family's burial ground.

"I think I may have a light problem," she answered absently, staring up at the leafy canopy. "Is it all as dark as this?"

"What?" MacGregor turned. "Oh, lights for the camera, you mean. It's pretty much the same everywhere out here. I expect you can work it out. Roland said that you were good with this sort of thing and had some fancy new kind of camera. And we can always buy anything you need."

Actually, what Roland had probably said was that she was good at making do and had the patience of Job when it came to rescuing photos on the computer. She wondered how he would feel about her making unauthorized purchases for this special job. Probably not thrilled. Maybe she could blame it all on MacGregor.

"Of course I'll manage. I'm a professional," she said loftily. "I have worked in some of the most famous cemeteries in— Oh my!"

MacGregor had tugged aside a curtain of honeysuckle and revealed a bedizened granite portico with a recessed wooden gate. The wood was so old it was nearly black, and it was heavily carved with a traditional funerary pattern of inverted torches, rose garlands and laurel wreaths. Again there came a feeling of déjà vu. Sleeping Beauty's castle would have been guarded by just such a gate, she thought, and Chloe's heart began to flutter.

MacGregor fished a giant key out of his pocket and stuffed it into the ancient box lock. The antique mechanism opened without the expected grate of rusted iron, and the gates themselves swung back without a shriek. Obviously, the gate's hinges were cared for, in spite of the plant life's overgrown condition. The plants were probably just a clever camouflage, which would suggest to a stranger a high degree of neglect.

Roger pranced on ahead of his master, but MacGregor paused before entering the dark space beyond. He held his arm across the threshold like a bar while he studied Chloe.

"I want you to understand something, Chloe. I don't let folks in here. Don't hold tours for the historical society and such nonsense. I don't have in photographers from the Smithsonian, though I've been asked a time or two. This is a private place for my family, and I want it to stay that way."

Chloe didn't understand why MacGregor should suddenly be nervous about showing her the cemetery, but she was willing to agree with anything he wanted. She would do whatever it took to get the job done without arousing her boss's ire.

"Sure. I understand."

MacGregor looked deep into her eyes. For the first time, the engaging twinkle was missing from his hazel gaze. Chloe was abruptly aware of a vein of granite running under his benevolent exterior.

She shouldn't have been surprised by the streak of hardness—all despots had them.

"I'm the keeper now. The guardian. These folks were my family. They were people once who were alive just like you and me. They laughed and loved, made war and babies. Some were heroes, some scoundrels. You ever hear that epitaph by Keats about *'Here lies one whose name was writ in water'*? Well, that goes for all these dead folks. All that's left of them now are these monuments and some crumbling old bones. I don't want them to end up being robbed of what little they have left. Flesh is forgotten, consumed. Bones, too, eventually. But these monuments live on."

"That's why I'm here," Chloe said gently, though her heart was pounding with some strange alarm. "I'm your insurance policy in case the unthinkable happens."

MacGregor nodded. "But my best insurance is that no one knows it's here. I want to keep it that way for as long as I can. Rory made me promise to talk to you about this."

Rory. Of course he was responsible for this new show of nerves on MacGregor's part. Obviously he didn't trust her.

"You have my word," she said gravely. "I won't reveal anything I see without your permission."

MacGregor nodded again and then turned and ducked under the low header that guarded the dark portal of the necropolis.

"Then come meet the family."

The first monuments on the other side were a row of sepulchers carved in the Greek, Roman and Etruscan style, decorated with urns and life-sized muses in various languishing poses. The poor maidens of the arts wept lichen tears down their anguished faces, and had their stony hands shackled in living ropes of passionflowers. The themes were primarily Greek, but Chloe had seen enough funerary monuments to recognize the work of Italian stonemasons.

"Oh my sainted aunt!" she whispered, staring up into a pitted gray face that was forever frozen in a mask of profound grief.

"Foggini," MacGregor confirmed with satisfaction. "He did Galileo's sepulcher. There's Picchi and Brancusi. And Granddad." MacGregor pointed as he spoke.

"Granda—Oh, your *grandfather*."

"Tamlane MacGregor Patrick. He was a little bit eccentric." They stopped in front of a vaguely neo-gothic marble tomb fronted with pillars and roundels of male and female masks representing the heavens and the earth.

"This looks vaguely familiar."

"It's by that Frenchie, Rodin."

"Auguste Rodin?" Chloe's voice was feeble.

"Granddad wanted *The Gates of Hell*, but Grandma wouldn't let him have it. She commissioned him to do this instead. *The Gates of Heaven*, she called it."

"I think I'm going to faint."

"I'm glad you know your art. You'll do a better job." MacGregor's face was smug, and another clear reminder that pashas, while sometimes generous, were not entirely saintly and benevolent. "Come along. I want you to see the Saint-Gaudens. He's just about the only American sculptor we have in here. I like him a lot, even if he isn't Italian."

Chloe liked him too. His brilliantly rendered marble angels looked happy.

They soon passed into a lower rent district where the lesser family and their pets were put to rest. There were Celtic crosses overgrown with ivy and vervain, surrounded by picket fences made of stone, or ironwork hedges drowning in clematis. Obviously, the boys hadn't been in with the pruning shears for a few months. That would make taking clear photographs of the monuments difficult, and perhaps even dangerous if Rory was right about the snakes, but the cat seemed to enjoy chasing invisible mice through the grasping bushes, and the feral plants lent the place a certain gothic air.

Chloe didn't stray off of the path in her bare legs, but she saw an array of arresting images that fired her imagination. There were the three-quarters eyes that were both the symbol of the Masons but also of the Holy Trinity. There were also lots of doves, suggesting that the inhabitants of those graves had either been Catholic or Jewish, and—sadly—the white lambs that marked the graves of children were abundant. There were a few anchors with broken chains that indicated some of the Patricks had been sailing men, and one out-of-place Muslim crescent.

"How large is the cemetery?" she asked finally, beginning to tire. A constant state of admiration was exhausting.

"Two acres. One hundred seven human graves and mausoleums. Ninety-three dogs. Eighty-one cats. Four horses—my great-grandfather buried his favorite team here. And one monkey."

MacGregor walked her slowly past aisles of eighteenth-century hands; praying hands, clasping hands, pointing and blessing hands. There were Saint Michaels and Francises and a bevy of Virgins. The end of the first corridor was marked with a particularly grisly carving of the Sacred Heart leaping out of Jesus's chest, confirming Chloe's impression that the majority of the Patricks had been Catholic.

"'For we do not wrestle against flesh and blood, but against the rulers, against the authorities, against the cosmic powers over this present darkness, against the spiritual forces of evil in the heavenly places,'" Chloe muttered, quoting Ephesians as she looked at a stone archangel who brandished an upraised sword.

"Is that the way you think of it?" MacGregor asked with a smile. "Then you will like this next part. Follow me and mind the clematis." He swept aside a thicket of vine with a large hand that would have looked at home carrying a machete.

"Whither thou goest."

The following section showed art typical to New

England and among the Presbyterians of Scotland: grim reapers with scythes and winged skulls. This section also was marked with the sort of candid epitaphs that spoke plainly of the deceased's faults and brought joy to the taphophiles of the world.

Calum Patrick 1741–1780
He was a terrible man,
Cruel to everyone except his wife,
His sons and his friends

Moira Patrick, beloved wife
1752–1774
Think on what a wife should be
For she was that and more

Andrew Patrick 1721–1770
He suffers no more

Edana Patrick 1740–1771
The angels took her home

Rachael Ryan Patrick 1723–1775
Ever tardy, even to the grave

Roderick Allen and James David Patrick 1725–1747
Hanged for seeking treasure that didn't exist
Here lie the ones responsible for this

Beloved Kelton Patrick 1791–1862
This stone is placed by a mournful wife who will
gladly join him soon

Ridiculously, Chloe felt tears gathering in her eyes. She heard a noise and turned to find Mac-Gregor sniffling dolefully.

"Here, girl." He offered a hankie. It was made of lawn and embroidered with a large MP. "This one always makes me sad."

"Thank you." Chloe felt like an idiot and was glad that Rory Patrick wasn't around to see her crying. The memento mori didn't usually affect her, but the art and atmosphere of this cemetery was overwhelming and should have moved even a Philistine. They stood in companionable silence for a minute or two, enjoying their shared moment of sentimentality.

"Come along. Let's get to the good stuff." Mac-Gregor wiped a sleeve over his eyes, and when it was lowered he was smiling again.

Chloe tried not to gape as she followed him. The cemetery had already rendered up the finest collection of funerary monuments she had ever seen outside of Highgate in London and some of the more famous sepulchers of Rome. The Patrick dead—even the animals—had not been stinted; the death houses were world class. What could possibly qualify as "the good stuff"?

She had her answer soon enough. The last section, set off by a wall of cedars, was the gothic horrors that Rory had referred to. The term wasn't entirely correct, as they were mostly in a style of gothic revival, which was even more overwrought than the original had been.

There was a ten-foot-tall statue of Father Time draped in a shroud, exhorting them to *"cast a cold eye on Death."* There was a tableau of the sea god, Triton, wrestling with a monster from the deep, an eight-by-eight slab that held a chess board with a white alabaster king checkmated by a black marble queen, and—strangest of all—a full-sized grand piano in speckled gray granite with keys picked out in ivory and obsidian. The lid was mercifully down tight.

Chloe cleared her throat. "What, no pyramids?"

MacGregor answered seriously, "I haven't chosen my own monument yet. Perhaps I should look into that. They must still know how to make pyramids in Egypt."

So much for injecting some levity into the conversation.

"You wouldn't have it made here?"

"No. Haven't you been listening, girl?" he demanded. "No one knows about this place. Just Rory's boys who do the maintenance, Rory, my nephew and me. This place is like a desert rose, born to blush and bloom unseen. Why, even Roland hasn't been beyond the gate! No one but family is allowed in here. Used to be that we'd let in the priest, but Father Martin passed on thirteen years back, and my Nancy was the last devout one. Now we'll just cremate and have a Mass later at the church in town. The church still doesn't like cremation but . . ." MacGregor shrugged impatiently.

The church's views on cremation had obviously been considered and then dismissed.

"Then I'm honored to be here," Chloe said seriously. "And I promise to do a good job."

"I'm sure you will." All of a sudden, Mac-Gregor's expression turned crafty. "Anyway, we may not be breaking tradition all that much by letting you in."

"No?" Chloe began a mental review of her ancestors, trying to recall if they had included any Patricks.

"Well, Rory's got to marry someday. It may be that you are the lucky girl. I've seen him watching you. There's some chemistry there. I think you would be a fine daughter-in-law."

The notion of distant cousinship vanished in a blink. She and Rory had chemistry? Only the kind that happened in gas chambers. She wondered if her own father was as clueless about her likes and dislikes.

"Well . . . thank you, but that's highly unlikely to happen." Chloe, who had passed beyond the ability to be verbally shocked by her host, said firmly: "Your son doesn't like me. And I don't think I like him."

"That doesn't mean anything! Rory doesn't like anyone."

"Well, it means something to me." She looked at her watch and changed the subject. "It's after ten. What do you say to rounding up the boys and taking a look at the slave cemetery?"

"If you like, but there won't be much to see until the boys have hacked a path through the brambles. The Patricks quit keeping slaves in the late 1700s and things have gotten a mite overgrown in the last couple of centuries. I've seen parts, of course, but it's just a jumble of crosses and stones. Pathetic sort of place—sad, too. Not like here. Maybe I should plant some roses out there, try to cheer it up a bit."

Chloe hadn't given the matter any thought, but MacGregor was correct about the family cemetery not being a sad place. It was a weird place, certainly, but not melancholic. Perhaps it was the company as much as the sculptures, astounding and absurd as they were, but Chloe felt both peaceful and safe. She wouldn't mind picnicking here, or even napping, which was not a feeling she had ever experienced in a cemetery before.

"Cruel as the grave," the saying went. The thought of being dead certainly wasn't appealing, but when you had to go, it might bring a measure of comfort to know that your mortal remains would be among friends in this little slice-out-of-time Paradise.

MacGregor led the way back through the cedars. The world got lighter once there were only the ancient oaks overhead.

"Tisiphone!" Chloe exclaimed, pointing at a stone. "You've got to be kidding. Poor kid, to be saddled with a name like that."

"At least it wasn't Alecto or Megaera," MacGregor answered without stopping to look.

"Or Medusa."

"*Chloe* isn't exactly plain homespun either. It would fit right in here," MacGregor pointed out, in what was probably meant as a compliment. "Besides, I think Tisiphone is kind of pretty."

He halted in front of a last mausoleum. The facade was a bookcase filled with hundreds of volumes of fictional work. The stone spines sported names like Dickens, Austen and Jules Verne. There was a bench placed to one side. The tomb belonged to Nancy Black Patrick. The recent date was suggestive.

"My wife," MacGregor confirmed, as though knowing her thoughts. He sounded slightly wistful. "My Nancy was quite a reader. I wanted her to have her favorites nearby."

"That's thoughtful." Chloe realized that her comment was odd, but the entire morning had been odd, and her assaulted eyes and senses couldn't absorb anything more. Also, her host was looking a little wan. It was probably time to be leaving. "MacGregor, I don't want to sound like a slacker, but would you mind if we put off seeing the slave cemetery until later? I need to make some notes while this is fresh in my mind."

"Fine, fine." MacGregor peered at her. "You're looking a little peaked, girl. You really should have eaten some breakfast. It's the most important meal of the day, and you aren't running to fat yet."

Chloe opened her mouth to retort and then thought better of it.

"You're right. I should have," she agreed meekly. "And I will tomorrow. But perhaps Morag will take pity on me and let me have some lunch."

"Morag hasn't got any pity. But Cook'll see you right. Oleander is one beautiful woman."

Chloe said a silent prayer of thanks for the beautiful cook. She was suddenly ravenous.

We understand death for the first time
when he puts his hands on someone we love.
—Madame de Stael

Chapter Three

Chloe took half of MacGregor's advice and ate a splendid lunch, but after a sumptuous meal that left her feeling a bit like the fattened goose destined for the Christmas table, she decided that a solitary stroll through the gardens would be in order. It seemed an especially wise thing to do, as MacGregor could be heard bellowing from the library. His curses hadn't been in wide use since Charles II had been on the throne, but they were still effective. As no one answered, she had to assume that it was either a cowering employee who had aroused his wrath, or he was on the telephone. Chloe didn't envy whoever was on the receiving end of such a tongue-lashing. Even from a distance, it raised gooseflesh on her arms. She happily fled the house.

Even having been through the mysterious

hedge before, it still took her a while of pacing up and down to find the gap where they had entered that morning. The break was hidden by some optical illusion caused by the overlapping vines. There simply was no marker that she could see that differentiated one bit of hedge from another. She was finally aided in her quest by the sound of men's curses—modern ones this time—and the clopping and the hacking of pruning shears and shovels. As she got closer to the voices, she noticed some slightly downtrodden grass only just recovered from a wheelbarrow's passage. That wouldn't last long, though, so she marked the gap with some fallen twigs before entering the maze.

The "boys" proved to be two brothers, Dave and Bob Munson, one of whom was a senior in high school and the other a college student. She hoped uneasily that Bob, the younger of the two towheads, was on some sort of work program and that MacGregor hadn't encouraged him to go AWOL for the day so that she could have immediate access to the cemetery. Then she remembered Rory had made the arrangements and dismissed her worry. Rory Patrick, the stiff stick, would never encourage carelessness or illegality among his employees. Also, for all she knew, maybe school had already let out for the summer.

"So, guys," she called out. She didn't offer to relieve them of the loppers and gauntlets, which were covered in bits of thorny bramble and poison ivy. "How goes the war against the flora?"

"We're winnin' the battle," Dave answered with a charming smile. Apparently his parents were reasonably well off and this job was just for pocket money, or else Rory paid dental benefits. "It's just slow going against these brambles. I'm gonna have to sharpen the blades again tonight."

"I bet. Well, I'm going to go get my equipment and start on the . . ." Remembering that no one was supposed to know about—or likely even discuss—the family cemetery, she finished: "I'll be on the other side. Mind if I borrow these shears?"

"Help yourself, ma'am. Sure you don't want a machete? Some of these vines are fierce. And then there are those snakes."

Chloe couldn't picture herself lopping off a snake's head. It was all she could do to kill the slugs that attacked her potted daffodils.

"No, thanks. We have a work policy at my company that says we don't use knives that are longer than the average human arm. I'll just keep an eye out for things that slither."

"Yes, ma'am."

Ma'am? Chloe shook her head as she walked away. Maybe it was time to update her wardrobe and consider a new hairstyle.

Lethargy warred with anticipation as Chloe went to fetch her camera bag, portable computer, battery packs, tripod, GPS—though she wasn't sure that she would use it—and MacGregor's hand-drawn map of the graveyard that showed where all the tombstones were. When she finally staggered into the maze she looked like a beast of burden packing luggage into the Outback.

It was oppressively hot under the trees where no breeze stirred, but she was absolutely itching to start work. This wasn't simply a case of taking a few casual snaps for reference; this was making a visual history of great art. She didn't kid herself that there would ever be a book in this, but she wanted to do a good job anyway. The monuments deserved nothing less than museum lighting treatment. She would use the digital camera for reference shots that she could check immediately on the computer and archive in the database when the time came, but the permanent and personal inventory would be recorded with her favorite old thirty-five millimeter film and camera. She might also shoot some slide film; it still had better resolution than either than either the digital camera or the print film could offer when it came to enlargements.

Chloe shoved her way through the clematis wall and then paused at the head of the granite avenue. It would have made sense to start with the monuments closest to the gate that MacGregor had left open for her—after cautioning her that she needed to tell him when she was through so that he could lock up again—but they were covered over in vines that would require a few hours of shearing to clear sufficiently to record all sides of the buildings. So, rather than trying to be cartographically methodical, she headed for her favorite part of the cemetery that wasn't hip deep in scratchy things and began there.

The shade was more dappled than solid outside the death house that belonged to Calvin and Edana Patrick. The square granite building was obscured only by a light fall of browned oak leaves on the shingled slate roof. The acidic leaves apparently kept down the moss and other vines that grew on some of the other monuments, for this house was relatively clean of parasitic plant life.

She found it surprising that so large a crypt had only two residents, but perhaps the couple had died before having any children. In the days of brisk epidemics, it was only too likely to have happened. Or they might have been brother and sister; the inscription didn't say. Personally, she didn't think that she would care to spend all eternity locked up with a sibling, but given the dates on the tomb, it was unlikely that poor Edana, being female—which in those days was considered another word for feeble-minded—was ever asked about the final arrangements.

Chloe consulted her map and saw that she was at tomb forty-six. She took her pencil and made a small check by it and then added the inscription above the door: *We all a Debt to Nature owe.* It wasn't likely that she would grow confused about which of these marvels she had already photographed, but she preferred to keep a running count of just how far along in a job she was in case a client asked. The tomb inscription was for her benefit.

She decided that she would need four shots of this monument with the digital camera, showing the detail on every side, starting on the south face where the small windows were. The edge of the roof was an unusual crow-step design, and she liked the benign-looking angel of death who adorned the central plinth.

Chloe had loaded her memory stick and was set up for the frontal shot when she noticed that there was a fine tracery of cobwebs all around the wide, solid wood door veiling the heavenly choir who sang around its frame. Her first impulse was to wipe them off, but she didn't have a cloth with her—she made a note to bring one next time, along with a broom, a stepladder and some gloves. Also, they weren't really hiding any detail of the architecture, and they added a certain eerie quality to the shot, which would show up nicely in the thirty-five millimeter photos when highlighted properly. She was being unprofessional in allowing artistic impulses to override technical ones, but in this case, it wasn't an actual impediment to sight, so she let her sensibilities have their way.

Anyway, she would have to come back later with a key to photograph the interior, if there was any statuary inside. That would be a job best left for early morning, though. By this late in the day, the interior would be an oast house, and she had no intention of subjecting herself or her cameras to a sauna.

Chloe hummed her way through her favorite Stevie Ray Vaughn tunes as she worked. Time passed quickly under the gloom of the oaks and cedars, and it wasn't until she heard MacGregor's footsteps that she realized that the light, such as it was, had shifted far to the west.

"I guess I forgot the time," she began, turning away from her tripod with a smile.

"Having fun?" Rory asked, plucking a stray oak leaf from her improvised coiffure, which was also going astray, being pinioned by nothing more than her pencil. Once again, Virtue towered over Wantonness. "I wouldn't have guessed you were a blues fan."

Chloe collected herself. She was surprised, but not entirely displeased to see MacGregor's son waiting for her. Sometime during her morning outing with MacGregor, she had decided that Rory actually had a large cross to bear in looking after both his dad and a large business, and that she would be magnanimous about his reserve and strange sense of humor—as long as it wasn't directed at her again.

"Actually, yes, odd though it seems," she answered, allowing herself to really smile at him for the first time.

Rory blinked once and took a half step back.

"Well, good." He sounded a bit wary.

Chloe pointed at the large iron key in his left hand.

"Did MacGregor send you to evict me?"

"MacGregor?" He looked at her oddly.

"Your father," she prompted him, and saw his brows draw together.

"I know who you mean. Most people call him *Mister* Patrick."

"Really?" Chloe's inner devil prompted her to say: "But not his family, surely. And MacGregor told me that he thinks of me as a daughter."

"What?" Rory looked a little startled. "He can't! Not already."

"Well, a potential daughter," she amended, saving her files and then closing the lid of the laptop and returning it to its bag. She wished for a moment that she had one of those new memory sticks that could hold more images before having to upload them to the computer, but they were both experimental and very expensive. And Roland didn't mind her being inconvenienced.

"Oh, damn." Rory sounded more weary than annoyed. "Not again. I thought we would have a few days before he started in."

Again? Chloe felt a slight pang at the thought that MacGregor might try to adopt every stray female who came his way.

"Come now! If you insist on this effete career as a flower man, you have to expect that your father would feel the need to try to arrange some opportunities for you to meet females," she teased.

"I meet lots of women, thank you very much."

"But are they the right kind of women?" she interrupted in a familial manner, zipping her tote closed. She managed not to laugh at his lowering brow. He was so easy to provoke. "You could save yourself a lot of grief if you would just take up a masculine sport like football or hunting. As long as you remain a shrinking violet, your dad is likely to try setting you up with masterful females who can mold the next generation."

"You'll stop laughing when you see that he's serious," Rory warned, then smiled nastily. "Did you know that you are standing in poison ivy?"

Chloe yelped and jumped for the path. It was only after she was clear that she saw she hadn't been anywhere near the noxious weed.

"Not real good at identifying plants besides flowers, are you?" she asked with a wry smile, which conceded that he had scored a hit by making her squeak and hop about.

Rory smiled back. This time his expression wasn't tinged with evil, but she wasn't sure that she liked it any better. He was lovely to look at, but she sensed that for some reason this man was not her friend.

"Maybe not. But I'm really good with irises. All of us effete guys are. You'd better hurry. You need to pretty-up for the company."

"Company?" she asked warily.

"Yes, my cousin Claude has graced us with his presence. Again. And this time he has brought a friend. MacGregor is not pleased. This would be a good night to be seen looking pretty and not heard."

"Why not just send me to bed without supper?"

"It would be kinder."

"What kind of *friend* is this?" she asked, shoving back her sweaty hair with a grimy hand and wondering if it was a well-dressed female with manicured fingernails. "Just how *pretty* do I need to be?"

"A dress will do. MacGregor isn't too well-versed about female apparel." Rory added as he began to turn away, "I wouldn't worry about pleasing Claude and his . . . muscular companion."

"No? Why not? I like muscular men as much as the next woman," she said, eyeing Rory's own lean limbs, which were actually much more appealing than any weight-lifter's body could be—but she would rather die than say so.

Rory's lip curled. "I gave you credit for having better taste. However, if you want Claude to notice you, then that is your affair. I know my cousin's taste though, so here's some advice. Unless you're independently wealthy he'll never look twice unless you flash some skin. Or else tuck a few twenty-dollar bills into your cleavage. Then you can have his undivided concentration turned upon at least part of you." He turned away.

"Thanks bunches. All you young Patrick men

sound so charming," she muttered, breaking down her tripod. "And thanks for lending a hand with my equipment. You're a real gentleman."

She raised her voice and called to Rory's retreating back: "You may as well wait here. You can't lock up until I'm done, and I'm not leaving until I get this stuff put away."

Rory stopped in mid-stride. She heard his curse under his breath and then he turned and walked back to the tomb. He was glaring at her.

"I don't know what it is about you that makes me forget my manners."

"You aren't seriously blaming me for the lapse, are you?"

"Certainly. I'm never rude to anyone else."

"Well, that's a lie," she answered cheerfully. "You are very rude to your father—"

"That is self-defense!"

"And I expect that you are probably rude to your cousin, too."

"Claude is a parasitic toad who only comes around when he—"

"And what is *my* crime?"

"Breathing," he snapped, and then started to laugh. His eyes creased into the charming folds that came from his father. "Maybe MacGregor is right about you."

"In what respect?" Chloe asked.

"Maybe you were a Patrick in another life. If I had a sister, I expect the relationship would look about the same."

"You think so?"

"With one notable difference, of course." Rory scooped up her tripod and camera bag, leaving her to gather the map, shears and computer. He didn't explain what the difference was, and she decided not to ask.

Morag served. Slowly. She was dressed, as always, like she was going to a funeral. That night the mood in the dining room made her couture acceptable. Two minutes in Claude's company had Chloe convinced that Claude Patrick was one of the planet's most unappealing human beings. The things that were wrong about him might not be noticed by some less discerning women, but Chloe had no trouble identifying them. Claude looked handsome enough, in the way of all the Patrick men, but his tendency to whine his sentences put Chloe's teeth on edge. She hated men who were babies. Her first short-lived romance with one had cured her of any desire to mother another Peter Pan.

Claude's friend, Isaac Runyon, was no treat either, but he was of another category of undesirable altogether. Claude was a jerk. Isaac was something worse. An air of violence lay over him like an extra skin. He looked and acted like a junkyard dog who was restrained only by the fist of a brutal master. Actually, he rather ate like a cur too, grinding his food with powerful jaws. His eyes were sly and greedy. She wouldn't be surprised if he was one of those nasty types who rode the bus at rush hour, using the crowded conditions as an excuse to dry-hump strange women.

Her best friend, Lynsay, had a ranking system for men, a three-tiered hierarchy for sorting potential dates:

A) Wouldn't screw him if he were the last man alive and all the vibrators were broken.
B) Would screw him, but only if no one ever found out about it.
C) Would screw him—in public if he wanted.

Actually, there was a D category too—would screw him in public, the news cameras rolling and her mother looking on—but Lynsay had yet to meet this hypothetical superman, and Chloe couldn't help but hope that she never did.

Her friend would probably rate Rory a C, but only because she didn't care much about personality and was tired of dating B's. Lynsay kept mental books on her relationship deficits and freely admitted that she often ran in the red. Most of her boyfriends only lasted as long as one of the shorter Alaskan cruises that she worked in the summer, but she was a great believer in the old "try, try again" thing. Chloe didn't keep books on her failed relationships mostly because she knew they would also be awash in red ink, and her personal motto ran something like: If at first you don't succeed, have the good sense to back away before someone gets really hurt.

Rory might be a potential C, but the other two were definite A's. She had no problem with things like thinning hair, short stature, or strange hobbies. She had even dated a guy with mild halitosis who walked dogs for a living. But idiocy and cruelty were deal-breakers for her, and intuition was telling her that these two were both. Chloe was happy to learn that they were only staying for the weekend.

Much as she disliked Claude's mannerisms, it did not affect Jolly Roger's opinion of their guest. Roger was fascinated with him, and spent a good portion of the evening stropping against Claude's legs and trying to chew on his shoes.

Claude clearly disliked the cat, and Chloe suspected that MacGregor kept the feline in the dining room precisely for that reason. Roger hadn't previously been allowed in the dining room at mealtimes, but his pheromone-induced attraction to Claude was causing the lord of the keep no end of amusement, so the beast would doubtless be permitted at the table until Claude left.

Chloe would have been amused by this, but she worried about what might happen to the cat when MacGregor wasn't around. Claude didn't strike her as the sort who was kind to animals. Perhaps she would try to lure Roger into her bedroom tonight. It would also be good if the cat were too stuffed to eat anything Claude gave him, she thought, slipping another bit of salmon under the table and chucking it in Roger's direction. The cat wasn't so besotted that he couldn't spare two seconds to gobble the poached fish.

Rory was on his good behavior and remained with them for the entire evening, though Chloe suspected that it cost him a great deal of patience to be polite to all and sundry. He managed this feat of forbearance primarily by treating everyone as just more dining room furniture and being sure to keep food in his mouth. Chloe unwisely made several attempts to draw him into a discussion, but was rebuffed every time.

His conversational aloofness was straining the tentative camaraderie they had established in the graveyard. Before dinner, Chloe would have been willing to take up a sword and knight Rory for his efforts to ride herd on his erratic father. Now, if she had a sword, she would take a poke at him. And at Claude and Isaac, too, though they would be poked a good deal harder. She might not be willing to lop the head off a hapless reptile, but she'd have no problem dealing with these snakes.

The cook had gotten carried away with the thought of having guests, and dinner was an especially long and elaborate meal that evening. While they ate it was easier to overlook the lack of conversation. Once the excuse of food had been taken away, the lack of social intercourse became painfully apparent.

Chloe hoped that the gentlemen might cling to the old custom of brandy and cigars sans female company, so she could excuse herself and go to bed, but MacGregor apparently didn't want her excluded from this masculine ritual, so she was poured a healthy post-prandial brandy with rest of the guests and passed the lidded silver cigar ewer, which she—and everyone except MacGregor—declined.

Chloe eventually managed to stop fixating on Rory's silence long enough to realize that the heir-apparent wasn't the only verbal laggard. Mac-Gregor was spending more time scowling than speaking while he smoked, something he did without any trace of guilt, possibly because it annoyed everyone else and was therefore a worthy endeavor. She wasn't holding up her end of the conversation either, but as she wasn't supposed to speak of the cemetery in front of strangers—and Isaac Runyon was definitely strange—she was at something of a loss as to what to talk about. So instead of speaking, she took shuddering sips of brandy and discreetly waved MacGregor's smoke away from her face.

Isaac finally took a stab at conversation, telling them about a new vodka and cranberry drink he had heard about in a Tijuana bar, called a Bladder Infection. Then he talked about a freakishly endowed woman he had met in the same bar. Chloe wanted to change the subject but couldn't think of single graceful segue.

As though sensing her conversational quandary and guessing that she was the weakest link in the chain, Claude looked Chloe's way, and with a nasty glint in his gimlet eyes asked the question she had been dreading.

"So, what brings you to Riverview?" He looked over at Rory and added offensively, "Or should I ask?"

"She's a nature photographer," Rory answered shortly, sparing her the invention of some lie. "She's come to do some work for the fall catalog."

"Oh." Claude appeared to lose interest, and Isaac—who had never had any beyond Chloe's breasts, which he watched as though she had in fact tucked some bills into her bra—was also willing to let a heavy silence fall.

Unable to stand the strained quietude and Isaac's fixed stare, Chloe rose to her feet and walked to the sideboard to fetch another slice of chocolate torte, which she didn't really want but would help her choke back the brandy and give her a moment's respite from the smoke. "I am so looking forward to this project," she said cheerily, pausing an instant to study the skull tattooed at the base of Isaac's thick neck. It smiled every time he looked up and creased his neckline. "Sure, I've done lots of catalogs before, but never irises. I had no idea that there were so many kinds! Bearded iris, Japanese iris . . ." Chloe paused, her mind going blank as Isaac turned to face her.

"The entire family of *iridaceae*," Rory supplied

helpfully, the faintest trace of amusement warming his face. "That includes crocuses and gladiolas."

"I have irises in my cameras, did you know that?" she asked Rory with a vacuous smile. Mac-Gregor raised his napkin and coughed suddenly. She went on, "It's called an iris diaphragm. It's the metal plates that form the aperture of the lens."

"Iris was also the goddess of the rainbow," MacGregor added, finally willing to be helpful conversationally.

Chloe again glanced at the less than dynamic duo of Claude and Isaac to see how they were reacting. Claude's delicate brows had drawn together in a suspicious frown, as though he was guessing that he was being mocked, and even Isaac was showing signs of rousing from his trancelike fixation with her chest, as she remained determinedly turned from his gaze.

"And, of course, there is the pigmented portion of the eye," Chloe finished, turning up her smile another notch. "A very interesting word, iris. So close to *Irish*, which is also a popular hyphenated word."

"Irish coffee," MacGregor suggested.

"Irish stew, Irish setter, Irish wolfhound, Irish terrier . . . ," she continued, ticking a list off on her fingers as she continued to smile blandly. Her cheeks were beginning to ache, and she was feeling rather like she was in a sketch parodying *Sesame Street*. She had never attended a stranger dinner party, and prayed that she never would again. If she had just a bit more courage, she would walk out.

"Irish moss, Irish potatoes, Irish roses," Rory added, still being helpful with the botanicals.

"Don't forget the Irish Republican Army and the Irish Free State," MacGregor chimed in gleefully, enjoying the game.

"There's Irish Bull, Irishmen," she went on. "Getting up your Irish, the luck of the Irish—"

"Irish eyes! Now there's a tune!" MacGregor broke into lusty, off-key song. " *'When Irish eyes are smilin', it is like a morn in spring—'* "

Claude winced, Isaac glowered and Chloe promptly joined in singing, also deliberately off-key, and after a one beat pause so did Rory, though he managed to competently carry the tune.

" *'When Irish hearts are happy, all the world seems bright and gay . . .'* "

Claude and Isaac were looking at each other in disbelief and growing annoyance. The bulls were just bright enough to know when they were being baited. The thought made Chloe grin. Maybe they'd take the hint and go away.

" *'When Irish eyes are smilin', they will steal your heart away!'* "

Chloe was still smiling when she looked over and found Isaac had risen from his chair and was looking directly into her face. Instantly her humor died away, and her attention narrowed its focus to the man in front of her. She felt her hand tighten around her fork, gripping it like a weapon.

Danger.

Suddenly she was sweating. Those flat gray eyes with bloodshot whites were as still as a photograph. They were terrifying, soulless, utterly inhuman. If eyes truly were the windows to the soul, then Isaac Runyon had nothing in him except the cold winds of a frozen hell. These were a dead man's eyes.

Nothing had ever frightened her more, and she found herself wishing that she had paid more attention to Granny Claire's lectures about warding off evil.

"That was grand!" MacGregor said happily as he jumped to his feet and headed for the door. His cigar was left to smolder on his dessert plate. "Let's go to the music room. Chloe, I will sing you 'Danny Boy' in Gaelic. I promise, you'll have tears in your eyes by the time I'm done."

"I can't wait," she whispered, backing away from the table and Isaac. It took real effort, but Chloe pulled herself away from the horrible visual communion with Claude's companion. Once the spell was broken, she practically raced after her host, clinging to her fork though torte and brandy were gladly left behind in the smoky dining room.

She slowed to a walk once she reached the hall and put a hand on the door frame to steady herself.

She listened intently and was relieved to hear only one set of footsteps following her down the corridor to the music room. There was a murmur of voices from the dining room, and then two other sets of footsteps headed for the front door. It didn't take an Einstein to figure out the group division.

Her relief at the separation was immense and physical. Slowly her heart calmed and the perspiration on her skin began to dry. She wondered sickly if Claude had any idea of the spiritual evil of his friend. Isaac Runyon looked like a man, but every instinct within her said that she had just looked into the mind of a conscienceless demon, a killer. Shivering, Chloe hurried after MacGregor.

Rory shut the door to the music room a moment later, and he looked over at Chloe and his father. MacGregor was bent double with not quite silent laughter. Rory was holding a struggling Roger in his arms and smiling reluctantly.

Chloe could only gape at them. Apparently they hadn't sensed the evil rage inside of Isaac. Hadn't realized that danger was stalking them.

"Claude and Isaac have decided to go into town for the evening," Rory told them, turning on a lamp. "They don't want to hear you sing 'Danny Boy' in Gaelic." His words provoked a fresh burst of laughter from his father.

"If only I had known! I could have gotten rid of Claude hours ago."

"You are impossible," Rory told him. "That ghastly caterwauling was a masterpiece of musical horror. Neither one of you came anywhere near the tune."

They don't know, Chloe thought, looking from one Patrick to the other. They really hadn't perceived that they sat at the same table with a devil and broken bread with him.

"I should have thought of driving them away with music before," MacGregor said gleefully. "Claude always did hate my singing. He used to cry when he was a baby whenever I sang him a lullaby. Why, I bet the two of them pack up and leave in the morning."

"I wouldn't count on it," Rory said. "Claude never shows up without a purpose, and he hasn't gotten around to asking for anything yet."

"I know what he wants and I'll give him some money if it'll get rid of him," MacGregor promised, his good mood restored by the thought of Claude's ouster. "Chloe can't do her job with those two spying around."

"No, she can't," Rory agreed slowly. "In fact, I think that she had better come to Botanics with me in the morning, just to add some cover to the story that she's here to work on the catalog." He looked at her and added with a slight smile, "You may just as well make yourself useful there as here."

"You're just trying to pick a fight," she answered mechanically, relieved that she wouldn't be laboring alone in the cemetery while Isaac Runyon was still around. That would have been asking a lot of her nerves. "But it won't work. I actually am curious to see your gardens. You don't know it, but I am a longtime customer of yours. And I would love to photograph the gardens too."

"Too bad that I'm not working on the gardens tomorrow."

"You aren't?" she asked, not really caring.

Rory stared at her, finally sensing her distraction and beginning to question its source.

"No. I'm antiquing pots."

"Oh. Well, I'm sure that's interesting too."

"That sounds downright fascinating," MacGregor stuck in, as he seated himself at the harpsichord. His white fingers played a little trill. Either the instrument needed tuning, or MacGregor's finger placement was slightly off. "In fact, I think I'll join you. It's been a while since I came down to see your operation. You could probably benefit from a little experienced business advice before you get on with the expansion."

Rory didn't look overjoyed at his father's plans, but MacGregor was busy playing the opening chords to "Danny Boy" and didn't see his son's lack of filial gratitude.

True to his promise, MacGregor sang the ballad in Gaelic. It was more an enthusiastic performance than a precise one, and his audience was largely unappreciative of his efforts. Half of the spectators lounged in a wingback chair and feigned sleep. The other half stood beside the piano and smiled politely as she turned pages in the music book, but Chloe's disturbed mind was about twenty-seven miles away, at her grandmother's cabin.

For some reason she was thinking of Isaac as the nightmare monster she had dreamed about the night before coming to Riverview. But obviously they weren't connected. They couldn't be. The monster was just something her mind had coughed up—a stress hairball. But when intuition opened its mouth, she knew to listen. Maybe she had overreacted a little back there in the dining room, but her psyche was insisting that this guy was bad news. She would take steps to make sure that she avoided Isaac in the future. She did not want to get any closer to the beast at the back of his eyes. She didn't believe in psychic premonitions—not really. And she would probably benefit from some of the modern pharmaceuticals that helped people with paranoid delusions. But there was such a thing as feminine intuition, wasn't there? And why subject herself to his obnoxious company when she didn't have to?

Chloe tuned back in to hear MacGregor singing about the Bluesman, Robert Johnson, selling his soul at the crossroads. She shivered. The tune was a bit too apropos, given what she'd been thinking.

While I thought I was learning to live,
I have been learning how to die.
—Leonardo da Vinci

Chapter Four

Rory waited until a civilized hour to leave for Botanics headquarters. Chloe suspected that this was due to an intimate acquaintance with Mac-Gregor's lollygagging tendencies rather than to spare her an early rising or an inability on his own part to face the day until the sun was well up in the sky. Chloe hadn't consulted the family Bible but she suspected that Rory's full name was Rory Stubborn Fortitude Patrick. He could do dawn risings with a hangover and one arm tied behind his back.

She didn't complain about the delay. Her sleep the night before had been uneasy, filled with dreams of being hunted by demons where she was trying to save two people, knowing all along that she would have to let one of them fall behind or they would all perish. Perhaps her thoughts had turned to sulfurous flames because of the temperature: the day's heat had lingered into the night. Whatever the cause, she was glad for the chance to eat a decent breakfast and pour a little caffeine jump-start into her sluggish system. Though not usually a large breakfast consumer, she nevertheless ate and drank with the steadfast devotion of one who was aware that her host was likely to get interested in something and decide that lunch was an unnecessary luxury.

The only danger to lingering at the table was a possible encounter with Claude and Isaac over the English muffins. But apparently neither of the men was a child of the morning, either, particularly when they had tied several on the night before, a likelihood which was safely gleaned from past behavior if not actually seen in this instance, or so she gathered from MacGregor's acerbic stray comments. To Chloe, this seemed to be a case of the pot calling the kettle black—or sometimes worse things, if she understood MacGregor's mumblings—but as she was growing fond of her employer, and he did pay the bills, she refrained from saying anything about his own bloodshot eyes and lack of appetite.

Patrick's Botanics was only a ten-minute ride from the main house. It was an impressive operation whose hothouses spanned five acres. It was large, modern and efficient, yet it managed to retain the same air of sumptuous comfort that pervaded the rest of Riverview. Perhaps it was the strains of Puccini's *La Boheme* throbbing on the gentle breezes produced by silent fans inside the immense hothouses—constructed, of course, in the overwrought Victorian manner that made their architecture more ornate than a wedding cake—that gave this impression of pampered wealth.

"*Ah!* Those Italians!" MacGregor beamed approvingly, beginning to look more chipper. "They have the best marbles, the best footwear and the best operas."

Chloe shook her head as she looked around, but it wasn't in disagreement. The outsides of the buildings might have been frivolous, but the interiors were not. There were massive tracks of grow-lights, clinically clean, stainless steel tables, and high-tech office chairs. Medical labs would envy this setup. Financial security was an amazing thing. There wasn't a shoestring *anything* in sight. These had to be the most pampered plants and employees on the planet, and she wished that Roland Lachaise could be there to see it. This was a level of work comfort to which she would like to become accustomed.

It was soon obvious that Rory had been in earnest when he said that he was antiquing pots that morning. There were pallets of them stacked chest high, just waiting for attention. After he, his father and Chloe had all donned white lab coats, gloves and paper shoe covers, he explained the process that his visibly nervous assistant was using to achieve an aged look. It was a simple but slimy one. Plain yogurt mixed with a thin gelatin was painted onto the outside of an earthenware pot, and then a hank of moss—in this case it was gray-green *asprella*—was shaken over it, planting thousands of nearly invisible moss spores into the goo. The pots were then placed in a cool, damp, and shady location while nature took its course.

Rory took pity on his fidgeting assistant, and removed MacGregor from the young man's orbit as soon as the explanation was complete. MacGregor did have a tendency to loom and make disquieting remarks regardless of who was at hand. Perhaps he forgot that the people who worked there were actual thinking beings and not just biological furniture to be arranged to his convenience.

Rory took them next to a backroom overhung with layers of shade cloth and showed them pots that were two days along, and others that were a week old. The pots that were only forty-eight hours into the process simply looked blotchy and diseased, but the week old spores embedded in the yogurt had transformed into a satisfactorily mossy covering. There were several species of moss whose names she didn't catch that were kept on hand for those who had pH problems in their yard caused by certain trees. According to Rory, there was a mossed pot for every location.

"And they'll stay like this as long as they are

kept wet, out of direct sun, and away from hostile plants of the *quercus* family. Most of these species can't survive near any of the beeches. Of course, a drop in the pH and many mosses come down with chlorosis and die," Rory said absently, as he consulted a chart hanging at eye level on a nearby support post. "But even that can add an aged flavor to the right garden style."

Chloe, at last recognizing a name, was about to ask if that prohibition of *quercus* included the local species of oak trees, but MacGregor finally had something to say and wasn't waiting for her to voice her questions about the effect of oak leaves on moss.

"Well, I'll be!" The man smiled, hefting a pot. It was the first time she'd seen Rory's malicious grin on his father's face. It made her uneasy. "What a wheeze. Do folks really buy these pots thinkin' they're antiques?"

Rory frowned and looked up from his notes.

"Of course not. It states clearly in the catalogue that mossed pots '*give the appearance of age*,' but that—"

"Nobody reads the fine print," MacGregor said, waving a dismissing hand. "People don't read at all. Congratulations, boy! I didn't think you had it in you. This explains why your little company is doing so well."

Rory's brow lowered at this insult, and Chloe hurriedly stepped into the conversational breach before return shots were fired. She tactfully redirected the discussion back to mosses; she didn't want the afternoon spoiled with verbal warfare between the lions, and Rory was beginning to look thunderous.

After a thoughtful look from the younger of the titans, who apparently sized her up and decided that her interference was well-intentioned and therefore pardonable, the trio moved on with their tour of the hothouse. The unpleasantness was soon forgotten. Rory was in his element there among the flora, and could speak at length without fear of contradiction by his father.

He cheerfully introduced them to a new species of moss just imported from Borneo, *Chaelomitrium weberi*, with which he was experimenting in the hopes of finding some commercial application—after it had been quarantined long enough to be certain that it was harboring no imported Borneo bugs which would be harmful to the environment. Great caution had to be used so that no alien species were released into nature.

"Looks like green spider's web," MacGregor said.

Rory nodded fondly. "Only a lot more aggressive, given the proper conditions. They can grow like wildfire. Put them in our growing medium and you can have what looks like a month's accumulation of moss in only two days."

MacGregor, quickly losing interest, grunted and moved along.

Rory didn't notice his father's inattentiveness.

Waxing rhapsodic on his favorite subject, he finally showed them his collection of prized Spanish mosses. Chloe peered obediently at the gray strands. But seeing that MacGregor's eyes were beginning to glaze over again, she moved the tour along.

The aquatic plants in the next building proved more entertaining, for they were still in flower and looked wonderfully tranquil and mysterious floating on the dark pools of water. The piped-in serenade had moved on to the first duet in *Lakmé*, and Chloe nearly groaned with pleasure.

Rory politely demurred when she asked to photograph his aquatic gardens, but once he was convinced that she was in earnest about this desire and not merely being courteous, he volunteered to show her the remaining hothouses personally, and to serve as her photographic assistant. He even unbent so far as to ask her advice about the selections to be featured in the fall catalogue.

Chloe answered happily explaining why some plants would photograph especially well. If Rory liked her work he might actually want to hire her to come take beautiful pictures in this temperature-controlled paradise, which was infinitely more appealing than the hot, tick-infested, overgrown cemeteries in which she had recently been spending so much time.

MacGregor followed, either curious about his son's business or desirous of orchestrating any quarrels that sprang up between his offspring and his co-opted employee. But the morning was disappointingly harmonious as Rory and Chloe found that they had *"two minds with but a single thought and two hearts that beat as one"* on the subject of aquatic plants, and the appropriate operas to insure optimal growth. Verdi and Rossini both got high marks for inducing photosynthesis. Common watercress and Wagner were rejected as being too plebian and heavy to waste time on photographically or aurally. Chloe even suggested that Rory sell CDs of the nurseries' favorite operas, an idea that he seemed inclined to favor.

Eventually a bored and fidgeting MacGregor decided that he had other things to do. He abjured Rory to bring Chloe back personally before the afternoon was too advanced. Rory assured his father that he would have Chloe home in time to change for dinner, and cheerfully waved his parent out the hothouse door.

"It isn't that I don't like his company. Sometimes," he condescended to explain a few minutes later. "But he makes the kids nervous. And I can't have that while they are cultivating spores. Unfortunately, he isn't terribly interested in plants—not even moss."

This was the most human Rory had ever been.

"I noticed that your assistant was upset, though I can't imagine why. I personally love to work with a lion breathing down my neck. It gives one an adrenaline boost and makes one feel alert."

Chloe didn't comment on the return of moss to their conversation. She liked green stuff as much as the next person, but couldn't get passionate about it.

"Doesn't his stomping all over your sentences and assuming you are up to no good make you nervous?" Rory asked. "Most people are terrified of him."

"Your father doesn't assume I'm up to no good. He doesn't really assume that your assistant is up to no good. It is only that he questions—"

"Without any cause!" Rory interrupted swiftly, as though she, too, had questioned his honor, or perhaps his masculinity.

"He only does it to needle you. Anyway, you stomp on as many of my sentences as he does."

Rory eyed her, but didn't say anything about her observation. They wisely went back to photographing water lilies, and managed to spend an entirely enjoyable afternoon in each other's company.

They were packing away Chloe's cameras when Rory broached the subject of her visit with an abruptness that, while characteristic of the Patricks, was a vast change from the aimless pleasantness of their earlier conversations.

"You don't really think there is any danger to the cemetery, do you?" he asked bluntly.

"Yes," she said simply. "I do. At least potentially."

"But those monuments are *huge*. You'd need a crane to get them out," he argued. "They aren't like paintings or even regular sculpture that someone could just carry away in the trunks of their cars."

"Not all of them would need a crane. Anyway, these thieves are smart and inventive. There was one statue taken out of a cemetery right in the middle of New Orleans that weighed seven hundred pounds. It disappeared in the middle of the day. The police still don't know how the thieves managed it."

Rory stared at her. She knew he was thinking hard, but couldn't guess precisely what about. It seemed likely that part of what he was cogitating over was an attempt to believe that people could actually do something so distasteful as steal from the dead. She didn't truly understand the thieves' brains, but still made an effort to explain the indefensible crime so he would take the threat seriously.

"Grave-robbing is probably the world's third oldest profession. I know that this is a repugnant thought to contemplate, but thieves steal when there is something of value and little risk. Cemeteries are good economics. They are in Egypt and South America, and now here. Tastes change, but grave goods are always popular. This year, the flavor is early American." She paused, but Rory said nothing, so she tried again.

"The New Orleans police recovered a million dollars' worth of stolen grave goods last year. And they reckon that is only about ten percent of the *known* missing monuments in that area. That is just one city. Savannah, Williamsburg, Boston—they've all been hit. And, Rory, the stuff that was taken isn't a patch on the humblest tombstone in your family's cemetery. That isn't a graveyard; it's the Louvre and British Museum combined. If Riverview is ever discovered by thieves, you'll have to hire armed guards and patrol it around the clock. Maybe put in a security system and get some guard dogs. These thieves aren't amateurs, and some innocent people have already gotten hurt trying to stop them . . . I'm sorry," she added. "I know that isn't what you wanted to hear."

Rory blinked and ended his inner communion. He smiled ruefully.

"No, that is certainly not what I wanted to hear. But I am already looking at a system for the house. They can give me an estimate for the entire property while they're at it. I don't know if motion censors will work though, given the wildlife."

"But it's just the cemetery you need to guard. I know the expense of electronics and guards would be—"

"It isn't that," he said, hoisting her bags with casual ease. "It's MacGregor I'm worried about. I don't think he would permit guards in the cemetery proper. And if he ever gets it into his head that someone has actually been anywhere near his precious graveyard, *he'll* start patrolling on his own. And then we'll end up with someone dead—probably a teenager looking for a quiet spot to enjoy a stolen beer and some necking with his girlfriend."

"I see." And she could. No second Sight was required to predict a tragedy if MacGregor did start policing the grounds.

"Look." Rory started for the door without meeting her eyes. "I'm not suggesting that you lie to MacGregor . . ."

"But?"

"But there's no need to tell him all the statistics, is there? And if you see any evidence of trespassing, you can come tell me first and I'll take care of it."

Chloe didn't even hesitate. The choice between confiding in an obsessed—perhaps even crazy— old man with a heart condition and his sane, responsible son was an easy one to make. Under the circumstances, even Roland would understand her decision. Really, she *was* looking out for her employer's best interests.

"Sure. I'll tell you first."

Rory looked back and gave a relieved smile.

"We'd better go."

Dinner that night was another long affair. Claude and Isaac were looking unusually shifty-eyed as they gobbled their food, causing MacGregor to glare suspiciously and comment nastily about freeloaders, when he spoke at all. The tone of the baiting suggested that Claude was in need of a large sum of money. Again. And, in spite of his words the night before, MacGregor was no longer inclined to bail his nephew out on this occasion.

In spite of her earlier hunger, Chloe now had no appetite. The spiritual miasma that clung to Isaac Runyon made her feel ill. Conscious of her obligations to be a good guest, she made an effort to start a conversation or two, but had so little success that she excused herself before the cigar and brandy course and fled to her room.

It wasn't that she had any dislike of fine food and drink, but even an excellent VSOP and a mountain of chocolate couldn't reconcile her to another minute spent in such obnoxious—and evil—company. She wished with all her heart that MacGregor would send the pair away. She did not understand how he and Rory could fail to perceive the malevolence that was in their midst. They made her so nervous that she could barely keep still.

What she truly would like to have done was cuff Rory for bailing out on the culinary ritual torture and leaving her alone, but there had been a frantic call from the nursery just before dinner about some new hybrids cocking up their rootlets and keeling over in their perlite beds, and like a surgeon or priest, he had gone racing back to Botanics to give aid and comfort to the dying stems.

Chloe had offered at the time to go back with him and perform last rites, but had been rebuffed. Kindly, but firmly. She knew why too. She was supposed to go stand in the breach and keep Claude from annoying his uncle into a coronary.

She scowled. The Patricks were making a habit of using her in a non-professional capacity, and while she didn't mind some of it, she was tired of being a human shield. It wasn't fair of her to blame Rory more than MacGregor for the situation, but she saw it as a case of diminished capacity. MacGregor was old and couldn't help being like he was. Rory, she hoped, knew better. Claude was *his* cousin—that made him Rory's problem, not hers.

The flight reflex died once she had a closed door between her and the rising tempest of the dining room. For a moment, Chloe toyed with going back to the nursery anyway and offering Rory some company while he attempted resuscitation of the rootlets, but she was tired and feeling miffed, and opted for a book and bed and a mild case of guilt instead.

But once between the sheets, Chloe found her mind feeling overshadowed by the weight of history, wandering back over the other Patricks who had lived in the house before MacGregor and Rory. Her reading of the previous day had shown that they were people with large families, large bank accounts, and large peculiar ambitions. They hadn't feared life, or death. Indeed, they had planned for both—and with more attention than they had paid to other, more common goals.

Given the family's age and wealth, there should have been Patrick statesmen and Supreme Court justices, captains of industry, *fame* to go with the fortune. But there weren't.

She got up and began to pace.

The plantation itself had managed the miraculous feat of avoiding the attentions of the twentieth century tourist industry that had been born with the creation of the automobile. This was mainly due to the careful screens provided for the never-ending Patrick wealth, accumulated by some unspecified means—she was voting for piracy or something else disreputable since the family records were so coy on the subject.

Chloe frowned. It was all so very odd. She had never encountered anything like it on her other projects. It wasn't just that the Patricks had spent a king's ransom in acquiring, perhaps illegally, statuary by the great artists of Europe; most great families from the pharaohs to the Tudors had done the same. But they had chosen that their immortality be achieved in funerary art that would never be seen by the wider world, and that suggested a familial arrogance that bordered on the pathological. Was that possible? Could this be a form of inherited obsession? And if it were a mental illness, then maybe they *were* conscienceless enough to be pirates. The Tidewater region had certainly seen a good deal of illicit trade in earlier times.

The theory sounded pretty far-fetched, but she

more than anyone knew that certain families could inherit . . . gifts. Tendencies.

She'd had a vision in the back of her mind when Roland first spoke of sending her to Virginia. Riverview would be like some of the other places she had worked in Georgia and South Carolina, antebellum mansions with wide porticos hemmed in with old oaks twisted with nutgall, surrounded by feral lilacs, festooned with spanish moss— spanish *pineapples*, she corrected, the thought of Rory's lecture about the wondrous non-moss easing the stern lines of her face. Places that were preserved, but not lived in. Or perhaps something like Williamsburg, which was inhabited by actors rather than real people.

But Riverview wasn't like that. It was more like Brigadoon, or some other magical place where time stood still. The twenty-first century might knock at the gates, but no admittance was being granted.

She wished that she might have met some of the previous owners. It would be like seeing a unicorn or a fairy. MacGregor Patrick came from some original stock. Perhaps if they brought in a spiritual medium . . . ?

The half-joking thought made her suddenly uneasy. MacGregor was already talking to ghosts. He didn't need to be encouraged down this path—and Rory would probably strangle her if she brought it up.

Her eyes wandered over to the painting by the dresser. She had noticed it before. It was a peculiar thing, and vaguely familiar in an unpleasant way. Almost modern in flavor, like some of the art done by fantasy and science fiction artists, though she couldn't imagine that it was. She leaned forward and squinted at the brass plate screwed to the frame:

The Death of Rebellious Absalom
Richard Dadd 1857

Chloe shivered and backed toward the bed, suddenly questioning the wisdom of her own desire for a little mental *séance* with the Patrick dead. They must have been a very strange family, collecting not just funerary art, but stuff like this painting. Dadd had been a nineteenth-century painter of immense talent who just happened to see fairies and hear spirit voices, which on one occasion sent him home to cut his father's throat. Judged to be insane, he had been confined to Bedlam and then Broadmoor where he happily went on with his artistic, spiritually guided career.

She wasn't sure of the exact date of his incarceration, but it was in the first half of the nineteenth century. To have acquired a painting in 1857, someone would have had to journey to Broadmoor Prison and commission the work. Supposedly all his artwork of that era belonged exclusively to Broadmoor, but it wasn't amazing that some wealthy Patrick had managed to get a painting anyway.

What *was* amazing was that they wanted one at all.

She stared at the tiny face of anguished David. It was mirrored in the face of the rebellious dead son and the stunted, stubby-limbed angels that surrounded them. They had nasty smiles that reminded her of Isaac.

In spite of the lingering heat, Chloe felt suddenly chilled. Those weren't angels that gathered over David! Of course not, Dadd didn't see angels. The creatures were imps. Malevolent, staring imps waiting to torment and torture their victim.

"Ugh!"

Going back to the painting, she lifted the canvas down from the wall and carried it across the room. It took a moment to shove her clothes aside, but she found the perfect storage place at the back of her wardrobe.

The door closed with a solid thump and she made sure the latch was securely closed. As an added measure of caution, she dragged a chair in front of the armoire. She didn't mind being near the dead and their attendant grisly reminders of human mortality out in the cemeteries, but she didn't want them following her to bed and pursuing her in dreams.

She stood for a moment, staring at the blocked door and belatedly debating the wisdom—and politeness—of shoving a valuable work of art into a cupboard. Chloe decided she didn't care about offending MacGregor or Rory. There was no way that she would be able to sleep with those dwarf demons staring at her. She would just explain to MacGregor in the morning where the picture was, so that no one would be alarmed at its disappearance.

Her heart was still thundering when she climbed back into bed. It was more than a little annoying to discover that she was actually nervous about sleeping under a particular work of art. It was crazy, but apparently superstitious fear was a virus inside her, latent until Riverview—-and maybe memories of Granny Claire—had brought it out. First there had been bad dreams, then a deep, unexplainable fear and loathing of Isaac Runyon, and now this squeamishness about a piece of art. She could only hope that this sensitivity didn't spill over into a distaste for cemeteries, because it would make things difficult if she started getting the whim-whams every time she stepped into a graveyard. Tombstones were the bread and butter of her work, at least for now. They weren't catapulting her to the top of the photographic world, but she was doing all right for having taken the road less traveled.

Shaking off her unease, Chloe reached for the pile of paperbacks on the bedside table. She hesitated a moment over her selection. She had started a mystery, but after her uneasy dreams the nights before, she decided that a romance might be in order. She wanted something soothing and uncomplicated, where the good guy always won. She took up the new Lisa Cach and started reading.

Though feeling keyed-up, sleep came upon her quickly after midnight passed. Her weary eyes closed against the lamplight and the paperback slipped from her nerveless hands.

He brought the shovel down with all his might, sinking the blade deep into the earth and shattering what he hoped were old tree roots and not a desiccated skeleton. This one was difficult, so much harder than the other, and he was growing tired. The failing darkness was bleeding the energy out of his muscles and bones. He feared that he would not have the strength to burrow all the way to hell, which was where this one belonged, dead or not.

Bringing Runyon to Riverview had been a bad mistake—a fatal misjudgment. The man had been greedy and wanted to take what wasn't his. He hadn't understood that there were some things that could never be permitted. To ask for money was one thing. Or perhaps to take a painting or some silver. But what he had wanted was impossible, and once he knew the secret, there was nothing for it but to get rid of him.

It was a shame that he'd used the shotgun. The stinking blood and bits of tissue were dripping into the ground. It would ruin the earth forever. But that was why he couldn't take the bits and pieces to the sacred place and hide them there. It would profane it— unsanctify the soil and disturb the ones who slept there.

He paused for a moment, breathing hard as he rested on the shovel. His ears were ringing. Maybe it was from the shotgun blast, but he kept thinking that he heard the sound of glass breaking over and over again. It was terrible. He wished it would stop.

But really, the glass was nothing—just a thing. It didn't matter, because no one would understand it. Nothing mattered except finishing his task. He had to put the wicked one back into the ground and then leave before it grew light. After a while, he'd forget. Many times he had done things for his father, his uncle, and for the rest of the family. He always managed. He would triumph this time too. And no one would ever know about his mistake except the ghosts, and they were righteous spirits who would never bear witness against him.

Trapped inside another nightmare, Chloe whimpered and twitched as shovels of dry earth rained down on her. She was bleeding to death from a horrible wound and wanted to scream for help, but was afraid that if she opened her mouth it would be filled with soil and she would choke on clots of grave dirt. Soon she was too weak to scream or move. And in a few minutes the air ran out and then there was nothing.

*Murder is a mistake—one should never
do anything one cannot talk about after dinner.*
—Oscar Wilde

Chapter Five

"If you are calling for the corpse of MacGregor Patrick, he's over here," a familiar but unusually grim voice said.

Chloe ventured further into the darkened library and saw a well-known pair of large, grubby work boots protruding from under the desk. Rory Patrick stood over his horizontal father, broad hands planted on narrow hips. MacGregor was snoring softly, but other than the gentle whistle passing between his parted lips, he might have been posing for an effigy to grace his sarcophagus—supposing he decided to have a decorated sarcophagus as well as a pyramid, which seemed a nearly inevitable conclusion given his heritage and outsized ego.

"What happened?" she asked, curious but unalarmed since Rory was so calm. Frankly, she felt worse than MacGregor looked.

"He had a duel with Misters Beam, Walker, and Daniels. I think he won, but it must have been a close contest."

Chloe walked around the desk and saw the dead soldiers lying on the floor. She whistled softly and nudged an empty whisky bottle with her toe.

"I haven't seen anyone in a *ménage a quatre* with Jimmy, Johnny and Jack since college—and they had to use a stomach pump to save the poor fool who tried it. Alcohol poisoning. Those bottles weren't all full, were they? Should we call for an ambulance or something?"

"No way." Rory smiled nastily and, mirroring her own action, nudged MacGregor with the tip of his loafer. He wasn't as gentle. "A stomach pumping might spoil a really prime hangover, and some doctor would likely give the old sot some pain pills for his head. No, this time I'm going to let him suffer through the aftermath without medical interference."

"I suppose he *will* have a really bad hangover. Maybe—"

"Bad as the day after a hurricane, if there's any justice in the world. It may be just the thing to cure him of this binge drinking. Nothing Doc Emerson, Morag, or I can say seems to make any difference." Rory forgot himself and actually sounded concerned. "This is probably Claude's doing. I bet he tried to get MacGregor drunk enough to cough up the twenty grand he needs. MacGregor is the soul of generosity, but absolutely hates being hounded for money."

As though recognizing his name, MacGregor snorted loudly, rolled his head, and then resumed his soft snores. His color was rosy rather than gray, but Chloe was still worried. Even with Claude's help, if the bottles had been full, there could be enough booze inside this old man with his weak heart to kill two males half his age.

"Do you want some help getting him to bed before you leave?" she asked finally, deciding that this was Rory's call to make. He was in the best position to judge what MacGregor needed.

"Bed?"

"Rory!" she scolded, genuinely shocked. "You aren't going to leave him on the floor, are you?"

"I suppose not. Morag might fuss about vacuuming around him. And *she* might call the doctor." Rory leaned down and grasped MacGregor by the front of his flannel shirt. He hauled him more or less upright. Some dead oak leaves and a few sprigs of crushed mint floated to the floor. Rory dusted his parent off with his free hand, muttering: "I wonder what the hell he was doing last night. He changed before dinner, didn't he?"

"Yes, I think so." Chloe answered with a twinge of guilt. She wasn't terribly certain what MacGregor had been wearing at dinner last night, having spent the meal staring at her plate, but she was fairly sure it hadn't been red and black buffalo plaid flannel. And certainly he had not been covered in pungent mint and oak leaves.

"Well, never mind." Rory grunted as he heaved MacGregor over his shoulder and then straightened from a squat.

Chloe was impressed with the physical display. There was nothing effete about the muscles that decorated Rory's lean body. MacGregor must have weighed around two hundred pounds, and that was two hundred pounds of flaccid flesh, which made the swift lift even more amazing.

"Let me get the door," she volunteered.

"Thanks." Rory paused before leaving the room. "Look, I don't think MacGregor's going to be up for any work in the cemetery today."

"I wouldn't think so!"

"Why don't you take the morning off? Get some rest. You look beat. Later, after Claude and Isaac leave, I'll come out to the cemetery and lend you a hand. It's only fair after your help yesterday."

"There's no need for you to come," she assured him, noticing that his face was a little flushed. "I can manage on my own. Anyway, why wait? Aren't Claude and Isaac gone already? They weren't at second breakfast."

She was learning the routine. A second meal was prepared at ten o'clock when MacGregor had houseguests. Wise houseguests showed up for it because they were unlikely to get lunch,

MacGregor preferring to drink that meal more days than not.

"They weren't?" Rory shifted. His father had to be getting heavy. "Well, I'll check on that. If they *are* gone and not just sleeping it off, we can go out whenever you want."

"Okay. I'll just straighten up in here a little," she offered, trying to assuage her vague feelings of guilt about MacGregor's condition. It was not her job to be his keeper; all the same, she had walked out on a man of whom she was rather fond and left him to wander into temptation.

And though it was wrong of him to have expected it of her, she felt that she had let Rory down too. That was probably why she had been having such terrible nightmares.

Rory grunted and then disappeared through the door. He didn't climb the stairs quickly, but he didn't pause to rest either. Chloe decided that it wasn't just the familial ego that was fed on raw meat and megavitamins; the Patricks had hard bodies to go with their hard heads.

Chloe gathered up the empty bottles and put them in the wastebasket. There were several dead leaves on the carpet and some clots of reddish mud, but for some reason the thought of touching them bothered her, so she left them for Morag, or whoever would be in to vacuum. All that was left to see order restored was to stack a few scattered papers and put them back on the desk. She worked slowly, turning them all right side up and placing them in neat piles with squared corners, and Rory was back before she was done.

Before she could ask about MacGregor, Rory said: "I guess you're right about Claude and Isaac. The guest rooms are empty. The beds are made up and everything, and I can't see Claude's car from the upstairs window. I suppose they took off real early. Maybe MacGregor paid off the whelp and then decided to drown his sorrows."

Rory looked thoughtfully at his father's newly tidied desk. A ledger and checkbook were sitting in plain sight.

"Good. I shouldn't say that, I know, but anything to get them out of here is fine with me!" Chloe nudged a gaping desk drawer shut. "Let me grab my camera bags and we can get started. I—"

The phone rang sharply, cutting her off mid-word. Even the Patrick's possessions were guilty of interrupting her, she thought, feeling more than a little cranky.

"Here." Rory opened the desk drawer she had just shut and extracted the giant cemetery key. He didn't hesitate to hand it over, a gesture of trust that she appreciated. "Take this and get started. I'll be along when I can."

The phone rang again. Rory went to lift the receiver, and then, noticing the dirt on his fingers of his right hand, reached into his pocket for a handkerchief.

"Okay. See you soo—" The phone, of course, did not let her finish.

"Fine. . . . *Hello?*" Rory didn't bark, but his greeting was far from convivial. Perhaps he didn't have a great deal of experience answering telephones. Probably Morag did that too.

Or maybe he had too much experience. Perhaps he handled his catalogue orders and—but no! He wouldn't be that rude to customers. Probably he was still worried and exasperated about MacGregor's latest drinking spree, and that was making him short-tempered. In any event, it wasn't any of her business, and she wasn't going to eavesdrop on a private call.

Chloe saluted with her right fist as she left the room, then noticed that her hand was also dirty. She peered at her fingers in the gloomy light. Something brown and sticky was all over the old iron key, and unlike the Patricks, she didn't carry a ready handkerchief. It looked like she and the Patrick funeral regalia would both need a wash-up before she handled her cameras.

Rory was off the phone by the time she staggered downstairs, burdened with the full complement of her high-tech tools. He was looking through the check register and frowning as she came through the door, but he put it aside as soon as she entered the room and came over to help her with her equipment. She gave him the freshly washed key.

"Where to? The slave cemetery is partially cleared now if you'd like to take a look."

"I'll wait for the guys to finish up in there. There's plenty to do in the family plot yet. The light's good, so I think we'll start with one-oh-four in the gothics."

"One-oh-four?" He was smiling, but it wasn't his usual malicious grin. In spite of his annoyance with MacGregor and Claude, some of the previous day's understanding and stored goodwill flourished between them.

"The chess set. Um . . . Adair and Eilidh," she translated, showing him the clipboard that had the gridded map. "It'll be too dark to work over there in the afternoon. I prefer to use natural light as much as possible. Flashes tend to flatten the image and—"

"*Mmmrreeeoow.*" A gentle paw tapped at her legs. As soon as Chloe looked down, Roger frisked over to the exterior doors and started pawing at the paned glass. It was a polite order to hurry.

"I think he wants out," Chloe said inanely. "Maybe he knows that I'm going to the cemetery. He seems to really like it there."

"Be patient, you stupid beast," Rory scolded. "We're coming. The idiot probably thinks Claude is out there somewhere. I caught him up in Claude's room, digging through the pillows and burrowing into the sheets. I had to shut the door to keep him out. I'll have to tell Morag to change the sheets first thing or he'll tear them to shreds. I'll catch up in a second."

Chloe grimaced at the impatient feline. "Usually cats are more discriminating in their tastes."

"They also eat mice and lizards," he reminded her. "They aren't *that* discriminating."

The sky, once sought, was found to be almost painfully blue, but there were some cottony clouds hanging around in the southern firmament that suggested afternoon rain, Chloe thought pessimistically. And worse, there wasn't a breath of air stirring in the leaves overhead or in the clumps of cinquefoil that clung to the shady patches beneath the sycamore tree. Hot, humid, and airless—three of her least favorite working conditions. Still, she didn't complain. After all, she could be hot, humid, and airless in a Florida swamp with alligators circling her.

The plushy decay of humus under the trees gave off a thick, sleepy smell when they disturbed it with the deeply patterned soles of their work boots, and even the avian warblers singing in the hedge sounded lethargic. The birdsong stuttered to a complete halt once she and the cat were inside the prickly cleft and brushing the vines with her wide load of canvas totes. The cautious birds didn't resume until the human and cat had escaped into the oak clearing on the far side.

Curious about their progress, Chloe made a slight detour toward the slave cemetery to see how the boys were getting on. The dried oak leaves crunched underfoot in an appealing manner and soon drew Roger's erratic attention. He came frisking over to investigate.

Her feet slowed to a stop. Suddenly and unexplainably apprehensive, Chloe waited just outside the cemetery enclosure to see if any ghosts would come. She held her breath for a count of ten, but none were stirring on that hot morning. If any spirits lingered here, they had apparently been mown down with the saplings and brambles, if they had ever had the nerve to rise up in the first place. What was left behind was a sad plot that had a certain dignity, if not the beauty, in common with the family's grander sepulchers.

Though there were no spirits about, Chloe still hesitated to enter the half-cleared cemetery. Something about it felt familiar and vaguely terrifying. She looked about slowly, noting that the grieving dogwoods had given in and dropped their blossoms on the humble graves during the night, and even the mighty oaks looked forlorn.

Whatever her qualms, they did not affect the cat. He apparently wasn't put off by the skinny crosses sticking up like ancient, pathetic ribs out of the matted earth, but went straight over to the south corner where discarded brambles were tossed carelessly into a heap, and began to dig. Chloe squinted and thought she saw evidence of disturbed earth beneath the brambles and perhaps a headstone lying flat on the ground. The boys had probably had to quarry the brambles out by the roots, possibly upsetting one of the markers. She really should go in and set it back upright, but she didn't know where the marker belonged and—

And she didn't want to. The thought of venturing into the cemetery was raising gooseflesh on her arms and making her feel queasy. It was ridiculous, but she couldn't force herself inside the fenced enclosure.

The newly opened ground theory was proven true, while Chloe stood at the gate, dithering. Roger had slipped under the vines and taken up furious excavation in the loose soil by the prickly canes. So intent was he that he was in danger of getting his fat tail tangled in the dying brambles. Chloe warned him to stop, but she was—as always—ignored.

"Roger, come out right now or I will come in and get you!" she threatened. But it was a bluff. She didn't want to go inside the cemetery to fetch him.

The cat began to turn in circles and then hunched down close to the ground.

Assuming he was obeying an urgent call from nature, Chloe politely averted her eyes and stepped back a pace, calling out again to the cat to come away, though she had little hopes of being attended since Roger would see nothing sacrilegious about what he was doing and was as stubborn as all the other Patricks. She continued to walk backwards from the cat's privy excavations with eyes averted, halting only when she sensed Rory behind her.

"Any ghosts out today?" he asked, echoing her earlier notion.

"Not a one," she said with forced cheer, even though it was eerie how he guessed her thoughts. "The boys have been busy digging up those brambles. I guess the roots went down deep. One of the markers has gone over. It isn't a cross or a regular stela with a deep subterranean post. At least, I don't think it is."

Rory looked past her.

"I wonder why they did that. It would be better to use a defoliant and then burn it." Rory snorted. "Will you look at that cat?"

Chloe lifted her eyes and saw Roger rolling ecstatically in the rich soil. She was relieved that was all he was doing.

"You'd think it was fresh catnip in there, not grave dirt."

As though understanding her amused words, Roger froze, let out a tremendous sneeze and jumped to his feet. He spun about once, his hackles raised in an alarming manner, and he went streaking past them toward the family plots. He was hissing at an invisible enemy inside the graveyard.

A phrase from an old malediction popped into Chloe's head:

I do feel beneath my feet the licks of hellfire.

For one odd moment, Chloe found that her mouth was dry and her muscles were tensed as though she, too, was preparing for flight from the tiny graveyard. She turned to face Rory, trying to determine if he felt that anything was amiss.

"What's wrong?" he asked her instead. "Are you feeling all right?"

"Yes," she lied, swallowing a couple times in an effort to relieve her parched throat. The sight of her companion helped. He had rolled back his sleeves and unbuttoned his shirt. He looked like the answer to a lover's dream—provided that the lover was dreaming of a half-naked chest dusted in red-gold curls. It was enough to jump-start her salivary glands and give her overstimulated imagination something else to chew on. "I guess the heat is still a shock. I must be acclimatizing more slowly than usual."

That was a weak excuse. The weather in Virginia wasn't that different from Georgia.

"You look like you've seen a ghost." The glance that passed over her was far from lover-like and adoring, though there was a certain sympathy in it. "Or some facsimile thereof."

"No ghosts." She forced herself to smile. "Maybe it was just the cat walking over those sorry graves. Or that awful Dadd painting in my room. I've put it away in the closet," she confessed.

Rory looked at her for another moment.

"Emotional sensibilities must be a liability in this line of work," he said, turning away and starting back for the family cemetery. He lowered his voice and quoted: *"There must be an end to all temporal things . . . They are entombed in the urns and sepulchers of mortality.'"*

This game she could play.

"Bracketing yourself in pretty high company, aren't you? Though I'll give you the fact that the Patricks' tombs nearly rival some of the Plantagents' lesser monuments."

Rory looked back over his shoulder and smiled pleasantly. "You recognized the quotation."

"Of course. By now, I've heard every quotable remark, ballad, and poem there is about cemeteries."

"That sounds like a challenge . . . I know!" Rory laughed and began humming under his breath.

Chloe joined in, singing softly and on key:

Cold blows the wind to my true love,
And gently drops the rain,
I never had but one sweetheart,
And in the greenwood she lies slain . . .

"'The Unquiet Grave.' You're really being morbid this morning," she told him, as he shoved aside the covering vines from the old gate and thrust the key into the lock. "If we are going to quote the famous on death then my vote is for Keats's epitaph—*'Here lies one whose name was writ on water.'* Your dad mentioned it the first day I was here. I always thought it so sad. Keats was only in his twenties when—"

"Damn." Rory pulled out his ready handkerchief and scrubbed at his hands. He then bent down and rubbed the lock with the stained linen. "There's gunk all over this thing. Dad must have come visiting last night and slopped booze all over. Watch out for the ants down here. They're having quite a party with the leavings."

Chloe looked down and saw that ants were indeed swarming over a large patch of dark soil. It reminded her of something . . . maybe a dream? She'd been having some real doozies lately. She didn't recall what she'd been dreaming about last night, but she'd woken up once, bathed in sweat and nearly certain the echoes of a scream and gunshots were reverberating in the damp air. But the noise, had it escaped her lips, must not have reached beyond her bedroom, because no one came pounding on the door to see what was wrong with her.

"I didn't know they liked whisky," she said, frowning.

"It might be some sweet liqueur. Keep an eye out for more bottles. He was probably too drunk to care about littering."

"Could he have really had anything else to drink?" she asked in alarm. "Seriously, Rory, you can die of alcohol poisoning. Maybe we should go back to the house."

"Relax. He was coming around when I put him to bed. As I expected, Claude did something to enrage him. The sot will be fine in a few hours. He always is." Rory's posture was as eloquent regarding his mood as any words. Chloe stared a moment at the stiff back and decided to drop the subject in favor of continuing harmony.

"Okay—what are you doing?"

"Hang on a second," Rory said, reaching into his shirt pocket and pulling out a small bottle of foul-looking liquid. He turned and waved it at her. There was an evil glint in his eye.

Chloe inspected the yellow oil with misgiving.

"Why? What is that?"

"Insurance of the homemade variety. It's an extract of citronella . . . and a few other things." Rory uncapped it and began smearing the stuff on the exposed portion of his chest.

She watched appreciatively as he ran quick hands over his torso and bare legs, but backed up a step as he advanced toward her and she caught a whiff of the pungent, ammoniac odor.

"No thanks," she said. "That smells like an outhouse."

"Hold still," he ordered, reaching for her arm. "I'll do you since you need to keep your hands clean."

"No, really. I have my own repellant—" But he didn't listen. So, rather than attempt an undignified escape that might damage her equipment, Chloe stood reasonably still while he ran efficient and impersonal hands over her legs, arms and the back of her neck. She pretended that she didn't enjoy it.

"I know it stinks," he said sympathetically, kneeling at her feet for a last pass over her calves. "But it's better than battling ticks and chiggers."

"Only marginally," she muttered at the top of his head.

His face turned up, lit with one his rare, charming smiles.

"All done," he said, rising to his feet and returning the nasty bottle to his shirt pocket. "You'll thank me for this."

"Don't hold your breath."

They found the chess set without trouble, and Rory proved a capable hand with setting up the reflectors. He had several questions about her digital camera. It was a Nikon F3 equipped with a Kodak 1.3 mega-pixel sensor. She had heard a rumor that they planned on marketing digital cameras to the home market soon, but couldn't imagine the average person bearing the expense when regular cameras were so much less expensive.

The monument was dusted over with golden pollen and assorted lichens, which made a colorful contrast to the rim of tiny stringed forget-me-nots that bordered it. The flowers grew weak and lanky in the deep shade, having only a few minutes of direct sun very early in the morning, but they still added a note of woodland charm.

The opportunistic clematis and honeysuckle hadn't engulfed the site yet, though they would certainly do so by the end of the season if no one cut them back.

Some tombs demanded awed whispers, but not this one. It was less a mausoleum than a macabre theme-park attraction. Only the fact that it had been hand-sculpted by a highly trained artisan elevated it beyond the army of plaster gnomes that flanked Riverview's drive. Chloe found that she was disappointed not to find any of Lewis Carroll's characters immortalized on the board. The whole cemetery was like a trip through the looking glass—indeed, so was all of Riverview.

She paused before shooting her first frame, again struck by a sensation of déjà vu, only this time it was identifiable. The tomb reminded her of an illustration in a book she had at home. It was a drawing of the exchange that Alice had shared with the White King when she complained about seeing nobody in the road. And the king had answered back that he wished he had such good eyesight: *"To be able to see nobody! And at such a distance too! Why, it's as much as I can do see real people, by this light."*

She shivered suddenly as the charmed feeling left her. *Able to see nobody by this light.* The words ricocheted inside her head, leaving her momentarily dizzied.

No, that was silly. She didn't believe in ghosts and goblins and things that went bump in the night. No rational person did. Except Granny Claire—and the soundness of her mental state was debatable.

Chloe began taking pictures. She worked carefully. Though the august Patrick dead were not hanging around the gloomy cemetery giving verbal instructions—or even psychic ones—they still managed to make their presence felt, directing her through the living Patricks to do a thorough job. This was probably the pressure she felt at the back of her mind.

"That's a wrap on the front shot," she said firmly. "I'm supposed to mark each grave with the GPS, but I'll do it later." She didn't explain why she was putting this task off. Her thoughts and vague worries about what she was doing weren't advanced enough to be shared, but she was having some second thoughts about the advisability of adding this cemetery to any database.

"Okay. What next?" Rory asked.

They moved on to 103 as soon as they were done at 104. It was not located directly beside the chess set but rather at a forty-five degree angle to the north. Chloe had learned that there were certain consistent axial orientations in all the great funerary monuments of the world, organizing them into neat patterns by the external synchronization of outside forces—usually the sun, moon or celestial constellations. But no such consistency was at work in the Patricks' bone yard. There were spirals and lines and zigzags of path darting all over the sanctified acres.

"I'm learning your tastes. You'll like this one," Rory said with a smile. "It's extremely whimsical."

"Oh!" Chloe breathed happily, finally having found her *Alice* figure. One hundred and three was actually an Etruscan goddess, but a young one. She was seated in an undignified huddle, her face appropriately sad under her *polos* crown, her skirt kited up at the knees in a childishly careless manner. A small plaque read:

> *Under this grave grazed on by sheep*
> *Lies an angel fast asleep.*

Beside the goddess was a stylized feline keeping guard that might have been a twin for the Lion of Amphipolis. She would have suspected that the lichen-covered beast was the original, but the fourth century statue had only been restored in 1937, and this grave was clearly marked nineteenth century.

Catriona Patrick. She had died before the Civil War.

They worked quickly, as the air was beginning to thicken and had taken on an ozone smell that suggested that a lightning storm was coming. What light there was under the canopy had become liquid, surreal, and Chloe wanted to take advantage of its unusual visual effects.

Rory checked his watch but didn't complain when she pushed her way deeper into the honeysuckle to get to tomb 102. He seemed to be genuinely interested in the technical side of what she was doing, and impressed with her thoroughness. Chloe didn't explain that she was being unusually thorough for personal rather than professional reasons.

Again, Chloe was delighted with the view of the monument when some of the vines were pulled away. The next statue was a mere three feet tall, nearly buried in honeysuckle, but it was an exquisite thing, a sleeping Eros, wings folded, head resting on a tiny quiver filled with golden arrows.

Here lies Deirdre Patrick
An envious Venus struck her down

"I don't believe it," she said in a hollow voice. "That's real gold, isn't it?"

Rory smiled wryly.

"Believe it. Deirdre had a gold fetish, which her husband indulged to the very end."

"Where is he?" she asked, looking about for the generous and eccentric husband who had provided genuine golden arrows for his wife's tomb, and then consulted her clipboard when no likely grave was found nearby.

"Gregory's over in the front section . . . with his first wife and their children."

"Oh."

"It wasn't his choice. His heirs made the arrangements. I'll point him out on the way back." Rory sniffed the air and looked up at the tree canopy. It was a useless gesture. Nothing could be seen of the sky. "I think we better get started. It's going to rain soon. Hard."

"Okay." Chloe took him at his word and worked quickly to get her shots. She had Rory hold a remote flash pointing at the glorious little arrows. She wouldn't put that shot in the official database, but she wanted one in which the beautiful eccentricity was featured. She was anxious to see the results in print. The peculiar light made the ancient stone appear to the eye like living flesh. Not human flesh exactly—it was too pale, too gray and waxy—but still it seemed organic rather than mineral. She prayed that the unique quirk of tone was preserved on film.

They packed up quickly after shooting Eros, as a damp wind began wending its way through the graveyard. It was strong enough to shake old leaves out of the trees and make the vines whisper eerily. It didn't surprise her when Rory started humming "Texas Flood."

They walked out by a different path so that Chloe could see Gregory's tomb. She noted on the way that Roger had been obliging enough to drag his moplike tail over the door of the first tomb she had photographed and cleared out the old cobwebs. The cat continued to strop at the mausoleum threshold as they walked by, ignoring them in favor of rubbing his face on the old wood and the remains of dusty webs that littered the sill.

"I think I'm going to need to get inside forty-six to finish the job," she said, pointing at the cat. "There are some statues inside the monument as well, aren't there?"

Rory hesitated.

"I doubt it. If there are, we'll have to get the keys

from MacGregor later. They're kept on a separate ring. We'll need to get a list, too, of where everything is. I used to play out here, but I haven't been inside the mausoleums in years and don't recall where everything is placed."

"Is there much art inside the tombs?" she asked, suppressing a shiver. She couldn't imagine *playing* in the mausoleums, though to a child who did not understand what death was, they might just seem like a city of eccentric playhouses and forts.

"Only the larger ones, like this. It was modeled after the entrance to the hypogeum of the necropolis of Crocifisso di Tufo," Rory said, demonstrating a greater acquaintance with the cemetery's history than she had supposed he had.

They paused to look at the pitched roof and the scene beneath of the slaughter of a Caledonian boar. On the side, there was another goddess atop a sea monster that looked for all the world like a carousel horse with a coiled serpent where its regular tail should be. The sea-goddess wasn't smiling and neither was her mount. All in all, it was not a warm and welcoming sort of tomb.

"I think I would have liked Dierdre better."

"So did Gregory. Wife number one was something of a dragon. French. Temperamental."

Chloe looked at the bronze plaque:

Madelaine Patrick (1822–1863)
We can say no more in truth
or we shall speak ill of the dead

"They all seemed to die so young," she said softly.

"The women did. The men, unless they met with the wrong end of a gun or knife, usually lived long, hedonistic lives."

"Oh, lucky you."

"There are worse things," he admitted, smiling. "We'd better go. We're about to have an ocean up-ended on our heads."

As though to emphasize the point, there was a flicker of bright light to the south that penetrated even the leafy bower. It was followed a few seconds later by the bass rumble of thunder.

Chloe shifted her bags higher up on her shoulders and started quickly for the gate. She wanted to wash the stinky yellow oil off, but in a bathtub, not the great outdoors.

"Roger! Where are you?" Rory shouted with a note of vexation. "It'll serve him right if he gets stuck in here for the duration of the storm."

But in contrast to his annoyed words, Rory headed back in the direction of tomb forty-six to retrieve the stubborn cat.

"I'll meet you back at the house," Rory called over his shoulder. "If you leave now you may beat the rain."

Chloe's answer was indistinct, but Rory saw her wave.

He backtracked quickly to tomb forty-six where he had seen the cat. Roger was still there and still pawing at the tomb door. Rory plucked a besotted Roger from the mausoleum's step and added him to the accumulation of bags slung over his chest and shoulders. The ungrateful cat complained bitterly about being taken away from the stone house.

"What? Did you hear something in there? A nice big cockroach? Well, it's your imagination. All the cockroaches in there are dead. You will simply have to make do with kibble for today. Or maybe Oleander has saved you some fish."

Roger glared at him and wrinkled his nose. He sneezed delicately.

"*Mmmmrrreeeooowww.*"

"Yeah, I know I smell bad. Chloe didn't like it either. Just be glad that the vet gives you those drops every month or you'd have to use something like this too."

The cat grumbled once, but settled down.

"Uh-oh." Rory held up a flat hand. Droplets covered it immediately. He hurried toward the gate.

Roger's renewed complaints about the falling water were more emphatic and involved a bit of claw.

"You can hide in my shirt if you can stand the smell," Rory offered the moaning cat, while struggling to secure the gate's lock.

"Let me do that." A pair of feminine hands took the key from him and turned it in the lock until the tumbler clicked.

Surprised, Rory stepped back a pace.

"You didn't have to wait for us."

"No problem. Digital Memories is a complete-service company."

Rory studied Chloe's face as she pulled the vines back into place. It was studded with tiny silver drops and her shirt was very wet. The water-logged cotton was clinging like a second skin, showing the details of her undergarments. He was not surprised to learn that she favored plain cotton over lace.

"I didn't think we were paying you that much."

"You aren't. But it's okay. The bags are waterproof and I don't melt," she said cheerfully, returning the cemetery key to him. She rubbed her hand against her damp shorts, leaving a tiny brown smear. "You know, it's inconvenient having it rain like this, but it's broken the heat, and it'll wash the dust off the graves. I should be able to get some great shots when it stops."

Rory stared at the smudge on her shorts. It appeared to be a lot like the ones on his handkerchief, except that the water had turned it red and made it look an awful lot like thinned blood instead of whisky-drenched dirt.

He looked down at the patch of darker earth that had been abandoned by the ants. The water was leaching the blemish away, but the twelve-inch oblong was still visible as a reddish stain.

He hadn't noticed any cuts on MacGregor's hands or arms while putting him to bed, but he decided that he would give his dad a look-over when they got back to the house. The old man would kick up a fuss, but it had been years since his last tetanus shot. If he had so much as a scratch on him, the doctor was coming straight out to give him an injection.

In any event, it was time they talked about his midnight outing. Rory wanted to know just what MacGregor had been doing and what he had seen while wandering about last night. He hoped that his father hadn't been spying on him again. His constant checking up was annoying. Rory knew how to handle their business, and his private life was *private*.

"Come on," Rory said. "I owe you a meal and a brandy."

"Thanks." Chloe smiled easily. "I could use both. It's actually a little bit chilly."

Rory glanced once at her sopping shirt, but wisely made no comment. They were finally getting along, and he didn't want to upset the new harmony with the woman who could prove a valuable ally. And perhaps something more.

There are four kinds of homicide; felonious, excusable, justifiable, and praiseworthy.
—*Ambrose Bierce*

Chapter Six

The wild threnody of the storm continued through the night and into the next morning. Chloe knew that she wouldn't get any work done that day, but nevertheless rose dutifully to make first breakfast, since with Claude gone there wasn't likely to be a second sitting.

She found MacGregor and Rory already seated at the table. MacGregor wasn't eating, preferring to inhale the steam rising from his coffee and perhaps divine meaning in the fragrant clouds that floated there. The news from the spirit world that morning couldn't have been good; he looked far too grim and weary.

Chloe glanced at Rory's dark face and then checked the chandelier above the table. The overhead lights were on, but the atmosphere in the parlor was so thick with gloom that she felt she was personally wading through the sticky black morass of MacGregor's lingering hangover.

Rory managed a preoccupied smile and word of greeting as she headed for the sideboard, but MacGregor, chin on chest, never broke his rapt communion with his pained, inner self. Apparently, he really did have the mother of all hangovers since he was still suffering thirty-six hours after the offense. Chloe made an effort to walk softly and not rattle the dishes.

"Are you going into work today?" she asked Rory, more to make conversation than out of any real curiosity. She kept her voice soft and low.

"I'll have to," Rory said unhappily. "We had a break-in."

"Last night?" She turned and stared. The previous night fell into that category of not being "*a fit night out for man nor beast.*" It didn't seem a likely time for a burglary at the back end of nowhere.

"Or perhaps the night before." Rory shrugged. "It was in the outbuilding where we keep the mossed pots. Everything is on timers. No one has been out there since the day you visited."

"Is it very bad?" she asked sympathetically. For Rory, having his business robbed would be as bad—and maybe worse—than having his home invaded.

"There was apparently a bit of vandalism. I'll know more when I've been in." Rory looked at his father. His expression was strange and she couldn't guess at its meaning.

"Oh no! I'm so sorry." Even as Chloe sympathized with the news, half of her brain was on MacGregor. No wonder Rory was staring. MacGregor didn't react at all to the revelation that someone had invaded Patrick property. Perhaps he was already aware of it and had ranted himself out, but such calm acceptance coming so quickly was out of character. It would have been more normal for him to be blustering and waving a shotgun, demanding that the sheriff make an immediate arrest.

"But it was only pots that were damaged?" Chloe asked carefully, wondering if Rory was holding back worse details so as to not upset his father. She took a muffin and returned to the table. Her own appetite wasn't at its best that morning. Storms often left her feeling stupid and sluggish, and today she was feeling especially mollusk-brained and unable to read the underlying emotional currents that eddied about the table. Maybe the ozone in the air was jamming her brain waves.

"Just pots," he said reassuringly, but his eyes again flicked over his father's slumped form. "It was probably some kids messing around. I'd have let it go, but the sheriff's already been called out and is taking all the employees' fingerprints. A little later, he'll come by here and—"

"I don't want that busybody here," MacGregor said, rousing himself from his stupor. He raised his head to glare at them with sunset-colored eyes. Chloe was shocked at how haggard he looked. The sybaritic, bluff MacGregor had aged a decade overnight and looked on the verge of the coronary Rory had been worrying about.

"But he must take your and Chloe's prints so that he can eliminate—"

"Fine. But we'll go to the gardens with you. I don't want strangers on the property right now."

"As you like," Rory said quickly, also noticing his father's drawn appearance. "But we'll need to go soon, or Bell will come calling."

"I'll set the dogs on him," MacGregor snarled, showing more of his usual spirit.

"We don't have any dogs," Rory said witheringly, also reverting to form. Chloe found the bickering a change for the better, but still didn't enjoy it.

"Why the hell not?" MacGregor demanded. "We used to have dogs!"

Chloe sighed softly and pushed away her barely touched muffin. *Patricks!* They made everything so hard! She couldn't fathom why she liked them.

"Let's get this over with," she said, rising. Knowing that she risked being rebuffed, she still went over to MacGregor's chair and offered him a companionable hand.

He stared blankly for a moment and then took her outstretched palm. He squeezed the fingers lightly and then let go. She could feel Rory's eyes on them.

"Don't worry, girl. I'm fine. No need for fussin'." MacGregor shoved back his chair and rose with something like his normal vigor. He marched for the door. "Just couldn't sleep last night with all that damned thunderin'. And when I did sleep I had bad dreams."

"*I could be bounded in a nutshell and still count myself the king of infinite space, were it not for the fact that I dream.*" Wasn't that what Shakespeare had said? Chloe couldn't stop a small shiver from coursing down her body.

"It was a real loud storm," she agreed tactfully to MacGregor's back. "You don't usually get them this early in the season, do you?"

"Not often." MacGregor clomped toward the hall. "Made Roger nervous too. The bloody fool howled his head off all night long. I finally had to shut him up in one of the guest bedrooms."

"Claude's room?" Rory asked, opening the front door, and a wave of damp air rolled in. The rain fell steadily, but already the temperature was beginning to climb.

"Yes." MacGregor paused to look at his son. "I believe it was."

Chloe had the impression that Rory intended to say something else about either the cat or Claude, but changed his mind at the last moment.

"Wait on the porch and I'll fetch the van," he told them. "No point in you two getting wet."

Rory sprinted off into the rain before they could answer.

It took Rory a moment to pull the van around to the portico, and it gave him time to think. He'd been in a sort of shock since Dave had called and told him about discovering the break-in. Often an entire week would pass without anyone going into those outbuildings. It was simply bad luck that one of Rory's newest employees had discovered the break-in before he did and had called the sheriff.

Suspecting what he did about the identity of the clumsy culprit, he wasn't thrilled that nosy Sheriff Bell had been called out to investigate. It was unlikely that the incompetent lawman would discover anything about the break-in, but one never knew when he might actually stumble onto some uncomfortable fact or another. And anytime Claude was in the area, the possibility of there being some uncomfortable facts to discover grew immensely.

There hadn't been any mention of blood at the scene, but it wouldn't be surprising if there were. It would have been a logical place for MacGregor to cut himself—if he was in fact the one who had broken in. There were other likely parties with as good a motive. Claude might be stupid enough to look for cash out at the greenhouses. Hell, Claude would do it out of sheer meanness.

But Claude was gone. It couldn't have been him. Not if the break-in happened last night.

"Damn." Rory didn't know what to think. MacGregor had flatly refused to let himself be examined for wounds, saying he was unhurt. He claimed that he had drawn a complete blank about the night of his bender—which was possible, of course, but Rory didn't believe him. Mac-Gregor had drunk himself blind on several occasions since his wife's death and had always been able to cheerfully recall every drunken peccadillo. It was more likely that MacGregor had seen or heard or done something upsetting and used whisky as a palliative after the fact.

The burning question, of course, was just what his father had witnessed that so upset him. Rory could think of one thing, and he prayed it wasn't what MacGregor was drinking over.

On the other hand, this vandalism wasn't Mac-Gregor's usual style. He had never attacked the nursery. Truly, Rory had thought that MacGregor was actually proud of what his son had built. Proud that his son wasn't some dilettante leech living off the family money.

But, of course, this only led straight back to the subject of leeches. . . .

If Claude hadn't gone from the scene on Monday morning, Rory would have suspected him of being the perpetrator of this midnight high jinx. It was definitely Claude's style: petty and stupid. But if Claude and Isaac had been up half the night raising hell at the local tavern, they would never have been able to pull themselves out of bed at dawn and head out to perpetrate more mischief.

And, of course, they couldn't have done anything later, not after they were gone. And they were gone. As MacGregor had pointed out, the sheriff would have heard if Claude were still in the area. He wasn't popular in town.

No, it seemed most likely that MacGregor had had a blow-up with Claude and made it plain that he wasn't giving him any money—at least not twenty thousand dollars. Nothing was missing from the checking account and MacGregor didn't keep that much cash at the house. And then, feeling mean and angry that his son hadn't been there to deal with Claude after he had promised to be home for dinner, MacGregor had tied one on and gone up to the nursery to smash some things. That's where he'd cut his arm, or maybe his leg, and bled on the cemetery key he always kept in his pocket. Then on the way back home, he had gotten to feeling guilty about what he'd done and had gone into the graveyard to talk to Rory's mom and receive forgiveness, leaving some of his blood behind.

It was all very understandable, if you knew MacGregor. But there was no way on God's green earth that Rory was going to explain this possibility to that gossipmonger, Sheriff Acton Bell. The only thing to do was to get rid of him as immediately as possible before he came around making more trouble at Riverview and accidentally found something. More than ever, he didn't want Bell near the cemetery. There was too much uncovered at present to allow anyone in. And Bell would make trouble for them out of sheer, jealous spite:

The envious boy who had gone to school with Rory hadn't outgrown his hatred of the gentry.

Rory pulled up to the porte cochere and leaned over to open the passenger door. Chloe Smith was standing beside his father, watching him with obvious concern and puzzlement in those beautiful blueberry eyes.

Their bright little photographer was yet another unknown commodity. She was observant, curious and smart as paint. He wondered how long it would take her to put things together, and what she might do when she figured out at least part of what was going on. She'd try to salvage MacGregor, most likely. Try to make him see the error of his ways.

It was in their favor, he thought coolly, that she felt protective of MacGregor. As long as she believed silence to be in his best interest, she would not talk to the sheriff about anything she turned up.

Chloe was shocked at how much the vines that lined the road had grown in the space of a day. She knew that scientific study had shown that plants grew forty percent faster during a rain event. And in some cases, with heat and an aggressive species the numbers probably went up even higher. But in the space of just two days, the honeysuckle and creeper had grown out onto the road far enough that they were flattening it with the van's tires as they drove by. They might have been driving into an equatorial jungle rather than a commercial nursery in Virginia. If this kept up, the Munsons would have to work full time shearing back the new growth in the cemetery so she could get her photos. Perhaps it was time to bring in some power tools——if MacGregor would permit them in the silent sanctuary.

The two Patricks were quiet during the ride, and didn't make comment even when they arrived at Botanics and had a brief look at the small pane of glass that had been broken in the greenhouse door so someone could unfasten the bolt. Chloe didn't stop to examine the damage. She was more interested in getting out of the damp, enervating air, and into the gentle moving breeze of the climate-controlled greenhouse.

A small man with a birdlike gait came hopping over to greet them as they stepped inside the hothouse. He was in uniform and wore a star which proclaimed him sheriff. He was followed by a small cloud of gnats.

"Mornin', Mr. Patrick. Mornin', Rory." The bright little eyes finally fastened on her. The man's ratlike face didn't go well with the beautiful strains of *La Traviata* that filled the room. "And you must be Miss Chloe."

"How do you do?" she muttered conventionally, when MacGregor failed to answer and Rory wandered away to look at the damage to the yogurt-dipped terra-cotta.

The little man stuck his paw out. It was far from clean and the gesture seemed aggressive, a test of some sort. She didn't want to accept his grimed digits, but good manners triumphed and she offered her own hand for a brief shake.

The sheriff clasped her fingers tight and wrung them like he was squeezing lemonade from a thick rind. Fortunately, he darted off after Rory before her joints cracked or she was called upon to make any further conversation. The gnats, fortunately, went with him.

"Officious bastard," MacGregor muttered, his brows beetling in an alarming manner.

"That may be so, but for goodness's sake, be polite," Chloe pleaded. "I want to get out of here as quickly as possible."

MacGregor blinked as though only just recalling her presence.

"Of course, you do, girl. *Bell!*" MacGregor raised his voice. "Come get your prints from Miss Chloe and me. We haven't got all day."

"Certainly. Ellis, James," Bell shouted at the deputies across the room. He waved irritably at the gnats. "Come take some sample prints from Mister Patrick and Miss Chloe."

Deputy Ellis was beanpole thin and a collection of jutting elbow and knee joints that flexed oddly when he walked, but he was efficient at taking their prints and didn't bother them with a lot of idle chatter. While the deputy went about his work, Chloe watched the sheriff talking with Rory. He reminded her of a yapping terrier, circling around a larger animal and just looking for the right place to get in a nip.

The sheriff was as brown as a walnut, and after a few minutes of listening to his conversation, Chloe was convinced that he was about as dumb as one too. He did ask a number of questions of them, but they were largely unrelated to the break-in, and she could see why MacGregor called him a busybody. The creature was a gossip of the highest degree and obviously collecting material to share with the coffee-shop crowd. Under other circumstances—like, if this were happening to someone she disliked—she would find the lawman amusing. But she was too caught up with the Patricks and their precious cemetery to find the sheriff anything but annoying.

Chloe wondered which of Rory's employees had summoned the sheriff; ten minutes in the same room with Rory and Bell had her certain that most of Rory's staff would never have called the inquisitive oldster to investigate the trespass and minor vandalism without permission. A couple of pots had been knocked over. If there hadn't been a tiny bit of blood spattered on the broken glass of the door, there wouldn't be anything to investigate. She was convinced that the exercise of taking everyone's prints was just that—an exercise meant to annoy, and to demonstrate the sheriff's power. There wouldn't be any usable prints left on the rough, mossy pots.

"The Creator must love idiots," MacGregor muttered at her side. "He makes so many of them."

Chloe coughed into her hand. Then, seeing the ink stains on her fingertips, she dug in her bag for a sanitary wipe. It wasn't her favorite product packaging to flash in mixed company, but she knew from experience with bleeding pens in shirt pockets that it would get the ink off.

"Here." She handed the smudgy towelette to MacGregor after hiding the wrapper.

She stepped closer to the deputies, attempting to overhear their conversation.

"So they had his pants down and his groin taped before you could say Hail Mary." The one called James dug at his ear with his little finger.

"Poor Tom," Ellis answered. Then he turned her way. Both men stared.

"Your friend plays football?" Chloe guessed, disappointed that they weren't talking about the break-in.

"Hell, no. He's an accountant," James answered. He looked her up and down, his finger still in his ear. The look stopped just short of being offensive, but Chloe couldn't take it as a compliment. He wasn't looking at her as though sizing up a criminal but rather as if trying to decide if she would look good in a wet T-shirt contest or at a monster truck rally.

"An accountant? Well, it's a more dangerous field than I'd guess."

Ellis answered: "He does sometimes play golf."

MacGregor joined them.

"Let's go. Rory, are you through? Chloe and I are leaving." MacGregor swiped at his hands in an ineffectual manner and then gave the used paper back to her. Chloe sighed and crumpled it up in her hand.

Rory looked up. Chloe could see him making some quick mental calculations. Guessing his cause for concern, she said: "I'll drive."

"Thanks." He came over and handed her the keys. He glanced at his father, then added: "I'll be back as soon as I can."

She stared at him.

"Is there any great rush?" she asked, and watched a brief stain crawl over his cheeks. She thought this was anger and not embarrassment, and felt more baffled than ever. This situation was annoying, but not worth genuine rage.

"No, of course not. I was just thinking that you might need a hand with the equipment today if . . ." He trailed off as a particularly fearsome squall began pounding on the roof with watery fists. "Guess not. Okay, I'll stay here for a while then and get this sorted out. If this storm clears up, I'll come back and lend you a hand with the cameras."

Chloe was aware of Sheriff Bell's busy eyes and pricking ears. She kept her face calm and blank and didn't ask any questions.

"The gardens will shoot better when the sun is

out and everything is dry," she said pointedly. "I don't think I'll do any work today."

Rory flushed again. The poor man was plainly more upset about the break-in than he was letting on, or he wouldn't have made a near slip about her real task in front of the sheriff.

"You're the boss. I leave the technical decisions to you."

"Good plan," she said, heading for the door. MacGregor was already in the van and twitching with impatience.

"Everything will be fine here, girl," he muttered as she got in. "Damned nosy bastards. But Rory will get rid of them. He knows what he has to do. It's family first, last and always."

The sun did come out that afternoon, evaporating the puddles left by the rain. Chloe waited for Rory for an hour or so, but neither he nor the Munson brothers came to the house. She began to be concerned that other vandalism had been discovered out at the nursery, and debated the wisdom of taking the van back to Botanics to find Rory.

Chloe went back and forth over the idea for another half hour, then the allure of the millions of little sparking water jewels glittering in the sun got the better of her. To hell with Botanics! It wasn't her problem and obviously she wasn't wanted.

It was too wet for the computer, but she grabbed

her 35mm and digital camera and headed outdoors to explore the gardens. She discovered almost immediately that the Patricks kept statues in
their pleasure gardens. They weren't the works of
art that graced the cemetery, but they had a certain
charm. There was one particularly genial rendition
of a Saint Francis up on a pedestal preaching to a
variety of oversized stone critters. His crumbling
robes were streaked with black, and he had a piece
of dripping green moss hanging from the end of
his beaky nose—a sight which surprised a giggle
from her. She looked about guiltily to see if she
was observed in her irreverence, then allowed herself the one vulgar shot of the cement saint before
scrubbing the green booger away.

She wandered happily through the roses and
late-blooming lilacs, but soon found her feet on
the path to the family cemetery. On her own time
and film, she wasn't even tempted by the slaves'
sad graveyard, but wandered immediately toward
the family vaults and the beautiful treasures there.
It was an Eden for a student of the arts and she
knew that she would never see so many treasures
amassed in one place again.

As she had half expected, the gate was standing
open beneath the honeysuckle shroud that had
grown in during the storm. MacGregor was in
there somewhere, communing with the dead. On
a hunch, she headed for Nancy's grave, and found
her employer sitting on the bench in the small
granite library. His red shirt was as conspicuous

as a hot-air balloon among the graveyard's watery grays and greens.

He looked a little better than he had at breakfast, but he was still far from his usual chipper self.

"Hello, girl," he greeted her. "Have you come to see my Nancy?"

"Among others. It's turned out to be a beautiful day, hasn't it?" She didn't make any comment about his choosing to sit on a damp bench under a dripping tree.

"That it has. Have you seen Roger about? The damned cat went off an hour ago and hasn't come back."

"I'll look for him. I think I know where he is," Chloe said, thinking of the cat's bizarre predilection for tomb forty-six. Cats were supposed to be able to see ghosts. Could there be one there?

"Usually I keep the gates locked," MacGregor said, running a finger along a stony spine and then over the shelf as though checking for dust on the stone books. "Too many people coming and going annoy the dead, you know."

"I'm sorry—," she began stiffly.

"Not you, girl. They don't mind you at all. No, I was speaking of the others."

"*Others?* You mean the Munsons. But you must have help keeping back the vines," she said gently. "You and Rory couldn't do it alone. Not without power tools and those would be so smelly and noisy."

"I don't know but what we shouldn't let the

whole place grow over. It would be safe then. In a few months, maybe a year, no one would ever be able to find it. Rory could open it back up when I die." He added abruptly: "I been thinking about it, and I've decided that I would like to be here with my Nancy instead of in my own tomb."

Chloe blinked at this announced change of heart. MacGregor was giving up his notion of a pyramid? He had to be feeling really low.

"You know why they invented mausoleums, girl? It was for the mourners who couldn't stand the thought of an earth burial for their loved ones. There is something very final—very cold—about the sound of dirt hitting a coffin lid. Who could do that to someone they loved? Or even their own family. You might want to put an enemy in the dirt, but your own blood?" MacGregor shook his head and added with a faint air of returning pride, "We don't have cenotaphs here either. We always bring our dead home. Always. Love 'em or hate 'em. If they're family. we bring 'em home."

Chloe grew alarmed. MacGregor really was in a morbid mood. She hoped that he didn't binge real often. Remorse on the morning after could also bring on a heart attack.

"Nonsense." Chloe took a seat beside MacGregor, wincing at the wet that immediately invaded her jeans. It was an impertinence, but she again took his hand into her own. "I know you're worried about someone discovering this place. But I don't think it will happen. The Munson boys are trustworthy. You know Rory wouldn't have them here if they weren't. And I swear to you—by everything I hold dear—that I will never tell a soul about this place and how special it is."

"I believe you, girl," he said, reversing their grip and patting her hand. He looked unbelievably sad and weary. "And I know that Rory will always do what is needed to keep this place safe. He is my son, after all. I just wish that . . ."

"That?"

"That we agreed more. That I knew what was in his mind. That we were more alike. Sometimes I can't guess what it is in his head and it makes me a little bit afraid of him. Nancy knew him better. She was a lot younger than me and always wanted children. I think maybe I left it too late to marry and start a family. If we'd had more time, Rory would have siblings to share the burden with. Nancy wasn't supposed to die so soon, and . . . Well, I don't know my own son and there's no point in denying it."

Chloe snorted and replied bracingly, "You're alike. Believe me, anyone can tell that Rory's your son."

"You think so? People used to comment on the similarity. He has my eyes and hair, you know," he added with a flash of pride.

"And your build. And your stubbornness. And your intelligence. So what's eating you? Are you . . ." Chloe hunted for a polite euphemism and couldn't find one. Anyway, she was too tired to bother being polite. "Are you concerned that jerk, Claude, might come back and do something bad?"

"No." The denial was immediate and firm. MacGregor smiled humorlessly. "Claude will never tell anyone anything about this place. That I am certain of. We don't need to worry about him." MacGregor's voice lowered. "No, he won't be saying a damned thing to anyone—ever."

"Well, good. Then we have nothing to worry about." Chloe wasn't as certain as MacGregor that Claude could be trusted, but she wasn't about to say so. And MacGregor was too upset to hear her suspicions about who had broken into Botanics.

Maybe it was time to start thinking about taking some greater security measures to allay MacGregor's fear. She would talk to Rory as soon as she could. He was right to be worried about his father's fascination with the cemetery; MacGregor's preoccupation with maintaining the graveyard's privacy at any cost was a TV docudrama just waiting to happen. Yes, MacGregor Patrick's veneer of modernity was thin. Rub it the wrong way and a ruthless pirate was likely to come through. And pirates were no respecters of society's laws. After seeing him around Sheriff Bell, Chloe had no trouble imagining him unloading a barrelful of buckshot into some innocent trespasser because the schmuck was showing disrespect for the Patrick dead. She was also less convinced than MacGregor that Claude would never say anything about the cemetery.

Chloe sat, squeezing MacGregor's hand and wondering how Rory had escaped the Patrick preoccupation with death and found his way into the world of computers and fax machines. She'd stretched the truth about Rory a little bit to comfort MacGregor. Rory wasn't a complete carbon copy of his father. Perhaps it was his mother's doing. Maybe she had been firmly grounded in twentieth-century principles of law and order, and had a love for the modern conveniences.

Of course, electronic trappings didn't guarantee that a man wasn't a pirate beneath the skin. What did she know about Rory, really? He'd been pretty ruthless when dealing with MacGregor's night of excess. And you didn't run a successful large company by being a marshmallow.

"You like my son, don't you?" MacGregor asked, as though picking up her thoughts. "You two have some things in common."

"A few. But don't go getting any wild ideas. We wouldn't suit."

MacGregor looked skeptical.

"I mean it, MacGregor. Lots of people like opera and flowers. You can't read anything into that."

"Well, now! Actually I can," he said, smiling happily for the first time in days. "But I won't trouble you with my thoughts since it makes you so skittish. You just run along, girl, and find Roger if you can. I'll be back to the house soon and we'll have some tea."

Tea? Probably with a shot of something alcoholic in it.

"Okay," she agreed, deciding against further warnings about his romantic fantasy. It was more important to cheer him up than to insist upon veracity. And time would take care of this ridiculous notion. She and Rory falling for one another? No, that wasn't in the cards.

Roger was where she expected, rolling and clawing at the door to tomb forty-six. He was looking a little greasy and bedraggled from his orgy of rolling. The summer rains had caused a new crop of moss or lichen to sprout on the stone sill, and the feline had covered himself in the slimy stuff.

"Yuck!" She held the cat away from her body as she inspected his limp form. Even his whiskers were sticky and he smelled a bit sour. "You're wanted back at the house, buster, but you're not getting inside until you're toweled off."

Roger moaned pathetically.

"Well, you should have thought of that before you went and got all dirty. What's with tomb forty-six anyway? It isn't the nicest one. In fact, it's damned gloomy." Her footsteps creaked over the discarded oak leaves. The desiccated remains were too wet to crackle. "Why don't you play in your own yard? There's a nice big bed of catnip right by the porch."

Roger began to purr. Chloe relented and tucked him into her shoulder. Her shirt needed washing anyway and she found the cat's weight to be pleasant and reassuring even if he smelled a little vinegary.

"Okay. I'll be your human litter-bearer—but just this once! I usually have cameras to carry."

She wasn't terribly surprised when Rory met her at the gate. He had obviously seen his father, as he had the cemetery key in his hand.

"I guess we need to be extra careful about locking up with vandals in the area," she said, shifting the cat so his claws weren't resting directly over her jugular vein.

"Hm."

The reply was absentminded and not terribly encouraging, but Chloe persisted anyway: "I was talking to your dad. I get the impression that he is worried—I mean, *more* worried—about someone finding the cemetery. He's talking about letting the whole thing grow over."

"It might not be a bad idea," Rory said, shocking her.

"What? But you can't!"

"Not until you're done, of course. But after? It might be best. MacGregor's been spending far too much time out here. It's morbid. He needs some other occupation. He has to let Mom go."

Part of Chloe knew that Rory was right, but she protested anyway.

"Occupation like what? *Bingo? The Rotary Club?*"

Really she was protesting the loss of all that beautiful art as much as MacGregor's forced separation from his beloved cemetery, which was self-ish, but she couldn't help herself.

"Why not? Other people do it when they lose a spouse," Rory said defensively. "He can learn to have other interests."

"Get real . . . Or better yet, get married and have some grandkids. That would really please him."

Rory snorted. "You get real. I have a business to run. I can't have kids just to entertain my father."

"Why the sneer? 'Other people do it. You can learn to have other interests'," she mimicked. Then, more seriously: "Really, Rory, you can't blame him for wanting your happiness. If you were just a tiny bit less stubborn—"

"MacGregor doesn't want my happiness," Rory growled with a shade of bitterness. "He wants a dynasty."

"He *has* a dynasty, and it's dying out. You don't know your father real well, do you?" She spoke without thinking.

"And you think you do?" he asked coldly, turning on his heel and walking away from her. "Believe me, you don't know him at all. You don't know any of us, so don't make judgments about who we are and what we need in our lives."

After a moment, Chloe closed her gaping mouth and looked down at the bored cat shedding on her chest.

"Well, Roger! What do you think that was all about? Did we just stab him in his Achilles heel?" She added, "Not that I didn't deserve it for being so presumptuous. So much for the peacemakers being blessed."

The cat didn't answer; he just stared over her shoulder, looking back at the gray mausoleum.

"Well, I think that somebody is still cranky about those broken pots, which is understandable. We'll have to cut him a little slack. Today."

The cat gave a soft chuff, but didn't protest when she took him out of the cemetery.

The graveyard is full of indispensable men.
—*Charles de Gaulle*

Chapter Seven

Chloe rushed through breakfast. There was no reason for her to linger at the table. The meal was as unpleasant as dinner had been the night before. Not that the food could be faulted; the fare was as excellent as it always was. It was the company. MacGregor still wasn't his usual boisterous self, and Rory was maintaining his . . . not *coldness*, but deep preoccupation with something other than his present companions.

Chloe tried not to be hurt at the discovery that Rory Patrick, who had been shaping up as one of the nice guys, turned out to have feet—and a heart and possibly a brain—of clay after all.

Her subdued request for the cemetery keys was granted, but there were no offers of aid from either of the Patricks, a fact that suited her. Until the spiritual gloom had passed, she would be better off working alone. It was bad enough to continue to have horrible realistic dreams every night, she didn't need the negative vibes during the day as well.

Rory did rouse from his self-absorption long enough to urge some of his smelly yellow oil on her. She didn't intend to use it, but accepted the offer without argument, deeming it easier than a debate. The two-tailed bashaw wasn't so far gone upon the road to thought that he didn't manage one suspicious look for her meek reply, but he chose not to inaugurate an argument in front of his father.

This fact was as interesting as anything else that had happened in the last three days, but Chloe firmly resisted the temptation to pry any further into the Patricks' affairs. So what if the fighting Patricks weren't fighting? She had a job to do and the rain had put her behind schedule. Anyway, she wasn't looking for any closer ties to the peculiar Patricks, was she? Her task was to get in, get done, and get out again as speedily as possible.

Chloe found the day's heat was lying in wait just outside the door, and it pounced on her with heavy feet. It was latent with the lingering humidity that hung suspended in the still morning air. It felt oily passing through her nose and into her lungs, and it insinuated itself into her clothing. But that, too, was something unpleasant that had to be ignored. The long pants and sleeves were necessary for the part of the cemetery she would be working in, so dwelling on her future heat rash was a pointless activity.

Roger raced out the door with her, nearly tripping her as she struggled with her assorted bags and clipboards, but he didn't follow her into the family cemetery. Apparently he had tired of the sport in there and was going back to dig in his favorite earth in the slaves' half-cleared graveyard.

Chloe didn't look in his direction. Her antipathy for the sad place was stronger than ever, and she wished passionately that there was some way to avoid doing that part of her job.

But once again, dwelling on future misery was pointless. She would have to take pictures of the place eventually, but not until she felt more like it, or she ran out of other tombstones to photograph. Maybe with time, her opinions about the place would change.

The gate to the necropolis was nearly blotted out with new creeper and honeysuckle vine. It was all she could do to hold the living curtain aside while she fit the key into the lock, making her wish that she had remembered to bring some pruning shears. She was peeved enough with Rory to ignore his wishes and to go ahead and lop back the plants where she was working. It would slow but certainly not stop them from taking over the familial burial grounds.

Her path to the southwest corner of the cemetery, slotted that morning for photographic immortality, took her by tomb forty-six. The little stone house looked rather naked and forlorn without Roger keeping vigil on the narrow sill. Chloe's footsteps slowed as she examined the tomb in the clear, early light. Something really was different about the place. The angle of the sun was causing some interesting shadows but . . .

Her eyes moved carefully, comparing the present setting with the one fixed in her head and found that there were two different images. Everything was in place from when she had last seen it. There were no trampled shrubs, no disturbed earth. It was just as it had been yesterday except . . .

"Get a grip." But even as she scolded herself, she was stepping over to look at the door's stone sill.

It wasn't morning shadow darkening the doorway. It was a fresh crop of moss brought on by the rain. The chlorosis that yellowed the other brave cemetery parasites hadn't set in yet. It was green and already beginning to take on the quality of dense, uncut velvet.

She wasn't a huge fan of moss, but Rory certainly was. Chloe reached for her camera. This close-up of the sill would make an interesting photo for her private collection, and perhaps it would serve as a peace offering. She did actually—sort of—owe him an apology for her comment the day before. They said a picture was worth a thousand words. Surely this would be sufficient groveling!

It was dark enough that she had no choice except to use a flash. She didn't want to spend a great deal of time on this pretty distraction, so she contented herself with a quick reading on her light meter and a couple of shots with different f-stops. It would have to do.

Chloe stepped back from the tomb, allowing the poor spider she had shocked into immobility with her flash to return to his task of webbing up the door. Roger had decimated his last effort, and she suspected that this would be the fate of the new silk home, too, but she wished the arachnid luck all the same. Forty-six needed some cobwebs. It was a building that cried out for webs and dead leaves on the roof, and patches of scabrous lichen creeping up its walls. Of all the tombs in the cemetery, it seemed the most *dead*. The thriving green moss was terribly out of place.

She worked through lunch that day. It was an exhausting stint, and she spent hours bulling her way through the months' accumulation of flora, using her tripod to stake the aggressive foliage back while she photographed her smaller finds. But she wasn't complaining because there were constant rewards for her labor. Whether the markers were those of blood Patricks or of their pampered pets, they were all extraordinary; touching, funny, beautiful. It was a pity that the place could never be opened to the public. Taphophiles would adore it—but, of course, it couldn't be opened. Thieves would adore the place too. No, they couldn't open it; not ever. It would be like allowing burglars into an unguarded Tiffany's.

Finally the sun moved so far to the west that working was no longer a practicality. At least, not in the family graveyard. There would, unfortunately, still be enough light in the slave cemetery to work for another hour or more. She weighed her options and decided that her desire to finish her job and escape Riverview outweighed her dislike of the other graveyard.

Chloe stretched a kink out of her neck and then hefted her various bags and headed for the gate. Out of curiosity, she detoured by forty-six to see how the moss was coming along. So far, so good. There wasn't even a hint of yellowing in the miniature grassy leaves. In fact, they looked magnificent. She decided that the weather must be optimal right then. The moss had crept several inches up the old wood door in the space of only a few hours. Its edge was squared and regular, like someone had applied it with a paint brush.

Amazed, Chloe put down her bags and reached for her camera. Rory would be curious about the progress of his favorite plant in the course of only a day. Outside of the controlled conditions of a nursery, she had never seen a moss grow so well. Maybe it was some species that he would want to culture.

Under the harsh light of the flash, the details on the tiny plants' structure sprung into relief.

Frowning, Chloe bent closer to the living velvet. She wasn't certain—and of course she was no expert—but this patch of moss looked an awful lot like Rory's new friend from Borneo. What was its name? *Weberi?*

But it couldn't be. How would the spores travel all the way from the nursery to the cemetery? No one came here except MacGregor and Roger. Unless the cat had gotten some in his fur and then rubbed them on the door . . . ?

But that wasn't reasonable. Roger never went to the nursery with Rory. At least, he hadn't since she arrived at Riverview and the Borneo moss was a fairly new arrival.

Chloe shrugged uneasily. Perhaps she had misunderstood when the moss came to Botanics. Roger might have brought the spores out weeks ago and they had just been waiting for a good rain to start sprouting. Maybe they needed weeks or months to gestate—or whatever it was that moss did before it grew in the wild.

The easiest thing to do would be to ask Rory to come look at the moss. It would make for a nice bit of neutral conversation, and maybe they could regain a little of their earlier harmony.

In the meanwhile, the horrid slave cemetery awaited.

Locking the gates behind her was a chore. She was certain that by the next day, she would need a machete to get inside. It was a pity that she wanted both the digital database and also her own shots, because if she could leave the thirty-five millimeter and its paraphernalia behind, the job would go a lot faster.

Well, she didn't need both cameras in the slave cemetery. The bulk of the bags could be left outside the gate. The setting sun was making for some dramatic lighting, but she would be content with just the shots needed for the database. Chloe took a deep breath of muggy air and forced herself to walk into the enclosure.

Roger trotted over immediately and stropped against her jeans. He left great muddy red streaks behind. Chloe didn't mind; she was already quite dirty and it was nice to have another warm body with her in the land of the dead.

"Hi, cat. What's a nice kitty like you doing in a dump like this?" The feline sneezed at her uncultured question and abandoned her.

Most of the markers had been wood and were long gone to compost. The rest were . . . awful. The rotting, crumbling stones looked like something from a Halloween horror house. It had never occurred to her that rocks could actually decay—but these were. They were rotting where they stood. Everything smelled dead. It was like walking into a nightmare.

Chloe shivered and then glanced briefly at the discarded pile of brambles, which could easily pass for some giant monster crouching in the dark corner, waiting for an unwary victim to get too near. She could hear Roger rooting around in his favorite patch of earth and tried to draw comfort from the fact that she was not really alone. Determined to get the job over with, Chloe left the cat to his work while she reloaded the digital camera with a new memory stick. She'd do one shot of each stone, working in a clockwise spiral. She had a small mister of water, should she need to dampen the marker to bring up a name on the few that had them. That would have to do; she wasn't touching any of the rotting crosses with her hands.

She stuck doggedly to her task, but her imagination continued to make it unpleasant. Every snapping twig that crunched underfoot became an unhappy bone. Every whisper in the vines was an unrestful spirit. Soon, she was walking through her first nightmare of Riverview, even imagining the rancid smell of new death on the air.

Chloe breathed shallowly, determined not to let her imagination and stomach chase her away before the job was done. If she could stick it out another ten minutes, the horrid task would be finished and she wouldn't have to set foot inside the cemetery ever again.

She wasn't bothering to take readings with the light meter, just used a flat flash with every shot. That would wash out the fiery oranges of the setting sun, but it was the best way to get an accurate and consistent shot of the rotting stones, and she didn't want to have to do the job again.

Two steps right—flash. Two more steps—flash. But the horrible smell was overpowering. She felt dizzy, almost too ill to go on.

Chloe turned ninety degrees and looked over at Roger through the tiny box of the viewer. Even the cat, sitting in a hollow of brambles, was painted with the peculiar colors of sunset. Red earth, red light, red soil, red fur . . . *Flash—*

But this time, there was something else there besides the ancient, fallen stone and a shallow pit. At first, she couldn't make it out. The flash had showed her some pale swags and scallops under the cats digging paws.

Flash—flash—flash. The vines were in the way, but now she could see more clearly. The scallops were bits of vertebrae sticking up through the earth-covered skin. The swag was really the bottom of a ribcage breaking through to the air.

Flash. A skeleton. The cat was digging up one of the slaves. Only, the smell was wrong. This was new death, not old. And she wasn't dreaming this time. It was real.

Against her will, the camera shifted a few inches up the rotting body to the lump that was the head. Dark hair. A skull tattoo on the bit of skin that still clung to the nape. She knew that tattoo. Knew the feeling of violent evil that floated in the air.

The camera finally dropped from her hands

and went silent. Only the habit of wearing a neck strap saved it from hitting the ground. She backed away slowly, colliding with stones, not feeling the accumulating scrapes and bruises on her spine and hips. Then it was the fence that stopped her. She slid along it, her hands clenching and then releasing each piece of iron that stood between her and freedom.

There was a gap—the gate. She stepped back. And collided with a warm chest.

She knew whose chest it was, but this time it didn't help. Still acting against her will, her hands clenched into fists and she spun around, hitting out in fear and hysteria. And she screamed and screamed and screamed.

Of course the police were summoned again, and this time there was no question about them coming to the house. They appeared promptly, Sheriff Bell and Deputy Ellis. They bore with them a second casualty wrapped in a blanket, the broken body of a gnome that Ellis swore had jaywalked in front of his car.

At any other time, Chloe would have laughed at the deputy's guilty expression. But she couldn't seem to find any trace of humor inside. She didn't have anything inside her—not hysterics, not fear. Nothing. It had all emptied out with her screaming fit in the cemetery.

Her memories of the last hour were not entirely clear. Rory had subdued her before she could do more than thump his chest. He'd been gentle in his manhandling. He hadn't slapped her or anything, not even when she had ignored his command for silence and kept screaming until the noise brought a frightened MacGregor on the run. The poor old man must have been shocked within moments of a coronary because he looked like a death's-head, but he had still managed to pick up her then limp body and carry her to the house while Rory went into the cemetery to see what had terrified her.

As soon as she had been given over to Morag, MacGregor had left her, presumably to return to the cemetery himself. It had seemed an eternity of smothering afghans and unwanted brandy and tea before Rory and MacGregor had returned to the house and confirmed her fears that she hadn't been dreaming. Isaac Runyon was indeed dead.

Morag had given her more brandy then, probably with the idea that if it gave Napoleon sufficient fortitude to cross the Russian steppes, it would give Chloe the strength to face what was coming.

Father and son had never looked more alike than they did in that moment. Both were gray of face and wearing their skin too tight across their bones. Their eyes were calculating, though, and almost cold.

But even in the distress of the moment, they had not forgotten her equipment. Rory had it all, even the clipboard. He looked at her, still swathed on the sofa, and attempted a reassuring smile. He said: "Don't worry. It's all here. I'll take it up to your room for you."

Chloe nodded gratefully. She didn't seem able to speak. Her vocal chords seemed to have been torn out with her screams. Rory approached her slowly, and very carefully lifted her digital camera over her head. She hadn't realized that it was still there and that she was clutching it like a teddy bear.

The sheriff and his deputies had arrived a few minutes later, and then the coroner. Chloe heard MacGregor mutter, "It's more crowded than a urinal at a football stadium." Chloe doubted that this was strictly true, but she took his meaning. She felt suddenly claustrophobic, overwhelmed by so many strangers in such close proximity.

The sheriff had tried to question her, but she had been unable to answer. She had started to say that she had been shooting her way through the graveyard, but had found her mind unable to form the words, paralyzed by fear of saying something wrong. Shooting was a bad word, she thought, under these circumstances. And she didn't want to say anything about her cameras until she had talked Rory and MacGregor. The police would want to see them and her thirty-five millimeter held film of the family cemetery.

Seeing her beseeching glance, Rory and MacGregor took turns explaining what had happened. Or explaining part of what she had been doing. No mention of cameras in the slave grave-yard or the family cemetery was ever made. Chloe was a guest, an employee of an old friend hired to do some work for them.

What kind of work?

Photography, of course. Hadn't they been told that when they were at the nursery? Chloe was working on the Botanics fall catalogue.

And that cemetery? What was she doing there?

Just looking at the old graves they'd uncovered. The gardeners had found them while clearing out the brambles. Too bad everything was so old and rotten. There was no knowing how old it was.

And the body turned out of the ground by the heavy rain and the digging cat?

Isaac Runyon. A guest brought to the house last weekend by MacGregor's nephew, Claude Patrick. The sheriff remembered Claude. . . .

A deputy disappeared as soon as he had a name, and Chloe was sure that he was going out to his car to use the radio. She wondered if Claude had a police record. She thought not, but Isaac would have one. She was sure of that.

. . . No, no, Claude had left early Monday morning before anyone was up. They had assumed that Isaac was with him.

And the crowbar, rope and shovel found near the grave?

Who knew for sure? But, yes, it did shed a whole different light on the break-in at the nursery. Maybe it hadn't been an act of random vandalism after all, but rather someone after tools.

Claude's name wasn't mentioned, but the thought of him hung in the air.

Could they be certain that the shovel, rope and so on had come from Botanics?

Perhaps they did. That would be hard to say, though. They looked like any old tools and could have been from anyplace.

And the gun?

What gun? A handgun! No, they didn't know anything about that. The deceased killed with a shotgun blast? Was the sheriff certain? Of course, the sheriff had seen many shotgun wounds. They weren't suggesting anything about his competence. . . .

Claude's whereabouts? No. They could give an address and telephone number for his main residence. A description of his car? Certainly. A bronze '58 Chevy Belaire. No, they weren't certain about the license plates. No, they couldn't think of any reason that Claude would have to hurt his friend.

Unless the friend had threatened him with a gun? They hated to say anything against the dead man, but he had seemed an uncultured sort. Mightn't he have brought the gun with him? There might have been a quarrel, or perhaps the two had just been out for some target practice—you knew how it was when some men drank.

The deputy returned. He had some news. Isaac Runyon wasn't just Isaac Runyon. Apparently he was also known as Icepick and someone called Shooter Bishop, both of whom had records—theft and aggravated assault, mostly. He was a violent man. Chloe nodded to herself. Of course, it didn't matter now. An Isaac Runyon by any other name still reeked of evil and remained just as dead. She could have told them that the creature was wicked, that she had seen it in his eyes and then dreamed about his death. But she wouldn't. No, it would take someone giving her a legal equivalent of the Heimlich maneuver to get her to cough up that part of her strange story. The law couldn't help her or the Patricks. She needed a shrink or maybe a witch doctor, and they needed an exorcist to cleanse their befouled land.

Maybe they needed Granny Claire.

The thought made her blink and then shudder. She didn't know which was the lesser of the two evils.

And what about the girl? This was asked with a nod in her direction, and Chloe again froze in place.

Shock. The doctor had been called. A good night's rest. Perhaps a sedative. No doubt she would be able to talk to them tomorrow. Not that she knew anything, but just for the sake of formality and thoroughness. Of course they would call. Just as soon as the doctor said she was fit to make a statement.

The doctor arrived as the sheriff was leaving. The two men exchanged words in the doorway.

A tranquilizer was offered immediately, and as Sheriff Bell still lingered, watching her with his bright gaze, Chloe took it. Then she closed her eyes on the nightmare of strange people and questions and waited for everyone to go away.

Soon the room was quiet. But Chloe intuited that she was not alone. She knew the feel of the Patricks by then, and both Rory and MacGregor were still with her. She guessed that their words to the sheriff aside, they probably wouldn't leave until they had talked with her.

It took a massive effort of will, but she forced her eyelids open.

"I'm okay," she croaked in a voice totally unlike her own. "Sorry for hitting you, Rory."

Rory's eyes assessed her condition.

"That's okay. I shouldn't have come up on you like that in the dark. So, how much of our conversation did you follow?"

MacGregor made a wordless protest. He looked as exhausted as she felt.

"Sorry about making you carry me, MacGregor. I guess I didn't show real well in this crisis."

"That's okay, girl. That wasn't a sight for a lady to be seeing—and I'm so sorry it happened."

Chloe agreed heartily, though she didn't think it was a sight that a gentleman needed to see either. Especially not an elderly one with a heart condition.

"Well, you'll have ample opportunity to repay the debt to my father," Rory told her. Then he added to his sire: "Sit down, before you fall down."

Chloe wasn't so far gone that she misunderstood what he was saying about her debt. "You aren't going to say anything to the sheriff about the family cemetery?" she asked MacGregor.

The two men stared at one another and then at her.

"No. *We're* not," Rory answered.

Chloe gazed at him, and for one instant wondered if the situation had been different—if one of them had found the body instead of her—would Isaac have been reburied and the police never called at all? That would certainly be the easiest thing for them. Rory's voice was soft, and his actions had been almost sweet, but the sugarcoating did nothing to hide the steel will underneath. He was waiting for her answer to the unspoken plea.

"I understand," she whispered. "There's no need to say anything, is there? The . . . the body wasn't anywhere near the family cemetery. It can have no bearing on the investigation."

"No, it wasn't anywhere near the other cemetery."

"But the shovel and crowbar? They came from Botanics." She went slowly, wanting this all to make sense.

"Probably."

"And he was going to . . ."

"Obviously, he was going to rob the cemetery—just as MacGregor feared. Possibly he brought them with him. Or he might have taken them from the nursery. It would explain the break-in."

Rory and his father again exchanged a look she couldn't read.

"He was going to rob the slave cemetery."

"So it would appear."

Chloe tried to swallow this. It wasn't going down smoothly. Why rob the slave cemetery? There was nothing there.

"And Claude stopped him?" Her brain tried on this concept, but in its damaged state, the idea didn't fit quite right. Her reading of Claude's character said that he was much more likely to have suggested that they both go and rob the family's memento mori. There wasn't enough of value in that poorer boneyard to make it worthwhile. She knew that, and they must have known it as well if they had any contact with the funerary thieves. They wouldn't want those rotting old stones, and there wouldn't be anything buried with the bodies. The only place that would interest the funerary brokers to the tune of twenty thousand dollars was in the family cemetery.

But perhaps she was simply so prejudiced against the missing Claude that she was misjudging his character. Maybe he actually shared the Patrick obsessive reverence for the dead. They had never really spoken together because of Chloe's fear of Isaac Runyon. She should accept MacGregor's and Rory's judgment about their kinsman. Shouldn't she?

"Apparently he did stop him," Rory answered again. "Permanently."

That part was indisputable.

"And then Claude just panicked? He took his car and ran away?" She turned to look at MacGregor. His gray face showed neither contradiction nor confirmation of her question.

"It makes sense, doesn't it?" he asked her on an odd note of pleading.

"And when they find Claude?" Chloe asked him softly. "What will happen then?"

MacGregor looked over at his son.

"If they find Claude," Rory said, "then they'll know exactly what happened."

"*If?*"

"I think Claude is hidden away somewhere. I doubt that Sheriff Bell will ever find him."

Hidden. Where the sheriff would never find him.

Chloe began to shiver beneath her afghan. She turned her eyes toward the window. She couldn't bear the weight of the combined Patrick gazes. It seemed safer to stare into the night.

"Okay, I won't say anything about the other cemetery either," she whispered, unhappily committing herself to the collusion. "I don't trust Bell at all."

"Let me help you up to bed." Rory's hands were gentle as he raised her to her feet, and for a brief moment she allowed herself to lean into his strength and warmth.

It might have been her imagination longing for comfort, but it seemed to her that he dropped a kiss into her tangled hair and breathed a soft *thank you*.

Or maybe it was *thank God*.

The day which we fear as our last
is but the birthday of eternity.
—Seneca

Chapter Eight

Somehow Chloe managed to get through her interview with the police on the morning following the murder without breaking a sweat or giving anything away. It helped that the room where she was interviewed was air-conditioned to the point of causing frostbite, and that Rory and MacGregor were omnipresent and prepared to act as watchdogs against any less-than-gentle questioning by Sheriff Bell—though at moments, she honestly wondered if Rory was watching her more closely than the police.

This was an odd notion, but when she had been shown some of the crime scene photos, particularly the one with the pistol in it, Rory had all but pressed noses with her as he waited for her reaction. Maybe, after her hysterics the night before, he had been expecting her to faint.

Of course, she didn't swoon. Didn't even come conveniently close. For once in her life, Chloe was happy for the lingering vestiges of male chauvinism that haunted Riverview and its environs. She greatly appreciated the fact that Sheriff Bell obviously believed that old chestnut about females being fragile flowers and rather too inattentive to their surroundings to recall any useful details in moments of distress. This meant that he did not press her very hard when she pleaded faulty memory about certain facts and events and refused to look at any other photographs of the dead man because it *upset* her.

The excuse of a temporary memory failure wasn't a complete lie. The details about the hours right after finding the body were a little hazy because they had gotten mixed up with her nightmare. However, the actual physical state of the corpse was branded into her brain. Remembering things—images seen through her camera—was part of her job.

And if she needed her memory refreshed, she had better means than the poor-quality police photos at hand to do it. The digital camera in her bag had a built-in display and could zoom in up to a 3 × enlargement of the photo. And the images would be even clearer once loaded onto the computer. If she loaded it onto the portable. Chloe was pretty certain that she had disabled the automatic backup software that would send her backlog of photos to the server at work when she returned to the office and docked the portable with the computer in the office. But, in this case, *pretty certain* wasn't certain enough.

The interview wasn't a long one, as no one had anything new to add to the previous day's statements, and MacGregor wasn't encouraging anyone to linger for coffee. Chloe was soon allowed to return to bed and sleep around the clock without interruption.

Now it was a new morning and she was still in her room, alone with her camera and a guilty conscience. Chloe slumped against her pillows and groaned at the thought of what was sitting in her bags.

Though she knew that everyone, from her police-friendly father right down to the less than stellar-intentioned Sheriff Bell, would say that she was wrong to hold back her own photographs of the crime scene, she did not mention them to either the police or the Patricks. She had taken the stick from the camera before going to bed that night and had put it away in a waterproof pouch where it would not get damaged or lost. It was a cowardly impulse, but she would have liked to have been rid of the horrid thing altogether. However, her conscience, which would not allow her to produce the documentary film, would not let her destroy it either.

For a time, in the dark stretches of the night when she had lain awake in a tranquilized haze trying to come to terms with what had happened, she toyed with printing out selected images onto photographic paper and bringing the sheriff the crime-scene photographs by themselves.

But once the police had those prints, they were probably just bright enough to ask for the original source material as well, and then she'd have to explain about the digital camera and the computer—where the family cemetery photos had been uploaded before she erased and reused the memory sticks—and she had promised MacGregor—*twice*—that she would never tell a soul about his cemetery.

"Damn," she muttered.

There was probably a way to selectively delete photos from the computer without leaving obvious gaps in the memory, but she wasn't at all sure how to completely get rid of all traces of the photos short of wiping the disk. And even if she reformatted the whole thing, she wasn't certain that the images would be completely lost. She'd heard about computer experts being able to retrieve stuff from erased hard-drives.

And even if she hadn't twice made that promise of secrecy, Chloe wasn't certain that she would give up her film to Sheriff Bell anyway. She was still in some weird state of shock, but she was thinking clearly enough to know exactly what would happen if she revealed the family cemetery to this particular police force. Not mincing words, Bell was ambitious scum who couldn't keep his mouth shut—and he wouldn't pass up the opportunity to look important in the world's eyes. She was convinced that consideration for the Patrick family, or its treasures, would never sway him from seeking fame.

Indeed, since he seemed to actually dislike the Patricks, revelation of their secrets would in point of fact look twice as attractive to him. He would probably call the tabloids—she felt it likely that he was the type who had their numbers taped to the drawer in his desk, and that he'd had them there for years just waiting for his big moment to come—and *The Treasures of the Lost Cemetery of Riverview* where *Family Curse Strikes Grave-robber* would be an overnight sensation in both the printed press and shortly after in the small screen.

Well, Sheriff Bell could just take his ambitions and get real intimate with them!

If word of the cemetery got out, by dawn of the next day, every grave robber and reporter with access to CNN or a radio would be on a plane for Virginia, making plans on how to pick over the bones of the living and dead Patricks, their preference of targets depending upon whether they were tomb raiders or paparazzi.

Perhaps worse still were the possible machinations of the politicians. Granny Claire was nuts about some things, but her views about the state government had always seemed very coherent and unflattering. Chloe wouldn't put it past the state to try to step in and declare that Riverview was some sort of state historical treasure and seize the land from MacGregor. She was a little hazy on the rules about eminent domain, but there had been some recent cases that went against land-owners, and it seemed that the avaricious politi-cians would find *some* way to profit from the situation. It was the nature of the beast to lust af-ter wealth—and there were millions upon mil-lions of dollars just sitting there at Riverview, unprotected except for that antler hedge, some thorny creepers, and one old gate.

Of course, the Patricks could sue for damages to their property, but the art in their cemetery was irreplaceable, and there probably wasn't enough money in the entire state—never mind the county—to compensate the family monetarily for the damage that would be done.

The bizarre story—and injury from sensation-seeking reporters—could spill over into Rory's business as well. They would find some way to link the break-in at Botanics to their story. *Curse of Riverview* they would call it, or something equally lurid.

And that, of course, was the least of the losses the Patricks would sustain. Seeing his family's graveyard disturbed by trespassers and robbers would probably kill MacGregor.

MacGregor might kill someone else, too, before he would let them near his Nancy.

Chloe rubbed her forehead, liking the last thought least of all. The image of a lonely Mac-Gregor sitting at his wife's grave would not leave her. But there was another vision there as well—a berserker MacGregor, standing on Nancy's tomb and swinging at reporters with a battle axe.

And what was there to weigh against these awful potential happenings? What argument would convince her conscience to go to the police with her unneeded film?

Well, there was the law of the land, which insisted that a man—*even an evil grave robber*—had the right to justice when his life had been taken by another individual. And it had been banged into her head by her parents, and by her present employer, that it was the duty of every citizen to assist the police in their work whenever possible.

Until this incident, she had always believed that this was true, wise, and a just policy—that rights or property should never be placed above the rights of people.

But now she was faced with a real-life conundrum, and she was discovering that this long-held belief wasn't as absolute as she had imagined. She was stacking up Isaac Runyon's lost life against MacGregor's well-being—and, she had to be honest, the treasures of Riverview—and not coming down squarely on the side of disclosure, law and order.

She was on the side of justice perhaps, but not that of the law. In fact, she almost wished that the police *hadn't* been called. That Rory had found the body and just covered it back up again.

"You don't mean that," she whispered, but her voice lacked conviction.

Things would be simpler if she could lay the matter before Roland Lachaise and ask his opinion of what to do, but there was no way that she could do this without betraying MacGregor's trust. It was highly unlikely that Roland would take matters into his own hands and betray his friend's secret cemetery to the police, but it was still a remote possibility and Chloe couldn't risk it.

Anyway, there wasn't any hope of ever convincing the world—outside of Granny Claire, perhaps—of the evil taint that had surrounded the dead man. And there was the crux of Chloe's other problem. She had been pretending that everything was okay, that her dreams were simply about being stressed and that there were no bogeymen lurking in the closets of her brain. And who could blame her? To admit to the possibility of anything else was all but unthinkable. It would make her like Granny Claire, the most miserable and mean human being she had ever met. But to deny the nature of her dreams now would be an act of stupidity, and there was no one other than her grandmother she could talk to about this.

Chloe's mind skipped back to another unpleasant memory. Granny Claire had been "helping" her curious granddaughter to "focus" her abilities. Unfortunately, her notion of the perfect place for concentration was a pitch-black basement full of things that rustled and squirmed. Chloe had screamed and screamed—at first in anger but then in fear—but her grandmother had not relented until a few minutes before her mother was set to return to the cottage. Chloe had been seven then. Of course, she was all grown up now, bigger and stronger than her grandmother. But even thinking about the old lady made gooseflesh break out on her skin.

Chloe took a gulp of coffee from the mug on her unexpected breakfast tray and stared out her bedroom window. The three-petaled trillium in the window box screened out most of the morning sun with its lacy pink petals. But Chloe knew that the day was advancing, seen or not, and that she needed to make some decisions.

If only her brain could lose its focus on this horrible event . . . but it simply kept returning to the same old problem and turning it over and over in her head, trying to make everything fit together in a single, neat solution. The brain and the gut battled endlessly. Instinct said one thing, societal conditioning another.

"Damn." It was ridiculous to feel guilty for doing what was *right*, even if it wasn't exactly legal, she assured herself. What could her photos possibly show the police that they didn't see for themselves when they'd arrived on the scene just a little while later? Rory surely wouldn't have touched anything once he saw the body—it wasn't like there was any doubt about whether he should have rendered first aid to the corpse!

Nor was it as if she had photographed a monogrammed handkerchief with Claude's name on it, or the murderer lurking in the bushes—*if this even was murder*. It was just barely possible that it had been an accident as MacGregor suggested. Not a hunting accident, but some other kind. Until the pathologist made his report, they wouldn't know for certain what had happened. The sheriff could have been wrong about the cause of death. Isaac's body had been . . . Chloe swallowed hard. It had been gotten at by *things*. It would take an expert to sort the remains out.

Why couldn't his death be an accident or at least self-defense? Maybe there hadn't been a shotgun, just the handgun they found with the body. And maybe there had been a struggle over the gun and it had gone off, and then Claude had just panicked. . . .

Well, that was a little unlikely as a scenario. If one accidentally shot someone, the first step was nearly always to summon help, not to bury the victim. Of course, they were talking about Claude, who in Chloe's opinion was only marginally entitled to the classification of human being. He might very well have shot someone and then run away in a panic.

But even with this rationalization, the scenario failed on another front. Isaac would have won any physical struggle against the smaller man. The weasel, Claude, would never have wrestled for the gun. He would have just turned tail and run if things had gotten sticky. He couldn't have come up behind Isaac and surprised him. The cemetery was full of dried leaves that crackled when you stepped on them.

It was also ignoring the evidence of her own dream.

Chloe sighed. She knew what she needed to do. Somehow, she had to find the fortitude to load up those images on the computer and look at them. Once she was certain that they had no evidence in them, she could erase the images and forget about it.

Yes, that was all she needed to do, a small, routine act of some five minutes effort. That was all. And she just wouldn't go anywhere near the Internet in case somehow the files were being saved in a backup program.

"No way," she whispered, looking at her camera bag and shaking her head. "I can't. I just can't."

Chloe shuddered. Looking at the images might be what she should do—but she simply couldn't face it. Not yet. She would give herself another day for her brain to return to normal before asking it to look again at those scenes of violent death, or to make any major decisions about what she should do in the unlikely event that there *was* something in the photographs.

What she really needed was the comfort of her familiar schedule. Work was soothing. She wished that it was possible for her to return to Georgia and her own modest home, but of course, with the investigation into Isaac's death still going on, she couldn't leave Riverview.

Anyway, MacGregor, and maybe Rory—*a little*—needed her here. If for no other reason than to finish the job she had been hired to do. Now, more than ever, she needed to get that database done. Discovery of the family cemetery was still quite possible, and they wanted a defense against that awful day when Riverview might be made known to the grave-robbing world.

A course of action decidedly on, Chloe threw back the covers and went to get dressed. Surprisingly, the thought of going to work in the family cemetery didn't disturb her at all.

Rory was waiting for her when she came down the stairs and silently shouldered his usual half of her equipment. She didn't ask how he had known that she would finally return to work that morning. It was enough that he was there to help distract her as she walked past the slave cemetery. Not that she would embarrass either of them by expressing her gratitude for his thoughtfulness. There was still too much strain between them.

"I thought I'd photograph two-twenty-nine today," she said as a conversation opener. With all the ugly things that were on her mind, idle conversation with Rory about the ancient dead was the only thing that didn't seem awkward.

"Chloe?" he asked gently. "Are you sure you want to do this? Maybe you would rather just take a walk and perhaps visit the nursery."

Yes, she would prefer that. They could take a long stroll and talk things over while they listened to Puccini. Rory was usually reasonable as long as MacGregor wasn't around. . . . For one insane moment, she actually thought about confiding in him and telling him of the photographs she had taken. But the first clear look at Rory's closed expression put the thought out of mind. In spite of his words, the man who was with her today was some close kin to the suspicious soul who had been so hostile the day of her arrival.

She was fairly certain what he would want her to do with the photos anyway. He would not want to risk exposure of the family cemetery, and he might actually be arrogant enough to take steps to see that the film, cameras, and even computer disappeared before it could go to the police. If he told MacGregor about it, the older man would certainly insist that they be destroyed—with or without her consent, though they would likely try to make it look accidental.

It irritated her to think that both men would make the blanket assumption that she wouldn't simply guide the police to the other cemetery if they took her film from her. But she had obviously been sincere in her reassurances of privacy at the start of the job, and they had her properly categorized as one of the loyal ones who didn't break faith on a promise.

And she couldn't fault them for placing privacy above assisting the sheriff to locate their own murdering kin. After all, she was doing the same thing and she wasn't even related to the Patricks.

"Well, if you want to work, that tomb is a good choice," Rory said at last, when the silence had gone on too long. He peered at her face and then took another of her camera bags in a show of rare consideration. Chloe wondered if she were still sporting a ghastly pale complexion. She knew there were dark circles beneath her eyes that even a full day's rest had not taken away.

"Yes? Why?"

"It's the alchemist's tomb. It's another one with touches of gold. Very whimsical. You'll like it." His voice and face began to animate.

Chloe raised a brow.

"Are you kidding? More gold just standing in the graveyard? I've never heard of such an ostentatious family—well, not outside of some of the more insane Caesars who were gods incarnate, and a few medieval pontiffs. Come to think of it, they were related to God too, weren't they?"

"Yes, or so they claimed. Unbelievable, isn't it, that we Patricks should be so blessed? And we haven't a Caesar or Pope among us."

Oddly, though she spent more time being annoyed with Rory than not, she still enjoyed watching his face when he spoke about the things that interested him.

"But you have your very own family alchemist. That's still an achievement of tall order."

"If you say so."

"Of course it is. Not just every family has one, you know. Mine certainly doesn't." They just had a witch or two.

"I know." His tone was dry and ironic. "I mean, I know that it's uncommon. Nothing would surprise me about your family though. You have the eyes of the mystic."

Chloe managed not to flinch.

"I thought you said they were like blueberries. Anyway, we are all wholesome baseball and apple pie types." *Except Granny Claire.* "Not like your kin. So, be honest. Is that how the Patricks managed their rise to wealth and power?" she asked, trying for a lighter note. "They discovered the secret of making gold and raised the family fortunes through alchemy?"

"Not hardly."

"That's a relief. How mundane that would be, making gold out of straw or something," she said with mock disdain. "I'd kind of been hoping for a leprechaun and a pot of gold at the end of the rainbow. That is a much better story."

"Sorry, but there are no leprechauns either. We make our own gold," Rory answered, with a slight smile for her lighthearted conversational efforts. "But not through chemistry. That particular experiment never panned out. Nor the one for the elixir of eternal youth."

"How about an elixir of love? That would be popular. Probably if it was bottled as an old family recipe, it would sell well at county fairs." Not that Patrick men needed any extra help; they were already possessed of ample charisma. The murderous Claude being the exception, of course. Yet even he had been handsome in his own way.

"No, not that either." Rory looked back and smiled. "My ancestors apparently lacked scientific discipline. We were more given to acting than thinking and careful research. I am the closest this family has ever come to using science for profit, and I am not all that close."

"You don't consider botany a science?" They stepped into the prickly hedge tunnel, Rory leading the way and taking down most of the spiders' new webs with his broad shoulders.

"No. Botany isn't cold and analytical, and I am not controlled in most of my research either." He shrugged, swatting at a lazy bee that hovered near his nose. "Anyhow, I'm not using much of my formal training at Botanics. It's instinct. My mother had a green thumb and love of plants. I simply had the good fortune to inherit her gift."

"Well then, how *did* your family make its millions? Rum trade? Tobacco? Ugh!" Chloe spat out a stray tendril of light green creeper what had wrapped itself about her mouth and was doing its best to gag her. "These darn things just won't quit growing!"

"They're plants," Rory explained kindly. "They do that when it's warm and rainy."

"Don't change the subject! I'm not done gossiping about your family finances."

"My apologies. You were wrong about rum and tobacco. We didn't trade in slaves either. What's your next wild guess as to the source of our wealth?"

"I was thinking piracy. There is the river, and there was lots of that going on in the Tidewater area. And that seems like a sufficiently dramatic sort of occupation, one that would appeal to your kin. Or they could have lit bonfires and lured passing ships onto the rocks."

Rory snorted. "Wrong again—you really do have lurid tastes. Anyway, though I am no expert on this matter, I believe that the bonfire trick only works with ocean vessels on certain stretches of rocky coastline."

"So, no pirates?"

"No. We did some shipping though, and grew some hemp in the eighteenth century," Rory said kindly.

"Hemp! Don't be ridiculous. No one got rich on hemp. . . . I think maybe your forefathers routinely looted the museums of Europe," Chloe went on, rejecting the other story as boring and therefore spurious. "Do you have any great thieves back there in the old family tree? A seventeenth century cat burglar? Or maybe one of your ancestresses was a mistress to Charles the Second and made off with the royal jewels!"

Chloe made certain not to look to her right as they headed for the family necropolis. Instead, she focused on the stands of wild rosy columbine that were beginning to bloom and kept her back to the slave cemetery where the yellow police tape fluttered in the timid breeze.

"Almost certainly we do have thieves in the family—and I believe there was one lady who had a connection with the Stuart lecher. But I wouldn't know the details. I'm just the gardener. Ask Mac-Gregor about our history. I'm sure that he'd be only too happy to entertain you with family yarns. He would probably give you a leprechaun and a cat burglar, even a pirate or two, if you really want them."

Chloe couldn't see Rory's face but she could hear the lingering smile in his voice as he fit the key into the lock and pushed the gate wide.

"So, who did the alchemist's tomb? I only saw the back of it but it looked Roman, if I am think-ing of the right one. Was it done by Gaspari? Or Sammartino?" she asked casually, pushing through the remaining creepers, which Rory had not pulled aside. They were in close enough prox-imity as she passed through the portal that Chloe could smell the soap Rory had bathed in. It was an appealing herbal concoction that reminded her of a florist's shop.

"No, that one is a Massari. The Gaspari is closer to the outer wall," he said, letting down the green curtain behind them.

"Hm . . . Massari, is it? That rolled easily off the tongue. You are a fraud, you know," she told Rory. "And I'm on to you now."

Rory froze in the act of shutting the gate behind them. "What do you mean?" he asked, his voice suddenly neutral.

"I mean that '*I'm just the gardener*' routine. Give it up. You have nothing in common with Joe Six-pack who pushes a lawnmower for a living. The average man on the street wouldn't know a Massari from fettuccini alfredo. And you like opera as well as the blues. That's hardly the music of the modern masses."

Rory relaxed. "I just have a good memory for Greek and Latin names. Goes with the territory." He turned his head and smiled at her.

It wasn't his best smile, being slightly forced, but Chloe found herself answering it anyway. They were both still very tense and had to make allowances for moments of awkwardness. At least he was warming up again.

"So how come there are no ossuaries here? You seem to have every other sort of burial option covered." For one instant her mind flashed on the horror in the slave cemetery, but she immediately pushed the thought away. She could not afford to get spooky now that she was again among the dead. They were friendly enough spirits here in the Patrick family boneyard, but it was most unwise to call ghosts—even kind ones—when you might be left alone with them. It was doubtful that Rory could stay all day. They were bound to quarrel again eventually and then he would abandon her.

The thought made her a little sad.

"Why bother? We have plenty of space for everyone in the family. And outsiders are not welcome." Rory started down an east-running path. "Can you actually imagine the Patrick patriarchs spending eternity in some crowded, common grave like the regular hoi-polloi? We put up the occasional cenotaph to our famous or patriotic neighbors in town to appease the tourists. That's democratic enough."

"You have a point. An ossuary would be far too common an end for any Patrick."

"Far, far too common."

"So, I guess this attitude toward the hoi-polloi means you never had any socialists in your family? No friends to the common man?"

"Not a one. We all enjoyed our luxuries too much to embrace any fashionable—and certainly not any *unfashionable*—political causes. We looked after our own, servants or family, but that was it."

Chloe wondered if that wasn't the literal truth. She hadn't found a single reference to a Patrick dying while serving as a soldier in a war. She would have thought that the usual pride and a thirst for valor would have infected some of the younger, more romantic males of the tribe, especially during the War between the States, but apparently in their civic pride they were as different from the average man as it was possible to be.

However, she had a feeling that whatever the differences to the common man, Patricks did have their full share of familial pride and that it could be damaged. Having Claude on the run from the police had to be weighing heavily on MacGregor's spirits, and possibly making him speechless with fury. He certainly had not spoken to her much in the last few days. She hadn't seen him except for the minutes she was questioned by Sheriff Bell.

The picture of MacGregor with an axe flashed across her brain and she wondered uneasily what he would do if Claude were eventually found and arrested for Isaac Runyon's death. It seemed possible that his reaction to the indignity would be so strong that he might actually die of shame.

Chloe caught an unexpected glimpse of tomb forty-six's crocketed roof showing through the thinning trees, and suddenly recalled the strange moss that she had intended to show Rory on their next visit to the cemetery.

"Wait!" she called, glad for the distraction. "There was something over here that I wanted to show you."

"What?" Rory returned immediately to her side. He seemed unusually alert and his voice a bit sharp as he questioned her. "What is it?"

"Just some moss. It isn't anything important," Chloe began. "It looked a lot like your Borneo moss, the one you showed us in the hothouse where the break-in hap—"

"Where is it? Which tomb? Or is it in a tree?" he asked hopefully.

Chloe smiled at the abrupt questions.

"Over on Calvin and Edana's place, number forty-six. It sprouted right after the rainstorm and was growing like a house afire. Every hour it spread another couple inches. I took some pho—" But she was talking to air. Rory's passion for moss was apparently alive and well, for he had reversed course as soon as she mentioned Calvin and Edana, and was walking rapidly toward tomb forty-six.

It was probably just as well that she hadn't mentioned her extracurricular photography. She had forgotten for a moment that she had taken those photos the same day as finding the body, and there was no point in starting his mind down that particular path.

Chloe shrugged off her renewed unease and followed after Rory. She was rather curious to see how the moss was faring now that warmer, drier weather had returned.

"Moss growing at this time of year?" Rory muttered. "Perhaps some spruce fir or filamentous fungi . . . but even if a *lycopodiam lucidulum*—"

"Your conversation sometimes leaves a little to be desired," Chloe complained. "And it is too hot for racing about with this equipment if all you are going to do is speak Latin and grumble to yourself. Anyway, it isn't spruce fir moss. I've seen lots of that. This looked just like that hairy Borneo stuff. I was even wondering if Roger might have gotten into the greenhouse after the break-in and brought some spores out here in his coat. You know how he likes tomb forty-six, and all the moss is growing down low."

"It's possible," Rory said shortly. "But very unlikely. Roger never comes out to Botanics unless MacGregor brings him. And MacGregor rarely comes around anymore. I've seen him more this last week then in the entirety of last year."

Thinking back to the small jagged hole punched in the hothouse glass, Chloe was inclined to agree with Rory's assessment. The cat would have been cut to ribbons trying to fit in that small space. It was also a long distance from the house for the bowlegged cat to travel on foot.

Though, he might have followed if Claude ever went to visit. The cat surely adored that ratfink.

They rounded the corner of tomb forty-six and Rory stopped. In the two days since she had been there, the honeysuckle had made great inroads on the granite sepulcher. But the path to the door was still sufficiently clear that they could both see the long strands of moss that were turning a sickly yellow on the stone sill and dark wood panel.

"Oh! It's dying," Chloe said with disappointment. "I thought for sure that it would make it. It looked so healthy two days ago—just like those pots in your greenhouse."

Rory grunted and kneeled by the narrow sill. He gently fingered the sickly strands that had laced over the lower door. He soon abandoned the moss and ran a finger over the dark wood of the door itself. He leaned in and sniffed it. After another long moment, he pulled away from the tomb and wiped his hands on his handkerchief.

"It is *weberi*, isn't it?" Chloe asked, confident of her identification now that the moss was filled in.

"No. It's . . . a *lucidulam*." Rory turned to stare at her. His lips twisted into a smile, and he held her eyes as he said steadily: "It is not the Borneo moss. It couldn't be. There is no way for that moss to get here. Anyway, *weberi* doesn't like granite. I told you that. It wouldn't grow there even if Roger carried the spore out here."

Chloe's breath stopped, and for a moment she was unable to look away from Rory's face. Something inside her twisted at his overly sincere gaze. She prayed that her complexion neither flushed nor paled, and that Rory didn't notice the sudden trembling in her legs.

Weberi didn't like clay pots either. He *had* said that. It grew on wood and had to be deliberately cultured in a manmade growing medium if it was to thrive on terra-cotta pots. That's what Rory had told them the day she and MacGregor went to Bontanics. *Weberi* might grow on its own on the ancient panel door of the mausoleum, but it would never have started accidentally on the stone sill. Not unless someone had smeared it with yogurt or some other medium. Rory was lying to her.

And that, she thought grimly, pretty much answered her question about whether to confide in Rory about her photos.

"Oh, really?" She swallowed to ease the dryness in her mouth and willed her lungs to work. She added lamely, "Well, it was pretty a couple of days ago. I thought you would want to see it."

Rory continued to stare at her. He smiled, but underneath she knew he was angry maybe not at her but at something or someone.

"Have you photographed it at all?" he asked casually, causing Chloe's heart to thunder. "Maybe when it was just sprouting? I'd like to see any pictures you have."

Chloe felt as sickly as the yellowing moss.

"Photographed it? It didn't occur to me. I'm sorry. Would you like me to take some photos now? It would only take a minute to load up the camera." Chloe was amazed at how calm she sounded as she evaded his question.

He was silent a beat and then said: "No, that's all right. Maybe later. We should get on with your work."

"Okay, whatever you want. Shall we go on to two-twenty-nine now?" she asked. "Or would you like to stay here and . . . take a sample of moss or something? Maybe clear it off of the door before it does any damage . . . I can easily go on alone."

"No. I don't need to take samples of this moss. I know what it is. Just a common moss. And it's fine on the door. It's dying quickly and won't hurt anything."

And it made the tomb look antique and neglected—just like the antiqued pots. But Rory didn't add this.

"Okay," she said again.

Unable to preserve her calm any longer while facing Rory's gaze, Chloe turned around and started back down the path to the alchemist's tomb. She felt weak-kneed and had a stupid urge to cry, so she was proud of the fact that her legs carried her without a single stumble and not one tear overflowed.

Of course Rory didn't need to take samples of the moss. He already knew it was *weberi* and that it shouldn't be there.

What frightened and hurt her was that he had felt the need to lie about it. Why lie unless it was important? Maybe it was making leaps of logic, but an untruth about this moss and how it came to be in the cemetery didn't fit in with the neat explanation for Isaac's death that MacGregor—and her conscience—were trying desperately to construct. She didn't know exactly what this meant, but she was certain that somehow the break-in *was* connected to Isaac's death. And it also meant that, even after all they had gone through, Rory didn't trust her enough to confide in her about this matter.

Suddenly, in spite of the air temperature being in the mid nineties, Chloe had a crop of goose-flesh growing on her arms, and it was spreading faster than Borneo moss.

"Are you feeling well, Chloe?" Rory asked,

coming up behind her so close that she could again smell his soap. He put a hand on her arm and turned her around.

Under other circumstances, she might have been tempted to look him in the eyes, to ask to be taken into his arms and held again. His embrace had been heaven two days ago when she had been frightened. Now she just wanted to get away.

"You look rather pale. Do you want to go back to the house and have a rest?" His concern sounded quite genuine, but Chloe didn't know if she could trust it. Her welfare was not his top priority. Botanics, Riverview and MacGregor—and maybe Claude—came first.

"It's the lighting beneath these trees," she answered firmly. "This green cast makes you look a bit like moldy cheese too. We'll need to set up the umbrellas and use the flash to get any decent photos. I hope the vines aren't too thick for seating the tripods. At least the ground will be soft."

After a moment, Rory exhaled and let her go.

"You're the boss," he answered. "I think we'll have to clear a space for the camera. Shall I start over here?"

"That's fine."

But it wasn't fine, and Chloe knew that she wasn't the boss. She wasn't in control, and never had been. She was just riding the Riverview tiger and praying that she didn't fall off and get eaten by one of the Patrick males she was trying to protect.

*I'm not afraid of death. It's the stakes
one puts up to play in the game of life.*
—Jean Giraudaux

Chapter Nine

Rory watched carefully as Chloe worked on setting up her shots of the alchemist's tomb. Her expression remained closed and her instructions clipped, and she didn't make eye contact with him any more than was absolutely necessary for the sake of manners when he spoke to her.

The morning had started pleasantly enough, with their conversation returning to the nonsensical teasing that Chloe enjoyed, and that he was actually beginning to like too. But their short visit to look at the damning moss on tomb forty-six had shut her up tighter than a bank vault at closing time. Somehow, she had known he was lying about the moss. And the lie had hurt and frightened her into a full retreat. Rory found that he didn't care at all for this sudden reserve after their earlier camaraderie, and it annoyed him that beneath the calm facade she was actually alarmed by him and determined to push him away.

He had to admit, so far she was managing to hold him off. She was certainly keeping her distance from him physically. If he got closer than an arm's length, she quickly moved away. Two days ago she had trusted him, had been easy to manage. Now he was a leper.

She was too damned intuitive. He'd had a bad feeling about her from the start. It frustrated him to know that his clumsiness was inadvertently liable for her new aloofness, and the possibility that he was responsible for causing her fear was enough to make him feel genuine pangs of guilt—something he had not previously had experience with, but recognized just the same.

Yet, what else could he have done but lie? They did not have the sort of relationship where one could simply assume absolute and unquestioning loyalty on the other's part. She was fond of Mac-Gregor—and perhaps a little of Rory himself—and had promised to keep silent about the cemetery, but that was before she had found Isaac's body. A promise and vague affection wasn't enough to take on such a big risk. For her own sake, he had to keep her out of things. In these circumstances, the greatest safety for all of them was to be found in her continuing ignorance.

It might have been different if they had found their connection before Isaac's body was discovered, if they'd already been intimate. Lovers lost in the euphoria of a new relationship often shared things, and that would have given him some acknowledged bond to make things easier. But time had been short before Claude's arrival, and they hadn't had the chance to become friends—let alone lovers. And now they probably never would. Once Chloe's bright little mind put all the bits and pieces together she would know everything that he did.

That would probably be the end of any hope for a future together.

Of course, it might be the end of even more than that if she decided that she had to go to the police with her suspicions. Rory's hands clenched as he considered the possibility.

He should send her away immediately, but that would probably only further arouse her reservations about him. She was extremely devoted to her work. For all their sakes, she needed to be allowed to remain at Riverview long enough to finish her job. If she did that, there might still be some questions in the back of her mind when she thought about Isaac's death, but she would have completed her task and would therefore likely be content to leave things alone.

And if she wasn't, Roland Lachaise could probably be counted on to see that she was kept very busy in some other state, especially if MacGregor put in a call for assistance from his old friend.

Things would probably also seem more normal to Chloe if MacGregor returned to the cemetery and assisted her in Rory's stead. However, for her own sake, he'd have to keep her away from his father. The old man was drinking heavily these days and could not be trusted to remain discreet. His nerves were forsaking him. MacGregor felt horrible about her finding the body—guilt was consuming him. Above all, he longed for his wife—his friend and confessor—and Rory feared that his father saw in Chloe a reasonable substitute.

MacGregor would never tell the police about what had happened to Isaac, but he might very well tell Chloe, the woman he dreamed would be his daughter-in-law one day. That couldn't be allowed to happen. Not ever. MacGregor, unfortunately, did not understand that.

"I think this about does it," Chloe said flatly, breaking the long silence as she began stowing her equipment. "The heat is really building now and I don't like to have the computer or cameras out in the damp air. Condensation is a real problem. I'll make an early start tomorrow morning and make up for lost time, and I'll leave the computer behind. Everything seems to be working so I don't need to keep uploading and checking the images on the screen."

"Fine. I'll be available to play your beast of burden," Rory answered, not offering the polite assurance that there was no need for her to hurry.

"That isn't necessary," Chloe said, still not looking directly at him. Her lips in profile were pressed tight and flat.

"Of course it is. I don't want you working alone out here."

"Why not?" Now she did look at him, a hint of challenge in her dark blue eyes. It was a real pity that the gaze she'd finally turned on him was not more affectionate. "MacGregor trusts me."

"It isn't a matter of trust," he lied. "It's simply too dangerous for you to be out here alone."

Rory watched her eyelids widen slightly. "How so? Claude is surely long gone," she remarked bluntly.

"True, but there are other snakes about. And a copperhead could be every bit as dangerous as my dear, departed cousin."

"Oh." Her eyes veiled before he could read them, and she turned away to zip up her bag. "Well, I plan to get started around seven tomorrow and work through to lunch. Will that suit you?"

"It will have to."

"Then it's a date."

It was foolish of him, given the bleak situation and her obvious annoyance, but Rory was obscurely pleased by her choice of words. "Yes, it's a date," he echoed. Then he added in a lighter voice: "Look at that damned cat."

Chloe turned and watched Roger leaping after a butterfly that fluttered through its floral *pas de deux* with an idiot poise even though his feline audience was about to eat him. The dance of life went on regardless. For the first time in hours, her face softened.

* * *

It was afternoon, hot and stuffy with the air conditioner turned off, but Chloe never noticed. She sat in her darkened bedroom and stared blankly at the wall, her thoughts tumbling over themselves as they sought to order the new information she had fed her brain.

Rory's lie in the cemetery had made her angry and supplied her with the impetus to finally face what she needed to do with her film. And now she had to accept the fact that the image glowing on her laptop was more disturbing than she had feared. It looked like the old saying was right—A little knowledge *was* a dangerous thing. And she hadn't one clue where to get any clarification, supposing she was daft enough to want it.

"Damn." Chloe flopped back on the bed and laid an arm over her eyes.

It was not merely the subject of the photo that was distressing her; minus the smell and the crawling flesh at the base of the neck, which had tried to warn her that genuine death was near, the scene of Isaac's burial when reduced to screen size was not so bad that she couldn't look at it. But there was also the little matter of the thing that *wasn't* in the photograph, an important little thing about eight inches long and four inches wide, and its absence was cause for a new, ugly thought.

And probably alarm, too, though she had not yet reached a state of panic. Some part of her—no doubt hormone-driven—simply refused believe that Rory could do something that seemed so bad without a very good reason.

Idiotically, she wanted more than ever to talk to him about what she'd found, to beg for an explanation and reassurance. But, of course, she wouldn't.

"Catch twenty-two."

Only it was closer to that exchange in a Sherlock Holmes story she'd read. The detective had said something like: "*Remark the strange incident of the dog in the night.*" And Watson had said: "*But the dog did nothing in the night.*" And then the supercilious Holmes replied: "That *is the strange incident.*"

She now had her own strange incident to deal with, and she'd have to face it alone. There was no one to advise her.

Chloe looked again at the computer screen. Altogether, she had taken four clear shots of the body, and there wasn't a pistol to be seen in any of them. There were ropes and a crowbar—even the handle of a shovel thrown under some bushes—but no handgun. Admittedly, she had shot her images from an angle different from the ones the police photographer had used, and without a powerful flash. But still, unless the police placed the pistol in the open for clearer viewing during the crime-scene photographs—something they should not have done, and she would never have thought possible, but for her dislike of Sheriff Bell—the pistol should have been visible in at least two of her photographs.

It simply wasn't there. Isaac hadn't had a gun.

And things got worse.

After looking at the digital photos, she had followed a hunch and loaded up her thirty-five millimeter film into her little black box and developed the negatives. Normally, she wouldn't have touched the film until she was in a proper darkroom, but she had this portable box for field emergencies—which this certainly was—and it was perfectly adequate for simple processing jobs.

These thirty-five millimeter images were also revealing.

Admittedly, she had not been able to compare finished prints, but what she did have in the way of close-ups suggested that the moss of the tomb and the moss on the pots at Botanics were one and the same. She was certain that *weberi* was growing—and now dying—on tomb forty-six in the Patricks' graveyard.

So, what did this mean? Had Isaac broken into Botanics to steal some rope, shovels and crowbar, then gone out to Calvin and Edana's tomb to rob it—thus accidentally spreading the *weberi* spore to the graveyard? Chloe's brow wrinkled as she pursued this line of thought.

And then, perhaps, Claude had caught him there and that was where the murder had happened? Had there been any blood . . . ?

But no, that wasn't quite right. That moss hadn't grown accidentally. Someone had put growing medium on the door and deliberately planted spores there. Why? To hide something? But what? Not the body . . .

Maybe chisel marks from where Isaac had tried to force open the tomb's door?

Chloe turned this thought over in her brain, examining it for flaws before embedding it to the known facts file. Things didn't fit together as tightly as she liked, but this seemed a possible thing to have happened, so she allowed herself to use this hypothesis as a base for her theory.

Determined to find an answer and restore order to her brain, Chloe sat up straight, and she applied herself to this progression of assumptions. Her instincts objected, but she ignored them. Was there any other evidence to support this idea? Anything else that wasn't actual evidence but was still suspiciously out of place and a good candidate as a missing puzzle piece?

"There was the key," she murmured. There had been those funny rust stains on the gate's lock and key four mornings ago. She hadn't thought of it at the time, but could that have been blood— Isaac's blood—on her hands? She swallowed a few times and willed her stomach to remain calm while she thought this through.

MacGregor was usually very particular about who had the keys to the graveyard and would not tolerate their careless use. But he had also been very drunk that night. Had Isaac somehow lured him into a bout of hard drinking, perhaps slipping a little something extra into the Jack

Daniels, and then taken the key after MacGregor passed out?

Perhaps. But that still left Claude out of the picture. How did he fit into this? Had he come downstairs and found MacGregor passed out, and, guessing what was happening, taken a shotgun and gone out to the family cemetery to stop Isaac? It seemed a drastic course of action to take against a houseguest, but it was just within the realm of the possible, especially if all parties were drunk.

"Claude's an idiot," she said persuasively to her roiling stomach. "It could have happened that way. Rory was gone, MacGregor was out cold—and Isaac was a lot bigger than Claude is. He might have taken a gun to back up his threats."

She ventured a step further. The next one wasn't as large a leap of imagination as the last had been, and she took it easily. Faced with the same dilemma she presently had confronting her, and being worried about revealing the family cemetery to the outside world, Claude hadn't risked leaving the body there, or concealing it in one of the tombs where someone—maybe the Munsons, maybe MacGregor—might notice the smell and find it. Without proper interment in a vault, someone would notice the rotting body. When heat and bacteria got busy dissolving flesh and bones, the hard reality of what had happened to Isaac's corpse when the soul—or Claude—shuffled off his mortal coil would become evident. Death took an odorous form.

Probably Claude didn't have the keys to the mausoleums. They were on a separate ring at the back of the desk. And he might have been afraid of being disowned if MacGregor found out that he had broken into a tomb and let a non-Patrick pollute the family necropolis.

So he had moved the body to the slaves' graveyard—not out of piety, not out of a belief that his former friend should lie in hallowed ground but because the ground, had been dug there once before, and he had thought that he wouldn't have to chop through tree roots like he would in the family graveyard or just about anywhere else in Riverview. And if someday the bones were found, chances were good that everyone would just think it was some slave's remains and not bother to report them to the police.

"Maybe." But her voice was growing more animated, and as Chloe warmed to the idea she began to tap her foot.

So . . . needing a shovel, and not knowing where else to find one, Claude had gone to Botanics and broken into the nursery to collect tools and some growing medium to cover up the damaged door. Not being familiar with Rory's mosses, he had grabbed whatever was handy and taken it out to the graveyard.

"I like it. This works." It wasn't a perfect fit, but Chloe strung the incidents together and went determinedly on.

Next, Claude buried Isaac. But being lazy—and

maybe pressed for time—Claude hadn't dug as deeply as he should have, nor packed the soil tightly when he was done. And when they'd had the hard rains on the next day, enough earth washed away that Roger was able to—

Chloe shut down that thought immediately. Her stomach was too uneasy to face what had happened after Isaac had been unearthed.

She looked over at the screen of her laptop and thought again about what *wasn't* there. She had explained the moss, but what was she to make of the handgun that was missing in her photos yet conveniently there when the police arrived?

She exhaled. There was really only one conclusion, and this part was a little easier to excuse since she liked Rory. The gun had obviously been planted at the scene after MacGregor had taken her away. Probably Rory had put it there to suggest self-defense to the police so that Claude wouldn't seem a total villain when the manhunt began. Police would take a dim view of a felon who tried to shoot his host, and wouldn't really blame Claude for shooting back.

She hadn't thought Rory fond enough of his cousin to take such a risk on Claude's behalf, but maybe this was about Patrick blood being thicker than water when the chips were really down. Or maybe Rory felt that he owed Claude for stopping Isaac from robbing the cemetery. That actually made sense.

And her dream? There was no way to know if

Isaac really had been dead when Claude buried him. If he hadn't been . . . then it was a terrible mistake. Awful. But it could have happened, given that people were drunk and it was dark.

Chloe let out another slow breath. Maybe she was missing some details, but this string of theories more or less held together, and it was a tremendous relief to have something plausible to offer her panicking imagination. Maybe the nightmares would now stop.

What Rory had done for his cousin was unusual and possibly wrong—but so was she wrong for not turning over her photographs to the police. They were, all three of them, doing their best to protect MacGregor and the cemetery.

Chloe grimaced. She didn't like to think that she or Rory shared anything in common with Claude Patrick, but it seemed that they did; MacGregor and the Patrick legacy.

"Of course," she said softly. She had it now. Rory wasn't protecting Claude because he liked him or because they were kin. He was doing this for his father. The two of them fought all the time, but deep inside they had to love one another. If MacGregor wanted Claude protected, then Rory would do it.

"Well, hallelujah," she said, with immoderate relief that her instinctive liking for Rory was not a betrayal of good sense. She wasn't being blinded by emotion and stupid supernatural hysteria. And Rory wasn't just high-handed and arrogant—

well, actually he was. However, this time it was for a good reason, a reason her mind and morality could accommodate.

And now that she understood why Rory and MacGregor were so uptight with her, and why Rory had lied to her about the moss, she could set about putting everyone at ease. There had to be some way to let Rory understand that she knew what he was doing, that he had her unspoken blessing for obscuring the trail between Isaac and Riverview's cemetery, and for giving Claude a running start from the law.

A tap on the window startled Chloe. A crow perched on her sill, staring through the window-pane. As soon as she met its gaze, it flapped away with a noisy caw. Behind it, the dogwood tree shivered. Chloe got up and went to the window, forcing the casement open. Sly air spilled into the room. A breeze had kicked up while she was working. The leaves outside her window pulled against their green tethers and whispered pleas for their freedom. Chloe pushed the breathless voice away and began gathering her negatives off the light box.

Somehow, without being blunt about knowing their secret, she would have to let Rory and Mac-Gregor know that this discomfort with her presence wasn't necessary—that she understood what had happened and was willing to help with Claude's escape by remaining quiet about her suspicions. She would put her betraying digital images away somewhere safe where no one would ever find them. And the others—hard as it would be—she would destroy.

It wasn't, she assured herself, that she was actually condoning murder. It was just that she understood completely about family loyalty. If this were her father being threatened, she'd do the same thing. And there was the fact that every fiber of her being wanted to believe that Rory wouldn't do anything that was really bad. This situation was causing a freak aberration of behavior. All of them were behaving in a slightly lawless manner. It couldn't be helped. And it would never happen again.

Knowing that she was crossing some moral line with this decision, Chloe nevertheless got up and took the strips of film that showed the *weberi* moss growing in the graveyard and on the pots at Botanics, and went into the bathroom. She emptied out the brass wastepaper basket and, opening a second window for ventilation, she took out the book of matches stored with the utility candles in the vanity drawer and burned the incriminating negatives.

The act made her feel a little ill because she had never deliberately destroyed her own work, but she was also strangely relieved to see the film bubble and melt. They were gone and could no longer serve as temptation or chastisement.

Returning to the bedroom, she closed the lid of the laptop with a shaking hand and ejected the memory stick.

There she hesitated, uncertain of what to do.

The stick should be erased, maybe even destroyed since it was possible that an image could be recovered from it, and it could get all of them in a great deal of trouble, if those images ever were discovered by the police. But it had a lot of her work on it, and with Rory appointing himself as her constant companion, he would notice if she started reshooting tombs and would probably ask the sorts of questions she was not yet prepared to answer directly. Not yet.

It bothered her that she had this lingering disinclination to trust Rory with her full knowledge, but complicity through silence was one thing; actually admitting what she suspected was another thing altogether. She wasn't ready to go that far with her commitment. The inner choreographer who was directing her dreams and intuition simply wouldn't let her do more than turn a blind eye.

Chloe looked down. It would be easier to keep the memory stick for now. She would just make sure that it was well hidden until she decided how to completely erase the damning images. She simply needed to read up on how to do it.

A warning gong sounded below stairs, reminding her that it was time to dress for dinner. Chloe didn't have much of an appetite, but dressing for the evening meal was a ritual that the family continued to observe. If Rory and MacGregor could go through the motions and put on a good front for the cook and Morag, then she could too.

She walked over to the armoire and opened the door. A pair of size-six bowling shoes had showed up in it the day before. She was careful not look down as she selected a dress, not because she didn't like the shoes, but because she might see the evil imps leering at her from the shadowed canvas that remained tucked away in the back on the cupboard. If there was one thing that her nerves didn't need, it was leering, malicious imps reminding her of a mad man's vision of hell and the Patrick ancestor who had admired it.

As a well-spent day brings happy sleep,
so a life well-used brings happy death.
—Leonardo da Vinci

Chapter Ten

Chloe's appetite returned with a vengeance and she greedily ate dinner, munching her way through *nicoise* vegetable salad, roasted loin of pork with rhubarb sauce, crab soufflé, and stuffed cantaloupe, then capped the meal off with an enormous helping of pecan pie.

Perhaps it was sacrilegious of her to eat so heartily when death had come so recently to the house, but relief was proving an appetite stimulant, and she couldn't see that her limited acquaintance with Isaac Runyon merited any degree of mourning.

In any event, her mouth wasn't needed for conversation. Nobody was wasting breath on unimportant topics, and no one was anxious to inaugurate a discussion on the one subject that was preying on everyone's mind.

Eventually her culinary gusto attracted even MacGregor's attention, and the two Patricks watched with first amazement and then horrified amusement as Chloe systematically packed away enough food to compensate for all her recent missed meals.

"My God, girl!" MacGregor whistled softly. "I'll have to start feeding you more often."

Finally, unable to eat another bite, Chloe pushed back from the table and took a deep breath—or as deep a breath as her constrictive clothing would allow. Her glazed eyes noticed MacGregor's pale hands toying with his cigar box, which sat next to the half-empty brandy decanter, and she said pleadingly: "Please don't. I know it's my own fault for being a pig, but I will likely lose everything if you light that awful cigar."

Rory laughed aloud, startling all three of them. The sound was disorienting. There had been no laughter in the house for days.

It was also the first time that Chloe had heard Rory do more than chuckle. The sound of his amusement was deep and a little slow, and semi-sweet, like good dark chocolate. The thought was almost enough to make her regret her gluttony.

"Come on." Rory stood up, and walking around the table, offered her his hand. His drawl grew syrupy as he teased. "You need to go for a walk, Miss Chloe, ma'am. Let us take a constitutional stroll around the veranda and watch the magnolias sway by moonlight."

Suddenly Chloe was laughing too—though with less volume than Rory as her gluttony had made her too heavy for large chuckles.

She turned to face MacGregor, who was still looking rather the worse for his alcoholic adventure, prepared to ask him if he would care to join them for a breath of air. But before she could speak, Rory's fingers tightened on her hand in silent warning.

Their eyes met briefly. *Don't ask him. Come with me. Now.*

"Why, thank you kindly, sir," she said lightly. "I should love taking a constitutional through the magnolias. If your father will excuse us."

MacGregor also smiled for the first time in days and waved them away. He was reaching for the brandy decanter and had the cigar box open before they left the room.

"Stubborn son of a bitch. He's going to kill himself," Rory muttered. But he didn't sound truly angry.

He led her down the hall, surprising her yet again by retaining her hand as they walked through the dim house toward the back porch.

"I think you have lured me out here under false pretenses," she commented when they reached the back parlor and Rory did not offer any other conversation or turn on the lights. "I don't recall any magnolias at the back of the house. What's on your mind?"

"I was saving you from yourself. One more bite

of pie and your buttons would have popped. Personally, I would have enjoyed the sight, but my father has a heart condition and we mustn't let him get too excited." His tone remained light.

"Fortunately this dress has no buttons. Just a tie, and that can be loosened," she said, freeing her hand so that she could do just that while they had the privacy of semi-darkness. It was a relief to slacken the cloth tourniquet.

Rory waited patiently for her to finish retying her sash and then opened the parlor door. The scent of sweet lilac was heavy on the evening air.

Chloe breathed deeply.

"This air is damn near as rich as that pecan pie, and better than any perfume ever invented. You could get fat just breathing it."

Rory shook his head.

"Take shallow breaths or you'll get indigestion. Come on. We'd better find you some after-dinner mint."

"I couldn't eat another thing!" she protested.

"It isn't to eat, it's to breathe." Rory again offered his hand to assist her down the stairs. It was an unnecessary courtesy, but perhaps he was worried about her high heels on the cobbled stone path, or her bulging stomach protruding so far that she wouldn't be able to see her feet.

"To breathe?"

"Yes, it's called aromatherapy. We'll go the herb garden and I'll pick you some mint to tuck in your—uh, dress."

Chloe looked up into his face, but it was painted with the last intense colors of sunset and she could read nothing there.

"Okay. I'm game. I've never had a mint bouquet."

"I'll pick you a bouquet if you like, but as with pecan pie, a small serving is usually sufficient."

"You only say that because you get pecan pie all the time." Chloe was arguing out of habit, but she actually felt wonderfully peaceful, strolling through Riverview's garden, holding Rory's hand and watching night overtake the sky.

"We are going to get eaten by mosquitoes, you know," Rory warned her. "Or you are. Mosquitoes don't seem to like me."

"Too tough and sour, huh?" Chloe shook her head sadly, but watched from the corner of her eye to see if Rory smiled. He didn't, but she saw a definite lip twitch.

"In the old days," he said reminiscently, "we knew how to deal with uppity women. There are only so many things a man could do to ensure good behavior from his woman, or children, or horses."

"Ah! The good old days. And what do you do now that beatings have fallen out of favor?"

Rory stopped walking and turned to face her. "Why, I suppose that I will simply have to rely on the most tried and true method of all."

"And that is?" Chloe grinned up at him, daring him to say something outrageous. But rather than answer in words, Rory cupped a palm beneath her chin and lowered his head.

For one moment, Chloe stared in confusion and then incredulity, but the moment his lips brushed over hers she relaxed and allowed the unexpected kiss to happen. With a soft sigh, she closed her eyes and permitted her lips to experience the moment. Around her, the lilacs applauded softly as though pleased with her decision.

Rory didn't invade her mouth, not even after she parted her lips. The kiss remained almost chaste. But for all its lightness and brevity, Chloe felt a strong magic all the way to her curling toes, and it was a moment after the kiss ended before she was able to refocus on the twilit garden.

"You Patrick men are dangerous," she said softly, shaking her head.

Rory's white teeth gleamed briefly.

"Not me, sugar. I'm absolutely harmless."

Harmless? How he lied!

"I must be rock stupid, agreeing to step out with a liar like you," she went on, tucking her hand back into his fist as they resumed their stroll toward the herb garden.

He answered in an amused force: "I really couldn't say, though I have suspected as much for some time." The smart remark earned him an elbow in the ribs, which he managed to evade, such retaliation being expected.

"What saved me from a full seduction?" she asked curiously, feeling safe to ask such a direct question in the growing cover of darkness.

"Your overindulgence at dinner," he said wryly.

241

"And maybe the lack of a full moon. One must do these things right. Southern gentlemen have a tradition to uphold, you know."

"Ah. Well, I suppose I shall have to remember to give thanks to the cook."

"Are you really giving thanks for deliverance?" His question was lazy, as though her answer didn't matter. And maybe it didn't. With Rory, it was always hard to tell.

"For the moment," she replied with equal conversational weightlessness. "I have been doing a bit of leisure reading about this, and I think that the outdoor seduction has been greatly overrated, along with barns, stables, and haystacks. I see nothing wrong with a bed and keeping my more vulnerable parts away from bloodsucking parasites."

"Hm . . . I'll remember that." Rory stopped at the small gate and lifted the latch. "Here we are. Let's find you some mint."

Chloe sniffed gently at the medley of smells that bombarded the air. "Over here," she said.

"I believe you are right."

They walked past the knotted border of thyme and flat-leafed parsley, with Chloe taking only shallow breaths of the heavily herbed atmosphere. They walked quickly past the horehound, marjoram, and into the less scented yarrows and salvias where the selections of mint were grown in their own row.

"Mint is a fine aphid deterrent," Rory remarked, breaking off various stems and gathering them into the requested bundle. "It also repels cabbage moths and flea beetles."

"How useful. Does it work against mosquitoes or ants?"

"Unfortunately, no."

"Men?"

"Not at all."

"Ah well! So much for a universal panacea."

"You can, however, tuck a sprig of mint beneath your pillow and you will dream of your next lover."

Dreams. She almost shivered.

"You're making that up just to see if I am dumb enough to fall for it."

Rory laughed softly.

"Put that mint beneath your pillow and we'll see what happens."

"I'll consider it. I could certainly use a change of dreams."

"Here. Try this."

Chloe accepted her small bouquet, breathing deeply of the pungent mints. She doubted the herbs' efficacy as a love forecaster, but Rory was right about it helping to settle her large dinner. Her stomach immediately eased.

"What is this one?" she asked, sniffing at a particularly strong-scented twig. "I think I've smelled it before."

Rory leaned close, to breathe in the leaves'

odor. It was nearly full dark and they could no longer rely on sight to guide them.

"That is a native species of *mentha*. You'll find it growing down by the river. It's a bit rangy when it isn't pruned back."

"Ow!" Chloe slapped at her bare arm. "Damn. I think those mosquitoes have found me. Maybe they like your mint."

Rory calmly unbuttoned his shirt and dropped it over her shoulders. The fine cotton lawn was short-sleeved, but the shoulders were big enough that it covered her to the elbows. Once he had her cloaked, he put a casual arm about her waist and urged her toward the house. In spite of the blood-suckers, they didn't hurry.

Chloe was keenly aware of the bare chest only inches from her cheek. It was warm and smelled like Rory. Sometime in the last few days she had grown accustomed to his scent and thought that she would recognize it anywhere.

The view was another matter entirely. She doubted that she would ever become completely accustomed to his bared body. The sight, however fleeting, interfered with her ability to think.

"Come this way." The hand at her waist urged her to a ninety-degree turn.

"We'll go in through the kitchen. But no more pie for you tonight."

Chloe could only trust that he knew the way into the working quarters of the house. They were walking toward four squares of soft light, but she couldn't make out anything more than the white of the oyster shell path crunching beneath their feet and the small humps of fragrant greenery.

They arrived in the softly lit kitchen, only to find it abandoned except for the cat and the detritus of meal preparation still strewn on the counter. One bread basket was actually lying on the floor surrounded by an explosion of crumbs.

"Roger!" Chloe scolded. "What have you been doing?"

Rory frowned at the mess and headed for the hall door. Since he didn't let go of Chloe's waist, she hurried too.

"Morag!" He opened the narrow door and yelled louder: "Oleander!"

Chloe was puzzled until she realized Rory wasn't calling for a shrub, but for the cook.

"Damn." Rory headed for the dining room. "It must be MacGregor!"

"What's wrong?" The pleasantness of their romantic stroll had vanished into the ether, and all that was left was Rory's alarm and the lingering odors from dinner.

"Rory!" a weak female voice called from the music room. "Come quick. Your daddy's had a fit."

Morag's stooped figure appeared in the door. She might have been worried about MacGregor, but was not so distraught that she didn't notice Chloe wearing Rory's shirt and the arm he had wrapped about her waist. Her lips grew straight like the cut of a guillotine, and her expression became disapproving and possibly even somewhat anxious. But why would she be afraid for Chloe?

"We didn't know where you were," Morag chided, finally looking away.

"A fit?" Rory finally dropped his arm from Chloe's waist and pushed the staring Morag gently aside. "Have you called the doctor?"

"Oleander did. She said to call an ambulance. Your daddy has to go to the hospital this time."

Rory grunted and went to kneel by his father. Someone had covered the reclining MacGregor with an afghan, as though preparing him for a snooze, but the gray face and wheezing lungs were hardly those of someone enjoying a nap.

"I'll be better in a moment, boy," MacGregor rasped. "There's no need for the doctor. Morag's just raisin' a fuss, officious old trout."

"You're lying on the floor, wheezing like a leaky accordion, and your skin is the color of cement. You need a doctor." Rory's words were harsh, but his touch gentle as he tucked the throw more tightly about MacGregor's shoulders.

"Where's Chloe?" MacGregor gasped.

"Save your breath. You don't need to be talking right now."

"I need to see her."

Chloe, who had just been making a tactful retreat from Morag's stern eyes, stopped in her tracks and answered softly,

"I'm right here, MacGregor. Don't worry. Everything's fine."

"Good. Come here, girl." The painful breaths went on for several seconds. MacGregor managed to open his eyes and turn his head. He looked once between his son and Chloe and then smiled. "Come closer, girl. Did you like your magnolias?"

Rory stiffened.

"I settled for mint," Chloe said, coming all the way into the room and also kneeling at Mac-Gregor's side. She had a moment of déjà vu. It was like the morning when she and Rory had found him passed out on the floor, right down to the old buffalo plaid shirt he was wearing and the smell of crushed mint floating on the air.

As matter-of-factly as possible, she shrugged off Rory's borrowed shirt and draped it over his bare shoulders. She could feel the tension that gripped him in the knotted muscles beneath her hands. "You need to do something about those mosquitoes. Your son has rhino hide, so they leave him alone, but they were after me from the moment I stepped outside."

"My mosquitoes have good taste," MacGregor said, closing his eyes as though talking with them open was too much effort and he couldn't manage both things at once.

There came the distant sound of an ambulance siren. Chloe was willing to bet that there would be more numerous gnome casualties, since the drivers were unlikely to know what to expect.

"I'll go out front and show them in," she said, rising to her feet.

"You stay here, girl. I'll set the dogs on them," MacGregor muttered. His voice was getting weaker. His eyes closed.

"Go," Rory said softly. "And turn on the lights along the drive. The switch is by the door."

Chloe felt her eyes flooding with useless tears, and she hurried from the room.

If the mosquitoes bothered her while she waited on the front portico, Chloe never noticed them. She was too busy trying to wipe away the steady stream of saltwater that trickled from her eyes.

"He's too stubborn to die," she said to Roger, who had stepped outside to keep her company.

She repeated the thought over and over again until the ambulance finally arrived, but in her heart she didn't believe it. Her continuing dreams of death had to mean something. MacGregor—ready or not—was going home to his Nancy, and she couldn't think of anything to do that would help him, or Rory, except to continue to keep her promise of silence about the cemetery.

As soon to kindle fire with snow as to seek
to quench the fire of love with words.
—*William Shakespeare*

Chapter Eleven

The hospital was exactly like every other hospital
Chloe had ever been in. They might change the
type of tile on the floor, or paint the walls different
colors, but all hospitals carried the same medici-
nal odors; and in the intensive care unit they had
the same subdued lighting where frightening res-
pirators hissed and clicked, and where nurses still
wore serious white uniforms. Other hospital staff
might sport colorful scrubs as they went about
their work, but in the places where people were in
danger of dying they seemed to always wear non-
frivolous whites.

In ancient times, white had been the color of
mourning and winding shrouds. The Gaels even
had a color that translated into English as *the white
color of death*. Chloe hated it. She made a mental

vow that if she ever got married, she wouldn't wear white.

The assumption was that MacGregor had suffered a heart attack, so the emergency room people had started therapeutic treatment immediately. The family physician arrived almost upon their heels, but after a quick look in on his patient, Dr. Emerson left MacGregor to the medical team in the ER.

Chloe had managed to shut off her tears by the time they arrived at the hospital, and Rory remained absolutely stone-faced, so other than the doctor talking to them about what was being done in the examining room, and one nurse offering them some coffee, no one approached with soothing words of encouragement, suggestions of watching TV in the lounge, or boxes of unneeded tissues. It was nearly one in the morning before word came that MacGregor had been transferred up to the intensive care unit. Rory immediately rose and headed for the elevator, so Chloe had trooped up to the third floor with him and started a fresh vigil there.

Rory was eventually permitted to see his father for five minutes, but after that they were urged to go home. MacGregor was stable and they wouldn't be allowed to see him again until morning anyway. And this could be a long stay, the white-suited nurse reminded them. The family would need its strength.

Chloe, though exhausted, didn't suggest any

course of action, leaving it to Rory to decide what he wanted to do.

Rory had taken a long look at the plastic chairs that lined the waiting room and then her face, which had lost all trace of the light makeup she had applied before dinner and probably showed the lingering effects of tears. She wasn't one of those lucky women who look cute when they cry.

"Damn it all." His gaze in an otherwise calm face nearly scorched her with its blend of frustration, anger . . . and something else that made her breath catch. Something raw, which she had never seen on another person's face, but she recognized for all that.

Hearts thundering, they opted to return to Riverview.

Neither spoke on the ride back to the house. The silence wasn't peaceful, but it wasn't hostile either; it waited in anticipation. Chloe's heart never quite settled back into a normal rhythm, and she finally noticed how warm the night actually was. Even in her sleeveless dress with the late evening air washing over her through an open window, she felt hot and prickly. To distract herself, Chloe tried counting the gnomes as they appeared in the headlights. Many were missing, smashed into dust by the ambulance bumper.

Rory didn't bother to put the van away in the carriage house. They abandoned it in the drive with the keys still in the ignition.

It did not surprise Chloe when she climbed

down from the van and Rory took her hand in his own hot fist and pulled her into the house. What did surprise her was that he led her immediately upstairs and into a part of the residence where she had never been. He didn't pause to turn on lights as they went. They stopped only when they reached a closed door, which Rory opened with a quick press on the latch.

The moon's glow leaking though the curtains showed Chloe that they were in a bedroom, and a vaguely herbal scent told her that the room was Rory's.

"Now would be the moment to say something if you don't want this to happen." Rory's voice was deeper than usual, and also a little rough. The sweet chocolate tone was missing, but she didn't mind. She was not in the mood for sweet.

Chloe still had many unanswered questions about the things that had happened in the last week, and also many things in her own head that she wanted to clarify, but at the moment, finding explanations seemed less important than giving in to her body's wants. Some divine madness had overtaken her.

"Would silence be considered assent?" she asked. Her own voice had altered. "I am not quite used to being this bold."

"I'd prefer a more direct answer."

"I feel stupid admitting that I'm shy," she said, clearing her throat. But Rory still waited.

He wasn't going to let her off of the hook. Apparently he really needed to hear her words of assent.

Chloe gave in. She slid her arms about his waist and rose up on her toes so that she could brush her lips against his.

"Then have it your way—*yes*," she whispered. "I want this to happen."

And she did. She was at least ninety-five percent sure.

Rory's arms closed about her immediately and she found herself being lowered onto a down bed. The tie of her dress was undone with a single tug, and since it had been too hot for a bra or stockings, she was unwrapped except for a pair of panties. They soon followed the dress.

As he had demonstrated earlier, Rory could remove his shirt with commendable speed, and his slacks were even easier to dispose of.

Chloe wondered, as Rory loomed over her, a dark silhouette against the pale ceiling, if there would be any of the usual awkwardness this first time, if they would have to speak of their needs or wants—give guidance to one another.

Apparently Rory did not think so, for he didn't say anything else to her, and after a moment she had to agree with his policy of silence. After all, their bodies were speaking in some mutually understood tongue, and what else was there to say that wouldn't confuse things?

Her eyes opened wide at the first brush of his

mouth against her breast, but all there was to fill them was the silver moonlight, so she allowed her eyelids to droop and used her other senses to tell her of her state.

She sank her hands into Rory's hair and tried to moor herself while the room spun away. Her skin thrilled and tingled and even screamed as Rory moved over her. Cheeks, lips, hands—they all felt different and wonderful. Normally, she preferred her mind to be in charge of her body, but that night she gave herself over to the sensations he provoked, and waded out recklessly into the deeper waters where Rory urged her to go.

It was glorious. It was also oddly terrifying.

Though she spent equal time touching, tasting and exploring Rory's body, for the first time during an act of sex she felt out of control. Once she let go of her cautious, logical rock, waves of a new sort of passion were crashing over her, making her feel helpless even as they thrilled her. This new sense of vulnerability was notional, because Rory in no way restrained her, but it seemed that the deep, swirling waters to which he lured her suddenly dragged her down into a foreign place and held her captive there. It was a place she could never escape without Rory's help—somehow he had become both her jailer and her rescuer.

"Chloe!" The weight of his wants pressed down on her in a relentless stream and she felt herself disintegrating, breaking into parts that could not think, only feel. Just a small part of her brain continued to speak and listen to reason, trying to understand what was different now from every other time she had made love.

The needs of her body were plainly enough understood, but what her confused heart called out for she did not know. It was more than simple affection or a desire for recognition. But its wants—for all of being desperate in their strength—were unrecognized. They were shouted down by the feeling parts of her body, which Rory skillfully controlled.

She shook her head slowly. This had never happened before. Her mind was always the master of her body—but not this time. The last thinking pieces of her brain were alarmed and attempted to form a confederacy of her splintered thoughts which might regain control of the situation.

"Rory?" Chloe writhed against the linens, overwhelmed by her body's response to him, but still not able to completely abandon herself to the moment.

"Hush," he whispered against her belly. "Trust me."

Trust him. But she didn't. Not entirely. Night might smother all other shadows, but not doubt.

The last few days had muddled the conduits of thought and stripped away old logical and moral checkpoints. New emotions raced down these opened channels and straight into her brain and heart where they jabbered at her in foreign tongues. Her body translated some of the new message, but not all. Much of it was still a mystery to her. But what was there for her to see was a tangle of grief and worry about MacGregor, excitement and passion when she thought of Rory, and—just a little bit—of something like fear. It was there in the sweat of her palms and the goose bumps that covered her upper arms. But what she feared, she did not know. Surely it wasn't that Rory would hurt her.

"Stop thinking. I want everything from you except common sense. This is no time for reason and logic," Rory said, and bit lightly at her inner thigh. Then he breathed deeply as though gathering her scent the way he had gathered the smells of mint out in the garden.

How would he catalogue her? she wondered a bit hysterically, as his slow exhalation tickled over her bare skin and she felt his teeth scraping over her.

But the answer to this question remained elusive and her body's demands grew louder than the other things clamoring in her brain. Finally, she did as he asked and stopped listening to logic. It was the only way to escape this desire. He sensed the change at once and laughed softly as she relaxed beneath him.

The pressure from Rory's hands told her that he wished her to move, and with only minor hesitation she rolled onto her stomach, allowing him to part her legs with his own. She lifted her hips out of the feathered tick and pressed against him. His breath tickled the hair of her nape, sending tiny shivers down her spine and spreading the goose-flesh down her arms.

A low moan told Chloe of Rory's pleasure as he pushed into her. After a few languid thrusts, he slipped a hand beneath her belly and slid it down to cover her sex. His work-roughened fingers closed over her, supplying the pressure she needed to end her body's longing and allow her to escape completely into the realm of sensation where reason could not follow.

She hoped she would emerge as Persephone had from hell, carrying seeds of reason and understanding in her hand, though, for a moment, she doubted that she would ever escape.

After the act, she lay in a lazy S, sunken into the deep tick with Rory sprawled behind her, an arm draped about her waist but otherwise not touching as they allowed their bodies to cool.

Chloe was too tired to wander back into her reassembling brain and start asking questions. Instead she closed her eyes and let her body sleep. Her last thought was to wonder what Rory was thinking, if he understood what had just happened any better than she did.

In many ways, it was as though her life had started only after she arrived at Riverview. She had entered some cocoon and hatched out transformed into another being. She still looked like Chloe Smith, but something inside had altered. Whether this was a good thing or not remained to be seen.

* * *

Rory was awake. His body was calm, replete, and he found it pleasant to stay still for a moment and study the spill of hair that folded down Chloe's fragile nape and spread out upon his pillow. It looked like tarnished silver thread in the moonlight, fragile as gossamer. Perhaps, in a while, he would wind his fingers into those strands and gather them up in his fist. For the moment, he was content to observe and appreciate.

The line of her spine was gentle, her limbs soft and slender, vulnerable in their nakedness—so much more delicate than his own flesh and bones. Even her fingers, which worked so cleverly when she was awake, looked as fragile as folding flower petals where they curled in toward her pale palms.

He could break her with ease.

His eyes moved down her body. He watched silently as her ribs rose and fell in an ever-slowing rhythm. The tidal movement as she gave herself over to sleep was unconsciously hypnotic.

How trusting she was, to slumber with a stranger.

Her defenselessness seemed to be speaking to him, demanding something of him—but he didn't know how to answer its requests. He had never looked at a woman and thought of her in terms of her beautiful fragility. The feelings her weakness stirred in him were vaguely frightening, partly because he didn't understand them. It was as though some part of his brain was making a secret plan that the rest of him was unaware of. Surely it was telling him that he must defend her innocence. He couldn't be thinking anything else.

Rory gave a mental shrug. He would reflect on this later; the present was too beguiling to waste on self-examination. *Much too beguiling!* He smiled slightly, pleased at finding the right word for the moment.

He rose onto an elbow and blew lightly on Chloe's nape, stirring the nearly invisible wisps that curled there. The soft disturbance made her grumble and wiggle down deeper into the bed.

He laughed silently. He should be feeling sad that MacGregor was likely dying.

Probably he would be sad, but later. For the moment he had other, better things to feel—other bonds that needed tending. In some ways, it was all very simple. He either had to make this women completely his, or he had to get rid of her. It was the only way to be safe. Rory knew which he would prefer.

He leaned over and ran a finger down Chloe's exposed cheek.

"Wake up, sleepy-head," he said softly, and then lowered his lips to the dainty ridge of collarbone that seemed to ask for his touch. He bit lightly.

"Hmmm?" Her lashes fluttered and her eyes opened. The irises looked black in the moonlight.

"I knew you were going to be greedy," she complained, closing those sleepy eyes. But in spite of her words, she rolled over to take him into her arms.

Rory buried his face in her hair, hiding his triumphant smile. Somehow, he didn't think that Chloe would like it. Women almost never cared for the triumph of naked aggression over gentler caring.

I am going to seek a great perhaps.
—the last words of Francois Rabelais

Chapter Twelve

Chloe awoke the next morning alone in Rory's bed. A quick look about the room told her that though she may have been thoroughly ravished, she had not been thoughtlessly abandoned. Her sundress had been picked up from the rug—a breathtaking confection of antique jeweled silk threads, which she hadn't had time to appreciate the night before—and draped neatly over the back of a chair upholstered in faded but beautiful tapestry. Her sandals were precisely paired on the floor beside the seat. There was no sign of her underwear on the chair or rug, but she hoped her panties were tucked somewhere in the folds of her skirt. One thing was for sure, she couldn't leave the room until they were found! She could just imagine Morag sucking them up into the vacuum and having to call for a repairman to unwind the elastic and lace from the motor.

Chloe shuddered. It was the kind of thing that got immortalized as dating legend disasters. She'd rather die than face Morag without her panties.

A quick glance at the clock told her that the hour was early, so there was hope that she could return to her own room before anyone noticed that she hadn't spent the night there. It wasn't that there was anything wrong with her sleeping with Rory—in fact, she suspected that MacGregor would heartily approve—but having Rory's ancient, puritanical relation know about their affair was rather embarrassing.

In fact, even without proof of her final fall from grace being discovered by Morag, Chloe decided that she would forgo breakfast that morning and just grab something quick at the hospital. She would miss the eggs Benedict and scones with clotted cream, but there was no need for Oleander to go to the bother of preparing a meal just for her when she was too nervous to eat alone under Morag's basilisk stare.

The thought of MacGregor in the hospital, deprived of both good food and company, was another spur to be up and doing. That had Chloe bouncing out of bed and wrapping herself in her sundress, which fortunately did have her underwear tucked neatly into a pocket. Shoes in hand, she dashed down the hall toward the wing where her own bedroom was, leaping from rug to rug so her feet wouldn't squeak on the glossy wood floor.

Rory had likely left for the hospital as soon as it was light, she decided while taking an extra-long jump and nearly ending up on the floor when the landing rug skidded into the wall. He had considerately not awakened her—which was very unselfish of him. She just wished that he had roused her long enough to say goodbye. Waking up alone in his bed was slightly disconcerting.

It was childish and spoke of unpleasant insecurities, but she wanted to see him in the light of the morning after—to reassure herself that all was well—and perhaps, if he didn't mind, she would even sneak in to see his father. This morning she felt very close to MacGregor as well as to Rory. It was as though the Patricks had imprinted themselves upon her in the night, embedded themselves in her brain and heart, and even in her eyes, which seemed to look at the world in a different way.

Or maybe she was just romanticizing things, she thought with a moment of self-derision. If there was ever a place that could induce romantic fantasies, it was Riverview. The place was like a contagion to the susceptible brain.

Nevertheless, she still wanted to see MacGregor, so she was going to find a way past the nurse's station.

A quick shower and a dash of makeup served as

a restorative, and she managed to get out of the residence without being tagged with a scarlet A.

As she had expected, the van was gone from the front of the house. Fortunately, she had the keys to her car and knew where it was parked. It was a little tight backing out between the supports of the carriage house, but there was no serious damage to either party, so she went on her way without stopping to see if she had actually left some paint behind on the old wood post.

Riverview Hospital looked less menacing than it had the night before, but it still managed to cast a pall over Chloe's spirits. This cold, characterless building was no place for MacGregor!

Chloe walked briskly to the ICU, hoping to find Rory, but as she'd expected, the waiting room was empty at that early hour.

Her next stop was the nurses' station. Chloe had made up her mind that if no one was there, she would simply walk down to 306 and let herself into MacGregor's room. However, being an intensive care unit, there was a nurse on duty, so Chloe was forced to stop and practice her best smile and wheedling skills.

"I am here to see MacGregor Patrick in three-oh-six," she said politely but firmly.

"Would you be his new daughter-in-law, Chloe?"

She never even blinked at the lie. It was wonderful that Rory had done this for her. He had guessed what she would want and arranged this for her. It was better than flowers.

"Yes, I am."

"Then you can go right in. The doctor still isn't allowing any reporters or police in, but extended family is fine and Mr. Patrick has been calling for you."

Reporters? She had almost forgotten about Isaac's murder. Of course the media vultures would be circling.

"Have there been many reporters about?"

"Just one." The nurse frowned. "But he has been annoyingly persistent."

"This isn't good. MacGregor will have fits if he sees a reporter."

"It certainly isn't good! Mr. Patrick is a very sick man. But don't worry. No one gets past this station without checking in first." The nurse's militant expression smoothed. "But don't you be nervous about seeing your daddy-in-law. Just remember to keep the visit short and don't do anything to excite Mr. Patrick." The nurse hesitated a moment and then added: "He has been wandering in his wits a little, so don't be surprised if he is slightly incoherent and testy."

Poor MacGregor, left all alone to deal with the real world. He was probably fuming.

Chloe smiled reassuringly.

"I understand. MacGregor won't upset me—or visa versa," she assured the nurse.

"Good. I'll send your husband in when he comes."

Chloe paused for a second, about to ask if Rory had been there already that morning, but changed her mind. A real wife would probably know these things.

She walked rapidly down the hall and pulled aside the privacy curtain that functioned as a door to the 306. The lights in MacGregor's room were dimmed, the monitors' beeping and blinking unobtrusive. Probably, given MacGregor's feistiness, they hoped to let him sleep as much as possible. Other than the hiss of oxygen from the tube in his nose and the IV stuck in his arm, MacGregor looked rather like his usual self.

It was only when she neared the bed that Chloe could see how sunken and bruised the flesh around his eyes and nose was. He looked so old—so ill. All his joyful vitality had drained away in the hours of darkness. The change was shocking and made her unutterably sad. Much of her lingering pleasure from the night before drained away.

Sensing her presence, MacGregor's eyes snapped open. They were bloodshot and slightly jaundiced, but they still had their usual animation.

"Hello, girl. Have you come to see your love?" he whispered, smiling a welcome whose beauty nearly broke her heart when she realized that it wasn't for her, but for his dead wife. "I've been waitin' for you, Nancy."

So this was what the nurse had meant by wandering in his wits. Chloe said nothing, hoping that in silhouette she would continue to pass for Nancy Patrick. She slipped her hand into Mac-

Gregor's palm and forced herself to smile even as she turned her face away from the soft lights and let her hair veil her.

"I'm here," she said softly.

"Love, I've been needin' to talk to you. I did a horrible thing. It was Claude, Nancy. Rory and I . . ." He trailed off with a small shake of his head. "We had to, love. The heathens were going to desecrate the family's resting place—our *home.*"

Chloe didn't move her hand, but she felt herself begin to go cold. She didn't know what distressed her more, MacGregor bringing up the unpleasant subject of Claude and Isaac, or hearing him talk about the cemetery as his home.

"Don't talk," she whispered, afraid of stirring up her own ghosts. Her imagination had been blessedly silent all night and morning. She wanted the nightmares to keep sleeping. "I understand. Please don't say anything. You don't need to think about this."

"I won't say a word, love. I'll never tell a soul. Wish Rory's little girl hadn't found the body. That shouldn't have happened. Never meant for her to get involved. I told the nurse she was my daughter-in-law. Maybe she'll come see us too. You'd like her."

Rory's girl. So MacGregor did know about them. Perhaps Rory had said something that morning. If he had been there. It seemed it was MacGregor and not Rory who had promoted her to family member so the nurses would let her in. A suspicion flitted by and concealed itself between two rational thoughts. Chloe considered tracking it down but was unsure she wanted any confrontations with her mind.

She swallowed and said again: "Don't talk. Everything is all right. Chloe's all right. She'll come see you later."

"Rory's a good boy. He knows where Claude is—he must. I told him, I'm sure. And he'll see he stays hidden. That's where Claude belongs, hidden away. He's a Patrick—it's only right that he be with family. Rory will see to everything. I did all I could." MacGregor's whisper was almost lost in the hiss of oxygen.

"Yes, Rory will see to everything. Don't worry," she whispered.

MacGregor tightened his grip until his fingers bit into her hand.

"You understand, Nancy, don't you?"

Chloe didn't really understand, but Nancy would. She forced herself to answer soothingly.

"Yes. Don't worry. It's all right," she repeated, unable to think of any new words.

"I had to do it," MacGregor murmured. "My father told me when I was young, I had to protect the family, no matter what. And Rory . . . He's my son. He'll always do what's right for the family. The law wouldn't understand about Rory, but we do. I would do anything to protect my son."

The room felt very close, and for some reason Chloe was having trouble breathing. It was as though the smell of disinfectant had clogged her nose and even the pores of her skin, which were beginning to ooze an unpleasant, nervous sweat. She knew that it was foolish to be shocked by MacGregor's words. Hadn't she suspected all along that MacGregor and Rory knew more about Claude's disappearance than they were telling the police? This penitence for not going to Sheriff Bell didn't mean anything—didn't change anything. It was out of character for him to be so contrite, but MacGregor was ill—near death—and he just wanted to square the books. That's all it meant. There was no need to feel like the world was about to implode.

MacGregor mumbled something else indistinct, but Chloe didn't ask him to repeat it. As soon as MacGregor's eyes closed and he returned to sleep, she pulled her hand away and left the room.

Chloe smiled automatically at the nurse on her way out, but didn't stop to talk. She wanted to be away from the hospital before she met up with Rory. She needed a few moments to compose herself. It was one thing to have suspicions about them hiding Claude, but quite another to have them confirmed. MacGregor's words made it all real. Rory was hiding a murderer.

It was a shock to pull up in front of the house and see Rory's van there. It disturbed her to see that gray brown moths had lined up on the sunny side as orderly as hieroglyphs in a pharaoh's tomb. They didn't so much as flutter as she passed by.

Still unprepared to talk with him or face Morag, Chloe slipped from her car and, leaving her purse behind, set off on foot for the river. That should be a safe and private location for a bit of meditation.

She tramped through the rough for a quarter mile or so, determinedly not thinking, just following her nose, which told her that some of the wild *mentha* Rory had mentioned was growing nearby.

As she strolled, she began to have a physical sensation that she was at a slight material distance from her own body, having an out-of-body experience without dying, or, more accurately, that she was being pushed aside because something else wanted to see out of her eyes. She noted this but was not alarmed. It wasn't the first time it had happened, though she hadn't opened herself up since her mother died. Her grandmother called this spirit-riding.

Chloe had chosen her walk seemingly at random, but for some reason, the longer she walked, the more this goal of finding the mint became important to her. There was no thought of turning back toward the house, even when she came to a long stretch of dried, chest-high grass that had to be forded with brute strength. A dozen feet in, something grabbed at her shoulder. She shrugged off a limb of a fallen oak whose leafless claws were curled in menacing fists that made her think of Disney's movie of Snow White.

Things rustled and scurried away, and the thought of ticks intruded on the edge of her consciousness, but it never crossed her mind to abandon her search. A sort of dreamy déjà vu moved her on. She knew this place . . . from somewhere.

Chloe only stopped walking when she reached a giant hedge that completely blocked the river. A closer look showed her that the hedge was held together with ancient barbed wire whose teeth were now dulled with corrosion and probably tetanus. Annoyed, but still blindly determined, she turned left at the green wall and started searching for a break in the dense shrubbery.

Go left. Here.

She turned. The smell of mint and water grew stronger and she followed the invisible trail, pausing once in a while to sniff the air like a bloodhound after prey. Through the silence there came a sharp snap of breaking wood that echoed through the air like a gunshot. Chloe froze in place and the sense of dreamy detachment left her, chased off by that one sound. She fell back into her body.

"So, what do you think? Do we try to pull her out? If we don't get her now the next rain will carry her away," a male voice said suddenly from inside the small, bank-side copse.

Chloe remained still. Though no longer wandering on autopilot, frustration at being thwarted so close to her goal rose in her like a wave. The feeling seemed more foreign now, definitely not her own.

Someone else answered, the words indistinct.

Damn! Her hands clenched. It was one of the

Munson brothers speaking, and at the sound of his voice a flock of starlings took wing and disappeared into the sky, taking their twitters and shrill songs with them. The feeling that something else was riding around with her left.

The sound of the birds' cries also broke through the last of her preoccupation.

What the hell was she doing in this tick-infested grass?

Chloe stood unmoving, one foot still lifted. She felt the remains of fear. Her mouth was dry, her body shaking. It was ridiculous, but for some reason she was anxious that the Munsons would hear her footsteps in the sudden silence following the pessimistic meteorological prediction. They might come looking for her. And though the Munsons had always been helpful and polite, it never crossed her mind to make her presence known and ask the way to the other side of the hedge.

A very strange thought presented itself to her. What she needed to do at the river required privacy. Even secrecy. She pushed back against this thought.

"They say rain by mid-week," the younger Munson added, breaking some more sticks as he shifted his weight. "Storm's comin' up from the south. Gonna be a big one."

Chloe was suddenly aware of how warm the morning had grown, and that she was slightly dizzy and breathless with the sun beating down on her unprotected head. Her lungs were laboring from her overland scramble and there were deep V's of sweat in the valley between her breast and in the small of her back.

She also had a number of shallow scratches on her arms and legs that were itching fiendishly.

Damn! She looked at her watch. Where had her brain been for the last two hours? She needed to get out of there and back to the house. She just had to hope that she hadn't tromped through any poison ivy while lost in her black reverie.

Chloe turned quietly, placing her feet with care so no crackling sticks would betray her.

"No."

It was only a single syllable, but Chloe recognized Rory's voice. It stopped her cold and raised the hair on her arms.

"Let the river have it," Rory said.

"It's an old Chevy—could be worth something," the boy suggested hopefully. "I swam down and had a look at her. No body damage. Don't know why they junked her."

"Doubt it's worth retrieving. The engine will be filled with silt, the upholstery shot. We'd have to hire a crane in to move it. It's just scrap iron, not worth the effort to haul it out." Rory's voice was calm.

"Okay. Thought maybe your dad would like it—sort of a get-well present."

"Cars aren't MacGregor's thing. Now, if you could find some more of those gnomes . . . I'm afraid that a lot of them have gotten broken lately."

The boys laughed.

"I don't think they make 'em anymore. They passed a good-taste law at the state capitol."

"I can't imagine why."

Chloe's hand fisted. Rory sounded convincingly relaxed as he chatted with the boy—but he *had* to know whose car this was and be worrying!

"Well, let's get back to the house. That blasted lawn needs cutting again," Rory said.

There were loud, crunching footsteps and a sharp rustling in the shrubbery. Stupidly, Chloe started to panic and prepared to run from Rory, but the inexplicably alarming sounds receded, assuring her that the three of them were headed away from her.

No one knew she was there. She was still safe.

Realizing that she had almost run away and what that meant, she trembled wildly. She had actually been afraid—*afraid of Rory*.

"Oh, God." Chloe's knees gave way suddenly and she found herself sprawled on hard earth, wild grass and mint crushed beneath her. A thick fall of trees had blocked the water while she was standing, but down there she could see the river through the dying branches. The smell of tattered leaves was thick in the air. The river made a sharp bend at this spot and had slowed to a muddy drool. The lost Chevy would be mostly hidden by muck, perhaps already eaten by rust. How had the boys found it? Probably fishing for river wrack.

Chloe pressed closer to the dead branches, trying to see. Of the car there was no sign. But there was a pile of green plums beside a badly bent sapling that she suspected someone had been using as a slingshot. Harmless boy fun, except it had brought him down to the river. Just like she had been brought down to the river.

On the other side of the canal, a flock—no, a murder; they called it a murder—of crows were feeding on some kind of carrion.

Chloe drew back.

"This is crazy. I'm jumping to conclusions. Maybe it isn't Claude's car in the river. There must be lots of Chevrolets in the area. I saw some driving through town."

But of course it was Claude's car. She knew it as surely as she did the smell of wild *mentha*. Some part of her damned hyperactive subconscious had brought her here.

That, or maybe Isaac's ghost?

"No. This can't be. Think! Why would Claude's car be in the river? There has to be an explanation."

Thoughts—one vision very ugly—flashed through her mind: Claude's body floating in the car. Suspicion was insidious and looking for a toehold in her mind. It asked her if Rory actually knew about her film. If he knew that *she* knew that there had been no handgun at the time of the murder.

She was so far gone that she actually wondered for one moment whether Rory had slept with her because he wanted her silent loyalty rather than her body.

But that was ridiculous—too crazy a thought even for her hysteria. She couldn't doubt the chemistry that had happened between them. It had been there from their first meeting, and he wasn't a dinosaur like his father. He couldn't actually believe that sharing his bed would buy her silence. For heaven's sake! They weren't married. And in this day and age a woman could testify against her husband.

Chloe took a few deep breaths of the crushed mint and began to deliberately quiet her breathing. As soon as she forced the flood of panic away, a reasonable explanation came to mind and aborted the worst of her incipient hysteria.

Claude wasn't in the car. The boys said that they had been down to look at it. No one was in the river. As for why the car was there . . . the car was in the river because Claude—or someone—had put it there. They knew the police would be on the lookout for a '58 Chevy Belaire, so Claude had dumped it in the river, trusting that the current would carry it away from Riverview.

Rory, if he even knew about the car before Bob Munson showed him the derelict, hadn't told her about this for the same reason he hadn't told her anything else. He was protecting his family, and he was protecting her from the dilemma of having to decide whether to go to the sheriff with what she knew. She was projecting her own guilt about not going to the police onto Rory, and the longer she went on living with the lie of omission, the further her trust was eroding. The fault was within her, not with Rory.

Anyway, there was every chance that he would tell her about the car the next time he saw her. The Munsons knew about it, after all.

"Of course." Chloe turned her face into the bruised mint and continued to inhale deeply, hoping it would have a calming effect on her nerves and stomach, both of which were still badly knotted. "But what am I going to do if he doesn't talk to me?"

It was then that she discovered another part of what had altered inside of her.

"Well, damn. How could this have happened so quickly?"

Chloe exhaled slowly. She needed to speak to Rory. Somehow, she had to find a way to tell him that she knew what was going on and not to worry because she wouldn't mention the cemetery to anyone—and all without actually saying anything so baldly. She didn't want to force an acknowledgement of the situation from him before he was ready. She told herself that she wouldn't do it because that was too much like blackmail. If he confided in her, it had to be because he trusted her—and because they were so close that keeping secrets was no longer a possibility. No other confession was worth having.

It might not even be safe.

But would that opportunity for honesty ever come? Probably not, if it were left to Rory. Who in his right mind would ever admit to helping a killer?

"Damn it all. It can't be that hard to drop a hint or two," she said wearily, tired of the guilt and being torn mentally. "He should trust me."

Probably she *should* go to the police and tell them about the car; it had nothing to do with the family burial grounds. That would get everything out in the open. But she already knew that she wasn't going to do it. That was part of the change. Like Rory, she would keep quiet and pray for another rainstorm, one large enough to create the kind of torrent needed to move a heavy automobile down the river and out to sea.

Chloe staggered to her feet, smoothing the dirt and furry seeds from her blouse and skirt. She realized that she smelled strongly of river mint. Though she liked the aroma, the idea of returning to the house drenched in its scent was vaguely troubling. It reminded her of the moment when her faith had failed her. It was sort of like having blood on one's hands or a stain on one's conscience.

"You reek of mint," Rory said into her ear, slipping an arm around her waist and pulling her back from Saint Francis so he could kiss her. "Have you been out playing in the herb garden?"

Chloe couldn't help it; she stiffened slightly when Rory drew her against his damp chest and nibbled on her neck.

The question he'd asked was a perfectly innocent one, but some inner perversity made Chloe choose not answer. Somewhere along the way, she and truth had parted company, and lying now seemed the normal course of action. If Rory wanted truth, she thought pettishly, he should have to begin by telling her at least some part of it.

Or was that childish and stupid?

"Chloe, are you all right?"

"Yes." She cleared her throat.

"You shouldn't be out without a hat," he said, settling his own onto her head. It was large and tilted over her brow. "You look flushed."

Chloe's stance softened.

On the other hand, since it wasn't desirable to live with half-truths and evasions, she promised that she would make an effort to clear the air. Soon.

However, she wouldn't start with the mint and what she had heard at the river. Something smaller would do for the first confession. It was always wise to test the water before diving in.

Sighing, she leaned into Rory's embrace.

"I was in the garden for a little while. I went to the hospital this morning and . . . and afterwards I wanted to take a walk. I've been wandering everywhere."

"You didn't go to the cemetery, did you?" he asked gently.

"No, I didn't." She turned her head and glared at him.

Rory laughed and, tipping up the brim of the hat, kissed her scowling forehead. His large, rough hand caressed her waist. She had to admit that it felt wonderful. While he touched her, it was impossible to believe that anything they had done was truly bad.

"I'll take you there later, if you want to work. I need to get cleaned up and go to the hospital first though. I'd ask you to come, but as you discovered, they are still only allowing family in for visits. Also, there have been some reporters snooping around and I don't want to expose you to that."

"I know about the reporters. The nurse told me." Chloe gave her inner voice a chance to speak up, but it didn't want to say anything about seeing MacGregor.

"Good. I don't want you getting waylaid."

"Well, I know what *you've* been doing this morning," she told him, brushing away some of the stray bits of grass that clung to his arms as she changed the subject. Casually, she added: "You smell of mint too. Have you been rubbing it behind your ears?"

"Do I? I've been staking up plants this morning. That rain set everything off on a growing jag. Even the herb garden is out of control. We've got hours of work left to do."

So, he wasn't going to talk about the river. She tried not to be disappointed.

"You probably won't want to send the boys to the cemetery then." It wasn't a question.

"No, I need them here." He gave her a last squeeze and then let go. "I'll bring some stakes along so we can pull back the creepers while you work."

Stakes, not loppers. He was still thinking it was best to let the cemetery grow over.

"So, you are serious about letting the cemetery be overgrown?" she asked bluntly.

"Yes." Rory's face closed up. "My father has been spending far too much time there. He'll have all eternity after he's dead. There's no need for him to be there now."

Chloe tried to read Rory's face. Was this desire to let the garden grow over simply a desire to protect MacGregor? Maybe he just wanted to put all the worry behind them. If he wanted to forget the slave cemetery, she could understand completely. She never wanted to see it again either.

"He loved your mother very much, you know," she finally said. "That's why he goes there."

"I know. And when he dies I'll see that he is near her. But until he's dead I don't want him hanging around the mausoleum. It's bad for his heart and mind. He needs to get a life. Maybe even to get married again."

Chloe shook her head. "MacGregor will never remarry."

"Well, he can date then." Rory ran an impatient hand through his hair. Leaves rained down. "He isn't *that* old."

"And what about you?" Chloe asked softly. "Are you going to get a life too?"

Rory grinned suddenly. "I'm working on it. I have no ambition to spend my life alone if I can find some woman foolish enough to tolerate my family. But what about you, o mistress of curiosity? Are you beyond all need for husband, hearth and home?" Rory turned away as he asked this, studying his newly mown lawn. "Are you maybe just using me for sex?"

Chloe blinked at the question. Was he making small-talk about *marriage?* Or was he seriously feeling her out?

"N-no. At least, I need a home. Hearth and husband are optional at this point," she said truthfully. Her emotions were mixed on this subject even on a normal day. At present they were too tangled to even attempt deciphering.

"Holding out for the best?" he asked lightly.

"Absolutely."

He turned his head and smiled down at her.

"Good. That limits the competition somewhat. Well, I still need to shower. Want to help?"

Chloe thought about it. Did she want to help him? Surprisingly, in spite of her upset and the weird thoughts popping out of her crazed imagination, she did.

"I'll do your back for you," she said, slipping her hand into his.

"I was rather hoping you'd do more than that."

"We'll see. Let's go in the side door," Chloe said, tugging on Rory's hand.

"Why?" he asked, but he obligingly changed course.

"Because I looked in the window and Morag's

dusting in the front parlor. I don't want her to see us."

"Embarrassed?"

"Yes. Aren't you?"

"No. I'm not." He sounded mildly surprised at her admission.

They stopped by the small door and tried the handle. It was locked.

"Well, I am. I skipped breakfast because I didn't want to see Morag. So, you go in and unlock this door for me."

"I'm really going to sneak you into my own house because you skipped breakfast?"

"Yes, you are—but not because I missed breakfast. I told you that I'm shy."

"Chloe—"

"No sneaking, no shower. I mean it."

"What do you think is going to happen if Morag sees us?" he asked with amused exasperation. "Are you worried that she'll figure out what's going on and say something to MacGregor? Do you think he'd fire you? Or disinherit me?"

"No. I don't think MacGregor would mind a bit that we . . . um . . . that we're seeing each other."

" '*Seeing each other?*' " Rory smiled and shook his head at her choice of euphemisms, but didn't press for further explanations. "You could always climb up on the roof and go in my window. That would avoid the first floor entirely."

Chloe dropped his hand and stepped back to

get a look at the low roof that covered the veranda. Holding Rory's hat with one hand as she tilted her head, she eyed the columns and slender white rails for footholds.

"I guess we could climb up the trellis by the parlor door. It might hold your weight."

Rory started laughing.

"*We?* No thanks. You need to learn when I'm joking. I'll go open the side door. Be right back— and stay off of the roof. You're no good to me if you break a leg."

"Ha!" she said to his back as he disappeared around the front of the house. "I knew you only wanted me for one thing."

He glanced back.

"Maybe. But it's a really big, important thing."

"I've seen it," she retorted, not daring to raise her voice too far. "And it looks a lot more *big* than important."

"Ha! Only a woman could say that. Every man knows it's the most important thing in the world. That's why we all want a sex slave, someone so besotted with us that she will do our every bidding."

A besotted slave. Chloe began to laugh. She wondered if Rory noticed that it held a note of hysteria.

It is with true love like it is with ghosts;
everyone talks of it, but few have seen it.
　　　—*La Rochefoucauld*, Maxims

Chapter Thirteen

Rory and Chloe returned to the hospital that afternoon bearing a bowl of the garden's magnificent roses as a gift for the vigilant nurses. No plants were allowed in the patients' cubicles in the intensive care unit, but the place had seemed so sterile that Chloe insisted that they bring something cheerful into the wing. It was also a nice way to say thank you to the nurses who were serving as watchdogs against the police and reporters.

As she had feared and half-expected, the same nurse was on duty when they returned, and Rory discovered that Chloe was now being welcomed into his father's room. The announcement was cause for a lifted brow, but he didn't question the beaming nurse about the change in hospital policy.

Deciding to implement her new guiding principle of telling the truth whenever possible, Chloe leaned over and whispered into Rory's ear.

"MacGregor told them that I was his daughter-in-law, and I went along with it." She pulled back and paced slowly, waited for his reaction to this announcement.

"He would. The old cuss is as unbending as tempered steel," Rory said in fond exasperation as they paused outside the curtain. He brushed a stray *Veilchenblau* petal from her sleeve and then looked her in the eye. "So, did you talk with him earlier?"

The question made her squirm a little after her earlier reticence, but she answered truthfully. "Yes." She hoped she wasn't blushing. It was hard to be brazen about lies—even ones of omission—when one's own skin gave you away.

"What did he say?" Once again Rory's eyes were watchful. Too watchful for the man she had just made love with. This was not casual interest.

Chloe's heart sank a little. It was like receiving confirmation from the doctor that one did indeed have an illness. And a truthful answer would either kill or cure their relationship.

"He thought I was your mother. He wanted her to understand about . . ." Chloe took a deep breath and lowered her voice another notch. "About what happened in the cemetery. About you helping Claude to get away from the police."

Rory blinked. The rest of his face remained passive, but she could almost hear the gears of thought grind to a halt, re-mesh and start to turn in another direction.

As the silence went on, Chloe wondered if she had made a mistake in being honest. Maybe Rory simply wasn't ready to trust her. Or to have her trust him. Such faith did imply a rather high feeling of intimacy on her part, and they hadn't known each other very long.

"He told you that we helped Claude get away from the police?"

"Not in so many words . . . but yes. That you were hiding him." Deciding to make a clean breast of things, she added: "Look, I already guessed about the break-in. The *weberi* moss in the cemetery was the giveaway. I guess Claude put it there to cover up where Isaac was trying to break into the tomb."

She waited for Rory to comment, but he didn't say anything.

"I know you planted the gun in the cemetery. It wasn't there when I . . . when I found the body." She stopped. Surprisingly, she still couldn't tell him about the film. Her statement got another slow blink as it was assessed. "And I know about the damned car in the river."

Chloe exhaled slowly and started to turn away, glad to have the confessions over with, even if it upset Rory.

"Wait." Chloe might be done confessing, but Rory was not through with the conversation, and he reached out a hand to stop her. "Where are you going?"

Chloe looked at the lavender blossom lying on the speckled tile floor, enjoying the feel of his hand on her waist even it was there for the wrong reasons, and said wistfully, "I'm going to the cafeteria while you see your father. Rory, damn it! I wish you would trust me. I told you before that I wouldn't say anything about the cemetery. Mac-Gregor might not have known who I was when we were talking, but the same rules of confidentiality apply. *He* trusts me—and I am more a stranger to him than to you. Why don't you have a little faith?"

It was Rory's turn to exhale. He pulled her gently into his arms and laid a cheek against her still damp hair. That was much better.

"Sorry, love. I didn't mean to seem distant and untrusting. I have to tell you that I would far rather that you didn't know anything about this, but since you do . . ." His shoulders lifted in what was almost a shrug. "All I can say is *thank you*. I don't know many people who would be so loyal to their word."

Chloe wrapped her arms around Rory and kissed the midline of his chest.

"Well, I'm sorry if I shocked you, but I'm glad that I told you. Now we don't have to keep walking around each other, playing guessing games."

Rory shook his head. "Around each other, no, we don't. But remember that no one else knows about MacGregor *hiding* Claude. It would be better if you could put it out of your mind and didn't speak of it again. Not even to MacGregor. Claude is a fugitive and it is safer if we don't know *anything*."

Chloe looked up into Rory's somber face and nodded.

"You are probably right. We won't talk about it anymore. Hopefully your dad has it all out of system now that he's confessed to Nancy, and he won't say anything either."

"It's for the best that we all forget about it." Rory kissed her nose. "Shall we go see Mac-Gregor now?"

"Okay." Chloe reluctantly dropped her arms. She felt cold without Rory pressed against her.

"Let's tell him the happy news." Rory sounded mischievous.

"What news?" Chloe asked suspiciously.

"That he really almost has a daughter-in-law. I'd rather tell him before Morag does."

"*What?*" They were still conducting their conversation in whispers, but her gasp was loud enough to draw the nurse's attention.

"Well, almost-daughter-in-law sounds better than *lover* or *girlfriend*. A few lurid details about our afternoon might get the old ticker going again. He's been worried that I don't like females, you know. Maybe you could put in a good word for me, testify to my heterosexual nature."

"You say one word about being lovers and we will *never* share a shower again. And don't you dare mention marriage. MacGregor will hound us mercilessly."

Rory's eyes twinkled. "It might be fun to watch MacGregor hound you. Are you sure I can't say just a tiny word or two? 'Cause I really am the type who likes to kiss and tell my father every last detail about my love life."

Chloe relaxed. "Everything has its price. You blab and you go without," she warned him, her tone severe even as she worked to suppress a smile.

"You're a hard woman, Chloe Smith."

"You have no idea."

MacGregor was awake and appeared quite lucid when he turned his eyes upon them. Chloe prayed that he hadn't heard anything that had passed between her and his son out in the hall.

"I hate all the damn whisperin' in this place. It's bloody gloomy," he complained. "The women are all ugly and stubborn—even worse than Morag. I want to go home."

"The doctor says maybe tomorrow or the next day if your heart stays stable and you don't have any more attacks."

MacGregor glowered at his son for a moment and then turned his attention to Chloe. His expression at once softened and he asked kindly: "Well, at least there is one pretty woman who comes to see me. How are you, girl?"

"I'm fine." Chloe smiled back at MacGregor and went over to take his hand. In spite of her warning to Rory about not saying anything to his father she found herself offering him some indirect encouragement. "You need to get better and come home. Morag is being mean to me."

"The old trout! And what is she doin' to you, girl?" MacGregor's voice was stronger than it had been that morning, but still not robust.

"Glaring. For some reason she thinks I have designs on your son."

"Does she now?" MacGregor smiled. "Well, good. It would be perfect if he had some designs on you."

"Well, I expect he does, the cad—but probably nothing honorable." Chloe watched Rory from the corner of her eye. He shook his head but was smiling slightly.

"Sadly, girl, that is the way of men. They see, they lust. If you are lucky, they wake up one morning and decide to make a good thing permanent."

"I'll tell you a secret." Chloe leaned closer and lowered her voice. "It works that way with women too. Sometimes."

"And you lust after my son? Are you sure that you couldn't do better?" MacGregor asked, enjoying this game. Chloe sent a quick glance at Rory, who stood at the back of the room, perfectly content to let her be the one to speak to his father. It was sad that even in this situation the two Patricks weren't able to really talk to one another, but at least she could be a temporary bridge.

"Well, Rory's okay," she temporized. "But I really have designs on Riverview—specifically the Limoges dinnerware we used the other night.

And the rose garden. And I want Oleander, of course. I'd even be willing to keep you around since you can sing. So, as a package deal, it seems like a good bargain."

MacGregor laughed, and the monitor beside the bed began showing greater activity. Chloe glanced at the climbing numbers and hoped that this wouldn't bring the nurse in to scold them.

"I am going to step out for a breath of air," Rory said. "Please feel free to plan my life without me."

"Okay, but it won't be the same," Chloe replied, smiling warmly. "You are so much fun to tease."

Rory smiled back and then slipped out the door.

"You are good to us, girl. We're not deservin' of your generosity, but I am grateful for it. And Rory is too."

Chloe waved a shooing hand, not wanting to talk about indebtedness.

"The nurse said you were here earlier."

"Yes, for a while."

"I don't remember seeing you, just my wife. They had given me something for pain and it made me imagine things, didn't it?" He sounded wistful.

"I think that your Nancy is probably always close by." Chloe gave his hand a gentle squeeze.

"But it was you I talked to this morning, wasn't it?" MacGregor's eyes bored into hers, demanding the truth.

Her policy of veracity was certainly getting a workout that afternoon. Chloe sighed. "Yes, it was."

MacGregor nodded. "I thought so. My Nancy would have been less sweet about things. She had a bit of temper about some matters." MacGregor looked down at the thermal blanket, but he didn't release her hand. Chloe had a feeling the catechism wasn't over. "And did you understand what I was talking about—with Claude?"

"Mostly." Chloe also looked at the blanket and tried not to fidget. This was like getting quizzed in the principal's office.

"And does Rory know?"

"That we talked? Yes. I told him just before we came in."

"Good." MacGregor nodded. "You'll see that he leaves Claude there then. There is no need to move him. He's with family and—" MacGregor stopped and closed his eyes. His face screwed up with pain.

"What's wrong?" But she already knew.

"Damn it to hell and back and again," he gritted out. The bedside monitor burst into panic mode, the lights jumping into the red and the alarm going off.

"Get a doctor!" Chloe shouted at the curtain. Her instruction was unnecessary; there were already feet rushing about in the hall. "Hang on, MacGregor. They'll be here in just a second."

A strange nurse pulled back the curtain and dragged a cart into the room.

"You'll have to leave now." Her voice was more than brisk.

Chloe looked down at the hand that still gripped hers tightly. The nails were tinged with blue. "MacGregor?"

"Yes—leave, girl." It took an effort but he forced his fingers to unclench. His lips also looked vaguely azured. "Find Rory and look after him—and don't forget what I told you. You leave Claude be!"

"I won't forget," Chloe promised as more people ran into the room and a nurse took her firmly by the arm and propelled her out of the way.

"Nancy!" MacGregor choked.

Chloe stood outside the door for a moment, but found the sounds beyond the curtain to be unbearable. Not knowing what else to do, she fled for the waiting room, hoping Rory was there.

She was terribly afraid that this time, MacGregor really was dying.

Death is an evil—the gods have so judged;
had it been good, they would die.
—Sappho

Chapter Fourteen

MacGregor was dead. The words, though not the acceptance of them, had been all that had occupied Chloe's mind for the last three days while arrangements for MacGregor's cremation and memorial service were made. Because there had been no one to go with her to the cemetery while she continued her work, even if she had had the heart to be there with MacGregor dead, there had been nothing to do except stay at the house where all Riverview mourned MacGregor's passing with old-fashioned crepe bows on the doorknockers and shrouded mirrors. Even the grandfather clock in the library had been stopped, so its chimes did not strike. It was creepy and depressing.

Roland Lachaise had arrived at Riverview on the day following MacGregor's death, but rather than being a comfort to her, her employer had looked so bereft that Chloe spent much of her time trying to comfort him on his loss instead of the other way around.

And, after all, why should he comfort her? He didn't know that she was also bereaved. There wasn't any good way to make clear the bond she had formed with MacGregor without explaining everything that had happened at Riverview, including Claude's disappearance and Isaac's murder. So she said nothing. Instinctively, she had a feeling that anyone who had not been in the trenches with them the last couple of weeks could ever understand the union that had evolved between her and the Patricks because of their shared wariness of Sheriff Bell.

Her days were understandably lonely, but she was all alone in the evenings too. That was much worse. Rory had not sought out her company at night since the day MacGregor died, a fact that bothered her tremendously, though she supposed that perhaps he stayed away lately because of Roland being in residence and having some misguided chivalrous impulse to protect her from her boss's displeasure at her unprofessional behavior. It was a nice thought, but Roland was bound to suspect something when she failed to return to Atlanta by the end of the week.

Whatever his reasons for avoiding her at night, Rory wasn't around a great deal at any other time either. And when he was . . . It wasn't that Rory was cold to her. He was always kind during the day when she bumped into him, but he was obviously distracted when they talked and he was often away at the nursery for hours at a time.

At first Chloe had blamed his daytime distance on grief and the emotional drain of the logistics of orchestrating a sufficiently grand passage into the afterlife for his father. But Rory was managing those details, and also running his business, without any apparent difficulty. And as time went on, and some of the emotional cloud lifted from around her brain, Chloe began to think again.

Was Rory was avoiding her? Not Riverview and its ritualized unhappiness, but her?

If so—*why?* Did he regret their affair? Or was it something else? Something connected with Claude and Isaac that hadn't been aired when they were telling each other the truth?

Of course, Rory had never said that he was telling her the truth. The admissions had all been on her side.

It was only after this suspicion entered her besotted brain, and she started thinking back with an eye for detail, that she recalled her last conversation with MacGregor. Given her undivided attention, a paradigm shifted, and the seed that had so painfully occupied her subconscious for the last week finally sprouted. It began to heave its tendrils of doubt out into her waking thoughts, and other, unpleasant explanations for Rory's avoidance of Riverview began presenting themselves.

The fruit of knowledge—or at least of her

supposition—was bitter. Once she tasted the crop of speculation, all her ugly suspicions and insecurities popped out again, demanding to be examined. Horrors propagated like weeds. She couldn't dig them out fast enough to ever get ahead, and Chloe was finally forced into asking herself some of the nasty questions she had shelved after becoming Rory's lover. Her tidy explanation of what had happened with Isaac and Claude, which had begun to crumble when it was subjected to mental pressure, was melted down completely in the crucible of logic.

Instead of fighting her intuition, she now began to listen to it when it whispered. And open to accepting unpleasant facts, she began to have strange visions every time she stood idle—snippets of scenes like trailers for a B movie. The most persistent image was of Roger rubbing at Claude, rubbing at Claude's bedroom door, then rubbing on the black door that led into tomb forty-six. It was like a connect-the-dot puzzle, or a math equation: a equals b, b equals c, therefore a equals c.

At first she wondered if she weren't receiving some guidance from beyond the grave, but forced herself to immediately eject such irrational credulities from her brain. She was *not* her Granny Claire, and she couldn't afford such superstition about the dead if she were to continue with her present line of work. If she believed that the dead could talk to her, could invade her brain with messages, she would never be able to set foot in a cemetery again.

But the spells—the mental pictures—persisted, and minus the presence of paranormal interference, no tangible reason for the strange and ghastly visions that presented themselves could be found. It was as if the apparitions had inserted themselves into her psyche and would not go away, not even when she slept.

Yet, in spite of everything, the nightmares and suspicions, she wished that Rory was there with her. Maybe his presence at her side would keep the hallucinations away when she slept.

And maybe, her conscience said sharply, she needed to know the truth to end the indisposition.

Proof either way was attainable, but for days she did not seek it out. The exorcism of discovery might work to end her visions, but it seemed too rude a thing to do while observing MacGregor's death.

And . . . she was afraid.

Of course, the very fear that made her hesitate to know the truth was also a shameful goad. Thanks to Granny Claire's insistence that Chloe was going to start having the Sight, would one day have to testify for the dead and dying, she felt she had to act to disprove the notion of psychic channeling. Having some form of ESP she could accept—but not messages from the dead!

There were other matters at stake, too. Could she walk away and leave her crazy fear unchallenged and still retain any self-respect? If she backed away from this situation, wouldn't the horror only mature and breed other fears when she went on to a new job and her imagination again caught fire? And more practically, if she let the cemetery grow over without investigating, if she never knew for certain what was in tomb forty-six, could she ever really forget what had happened here?

But on the other hand . . . Chloe got up and took a turn about the bedroom, feeling confined and restless.

Could she live with the answers if her new fears proved factual? And whatever would she say to Rory if they were correct? True or false, could she ever face him again after proving her lack of trust? There was historic precedent to consider. The messenger often got blamed for bad news.

Chloe looked out her bedroom window. It was dark enough for twilight, though it was only just past noon. The clouds overhead brooded. The storm the Munsons had predicted earlier that week had finally arrived, and the Atlantic billows were swollen with rain. She could only wonder why the tempest hadn't broken yet. Perhaps it waited on MacGregor. Maybe the storm would hold back its violent tears until after the memorial service.

Maybe it held back so she would have a last chance to tell someone about the car in the river.

It was a foreign thought. Chloe shivered.

"Gran?"

"And why haven't you come to me about this nasty problem?" the voice of Granny Claire asked, as the light in the room dimmed. Chloe was willing to bet that though these bulbs had dimmed by half, the rest of the house remained bright.

Of course, there was a better explanation. She was imaging things. Chloe didn't turn from the window. Her grandmother wasn't really there—couldn't be there—so it didn't matter if she refused to look behind her.

Still, hallucination or manifestation, she felt compelled to answer.

"Take a wild guess, Gran. Why wouldn't I come to you in my hour of need?"

"Because you're still young and perhaps as stupid as I always feared."

"Yeah, that must be it. It couldn't have anything to do with you being nasty and hurting me every chance you got."

"Nasty I may be, but I know one thing. You can't order this power, girl. All you can do is find order in it. There are tools that can help. I can help, if you quit being stubborn and ask me. . . . I can't believe you're my only heir."

"Fine. Then, help. Tell me what to do."

"Not so fast. What do you want—truth or happiness? And try not to be a fool. Tell me what you really want."

Chloe's brows pulled together. The nasty voice

certainly sounded like Granny Claire was actually in the room.

"Of course it's really me, you idiot girl. I don't have to *be* there to *be* there. It's all part of being psychic and sharing blood. Did you listen to anything I told you?"

"Fine, you're here but not here," Chloe whispered desperately—to her grandmother, to her subconscious, or just to her imagination. "I want truth then. If you know it. Tell me what happened. What does Rory know?"

Her grandmother snorted, and Chloe could feel her anger and contempt like a physical blow.

"I'm disappointed in you, but hardly surprised. You're afraid of losing Rory and so you lie—even to yourself. You don't want the whole truth, so it's a coward's truth you shall have." The room darkened further. "You can quit worrying. You're safe with your young man. He's as innocent as you are in this matter. You can be happy, too, if you ignore anything unpleasant that comes bubbling up in your dreams. He's very wealthy. Keep your mouth shut and grow some irises and live in a dead man's mansion."

Chloe snorted. "Like that will work if I keep dreaming."

"If you're going to be an ignorant fool, you may as well be a rich one," Gran insisted.

"I'm not a fool—and anyone would be afraid to know these things. Anyone normal. Go away," she said. "I don't want you or your Sight. Neither has ever helped me or made me happy."

"Suit yourself. You always do. But the Sight is there to stay. You're going to have to make peace with it."

And as suddenly as she had arrived, Granny Claire was gone. Chloe looked down at the courtyard as the room behind her returned to normal brightness.

Inner vision gave way to outer vision, and she finally grew aware of what her eyes were seeing. There was a harsh wind waiting out there. With no rain to toss about, it had discovered some autumnal leavings to sport with, and it drove the desiccated remains before it with dry clatters. They rose up in giant arcs, graceful and tawny with the odd storm light showing through their skeletal veins. One dead maple pressed itself against the glass and clung there desperately as the wind tore at it.

She laid a hand against the pane, her fingers trembling slightly as she traced the curled edges of the buffeted leaf. Poor thing, naked and shivering, forced to hard places against its will. It reminded her so much of her own helpless situation.

Only, she wasn't helpless. Not really. That was just her reaction to an old ingrained fear of her grandmother. There were two hours yet before the service. Plenty of time to go to the cemetery. If that was what she wanted to do.

Granny Claire was wrong about her. She wasn't a coward. Chloe sat down abruptly and pulled off her heels and stockings. God help her, but she *had* to know if her suspicions were true. She wouldn't tell Roland—wouldn't tell Rory—she would just go and find her answers.

She would deal with the consequences of knowledge later.

Chloe stared at the strange light that filled up the rustling woods and bathed the monuments in a green haze. She wondered distantly if the nightmare color was all in her head. There was certainly a shrieking disharmony between the peacefulness of the abandoned cemetery and the horrible suspicions in her brain.

Today she didn't linger at any of the monuments, especially Nancy's library. She was on a mission and went straight to Edana and Calvin's tomb.

The dark vines along the path had grown feral and had lost all sense of their former borders until they overgrew most of trail to tomb forty-six. This new storm would trigger more hysterical growth. In a week, the cemetery could be swallowed. It was what Rory wanted.

Chloe sniffed the rank and musty air. It reminded her vividly of the nightmare she had had before coming to Riverview. The air was full of the smell of ghosts and other hauntings . . . and it was new. Until a week ago, the cemetery had been a peaceful place. Now restless spirits walked.

It seemed an omen that Roger was already there at the lordly gray death house, waiting for her on the steps, tail twitching impatiently.

"Have you been waiting long, cat?" she whispered.

Her hands shook as she pulled out the stolen key and walked carefully over the creeper-covered path. She half expected the vines to wrap about her ankles and drag her back from the tomb. Yet nothing touched her as she walked, and she made it to the dark wood door that separated the dead from the living without being molested. She paused there, giving herself one last chance to turn back, not to violate the trust that had been placed in her, the chance not to know the horrible truth.

What was it that Oscar Wilde had said? Something about it being *"always with the best intentions that the worst deeds are done"*?

But violation or not, she still needed to know what was beyond the door. For her sake—and for Rory's—she had to know.

"Mmmmrrreeooooow." Roger batted at her leg, chastising her for the delay.

Chloe shoved the old iron key in the lock and turned it hard, though the force was unnecessary. The lock opened without a sound.

She laid a hand against the panel and pushed steadily. The dead moss bandage tore with an unpleasant noise somewhere between shredding cloth and ripping paper. Above her, the oaks shuddered and moaned.

Beyond the door there was only gloom, darkness barely relieved by the odd green light that filtered through the leafy canopy overhead. She looked first at the door. It bore no sign of damage under the moss. No one had attacked it with a crowbar or shovel. It was pristine except for the yellowed moss. If anyone had gotten inside, they had used a key.

Next, she peered at the floor. Her nose had grown sensitized to the smell of death, and sure enough it was there. Small deaths, but many of them. A greedy arachnid had set up its web near the door and spread its silk trap with gay abandon. The ants and other crawling insects had provided it with a smorgasbord, and evidence of its gluttonous feasting littered the floor.

Why were there ants in this old tomb? There should be nothing left for them to eat here.

She watched the giant web billow with the inrush of damp air. There was no eight-legged horror in it now. Still, she loathed it. Avoiding the sticky trap, Chloe pushed the door wider and stepped into the crypt.

Roger immediately followed. He was not fastidious about the treacherous silk but trudged right through, dragging the chitin-encrusted cerement behind him. She tried hard to suppress the image but still thought of a shrouded zombie lurching from the grave.

As expected, there were three brick vaults in the wall. All were cloaked with cobwebs, some old and gray and some new and white. The first two openings were bricked up in an intricate pattern that resembled the herringbone of a wool coat. The powdery mortar beyond the ancient, abandoned webs was crumbling from the years of intense summer heat, and in some places was missing altogether. There were no obvious markers to tell her which grave belonged to Edana and which to Calvin, and she did not look for them. The long dead Patricks were not what brought her there.

Chloe forced herself a step closer to the third crypt, where Roger sat covered in wisps of gray cobweb. This one didn't belong. It had been bricked up in a less careful manner, the style a simple running bond. She didn't need to peer closely beyond the new silken veil to see that the mortar on this vault was fresh and covered with more dead *weberi* moss, which—so damningly when one knew the truth—didn't like to grow on stone but looked so wonderfully aged when it was dead.

So, now she knew.

Unable to think coherently about what she had found, Chloe looked at her watch and tried to make sense of the glowing numbers. Finally she was able to arrange them into a familiar pattern and understand that she had less than an hour until the memorial service. She needed to go back to the house, return the keys to MacGregor's desk, and then change back into her black dress and stockings.

Carefully, she retrieved the cat and locked the

old black door behind her. She did her best to mend the shredded moss, then laid several long creepers over the sill. She didn't know which she was doing; hiding the evidence of her trespass, or simply hiding the tomb and its residents.

"Come on, Roger," she whispered, her vocal chords sounding rusty and pained. "We have to go now."

As though he understood her and was now content, the cat started down the path to the cemetery gate. Chloe followed close on wooden legs. Around her, the trees and creepers shivered as the wind whispered through them.

Rory's restless eyes continued searching for Chloe even as his head nodded automatically to Roland Lachaise's reminiscences about his father. He had been looking for her since they returned from the church. They had been separated at the chapel and other than seeing her climb into a car with Roland, he had not had so much as a glimpse of her since.

Determined to find her, Rory planted himself in the center of the music room where he could see all doors. It was an odd place to receive condolences, but he didn't care, for his vigilance was finally rewarded with a glimpse of Chloe descending the main stairs. She looked exceedingly pale and her gaze was unfocused as she pushed politely through the crowd that chattered in the foyer.

Rory felt a piercing guilt that he had left her so much on her own while dealing with the minutiae of death. Obviously, MacGregor's demise had affected her tremendously. He shouldn't be surprised at this. After all, she had been willing to withhold what she thought was important information from the police because of her affection for his father. Rory experienced another small twist of pain. This felt more like jealousy, though, than guilt over his behavior, and it angered and shamed him that he had slipped so far as to become illogical. Chloe had clouded his judgment.

The fact of the matter was that he didn't know what she would do now that MacGregor was gone. In spite of their being lovers, large parts of her were held back from him. Would her vow of silence remain? Would she stay at Riverview? And if she did, would it only be to finish her job—a job he wanted stopped? The cemetery could never be added to that national database. It had to remain hidden, forgotten.

"Lovely memorial, my boy! MacGregor would have adored all the attention. I am glad that so many of his friends could come."

Rory nodded again, ignoring Roland, eyes still on Chloe.

The services had been simple and well attended by local people, but he hadn't a clue what had actually been said. Rory had focused all his attention on the flowers at the altar, the smell of hot wax, gladiolas and spicy stock filling the air with the expected ritualized scents of death. Whatever lies—or even truths—the young priest said of

MacGregor were irrelevant to him. One greater truth had superceded them all.

It was the reality that would likely take Chloe from him if she ever discovered it. It was the mark of Cain on the Patricks. It made him feel guilty whenever he was near her. He didn't know if he could bear to see her face if she ever knew the truth of what had really happened. How could he stand to watch the affection fade from her eyes and fill up instead with fear and loathing?

Rory grimaced. He should have sent her away immediately. Now it was too late. She was involved up to her pretty little neck, her innocence forever spoiled by knowledge she shouldn't have.

Regardless of his feelings and his father's wishes, he knew what he needed to do. It would have to wait until all the guests were gone. Only Roland was staying at the house, but the man was observant and in tight with Morag. It was better to wait until there were no outside witnesses. Still, with Chloe so insistent and curious about everything in the cemetery, Claude would soon have to be moved somewhere else—perhaps into the river when the tide was high and the waters raging.

Then, they would see what happened—if Chloe could let the matter of Claude's disappearance go. If she couldn't . . . Though he hated to even consider the other options, he would have to decide what else to do about Chloe. The list of choices was short and unpleasant.

License my roving hands, and let them go.
                    —*John Donne*

Chapter Fifteen

The storm was a wild threnody, the rain a canorous violence that cleansed the land. Chloe sat curled in the wingback chair by the window and watched the heavens explode with brilliant light while the rain beat out its violent dirge against the old glass that still refused it entrance. She debated for a while about whether to go out into the storm herself to attempt purification by stormy baptism, but she had decided that it was fire that would burn the ugliness out of her mind. She knew now what she was going to do. She was simply waiting for the rest of the house to retire to bed before seeking Rory out.

Chloe smiled a little as she thought of Roland's favorite maxim—it was from *Ecclesiasticus*: "Let thy speech be brief, comprehending much in a few words." It was apt. What she wanted from Rory was at once very simple and very complicated.

Words had many shadings—one could even lie by omission. And to ask for the truth was no help. Truth was a chimera. There were so many kinds of truth: religious truth, statistical truth, moral truth, legal truth, emotional truth. . . .

It was only the last one that she was concerned with tonight. And to know what Rory truly felt would not require any words. Indeed, words would probably only confuse the situation.

Once this question was answered, then she could decide which other truths—legal, moral, and so on—she wished to address. If she were lucky, the flames would be hot enough that nothing would rise from their ashes and there would be no more decisions to be made.

She watched the light show as it retreated into the distance, then listened to the wind's melodious howling for a few minutes more before it also faded away. Then she stood up and went to find her slippers. The floor beneath her feet was chill and vaguely damp and she disliked the feeling. It reminded her too much of her now familiar nightmare about the bitterly cold ground swallowing her legs as it gulped her down into the bony soil. She would not be able to enjoy Rory if she could not ignore the dream.

Chloe paused at the armoire, hearing footsteps in the hall. The tread was familiar, though quieter than it was during the day. The mountain had come to Mohammad.

Chloe exhaled and turned to face the door. The

latch lifted, and as though summoned by her thoughts, Rory stepped silently inside her borrowed room. At first he was a shadow, but soon proved to be not just a wishful dream but the man of flesh and blood.

She moved toward him quickly, unable to suppress a small involuntary cry. The door closed and in an instant they were on the floor, which no longer seemed cold. Hot hands were beneath her robe, stroking skin as though they were in a speed trial that required him to touch all surface area in a limited amount of time. He seemed as wild as the storm, as rough and as charged with unexploded energy as the air outside the house.

The tie at her waist was pulled from its loops and the overlapping panels shoved open. She had not bothered with a nightgown, coy seduction playing no part in her plans for the evening.

Though she had not intended to speak, a few words slipped unbidden from her lips as she pushed his discarded slacks to the side. "It's about damn time," she muttered, sinking her fingers into his hair. The auburn blaze was hidden by the tract of darkness provided by the bed's high mattress, but she could feel the familiar texture of silken fire beneath her hands. It wasn't something that she would ever forget. He was burned into tactile memory.

Rory laughed silently, and paused long enough in his inventory of her torso to drop a kiss on her nose. "Sorry. I was unavoidably detained."

"By a flying saucer full of emasculating aliens?" she suggested with a trace of sarcasm. "Nothing less will do. It's been *days*. I was beginning to think that I was the world's worst lover."

Rory smiled at her, his teeth showing white. "I wish it was something so exotic. No, it was Morag, then Roland, then Sheriff Bell—and it was me." He groaned then and lowered his head to her neck and then down to her breasts. Chloe let him go. "I was being an idiot, trying to stay away until the time was right."

"That was idiotic all right, but possibly you couldn't help it." She managed this concession. She had forgotten that the police would still be actively looking for Claude; they wouldn't stop and mourn with the Patricks. If anything, Mac-Gregor's death might make them twice as annoying. Rory was the last Patrick who might know anything about his cousin.

"But it wasn't only that which kept me away, I swear it. Everyone has come to Riverview to see me tonight. Do you think there is a conspiracy to keep us apart?" he asked as he turned his head from side to side, sampling her flesh with tiny nips and then dragging his cheek along the path of his assault.

Chloe laughed without humor. "Oh, yes. There's a conspiracy and I know the members— only I wasn't asked to join because it's a males-only club. No girls allowed."

Rory paused for one instant, surprised by her

answer. "Yes, maybe there has been a conspiracy," he said. "But it's been disbanded. I won't be that foolish again."

After that, he didn't speak another word.

The floor was abandoned in favor of the bed's comfort. Chloe had always known of Rory's strength. She had watched him lift and carry his father up a long flight of stairs, but it was still amazing when he stood up from the floor with her weight suspended in his arms and not giving so much as a grunt.

It was all in the configuration of tendons, she told herself. She could go to the gym and lift weights for a dozen years, but she would never have that kind of strength in her body. Her weaker joints would not allow it.

The sense of helplessness that being lifted into the air engendered was at once terrifying and also arousing. In punishment for causing her new fear, she bit Rory on the shoulder. He rolled, pulling her on top of him. The invitation was plain and she accepted gladly. Down she slid, enveloping him, taking him all the way into her and stretching her legs out until their pelvises ground together, increasing the pressure on her abdomen and in turn upon Rory.

Chloe laughed, this time breathlessly, and asked: "Did you ever name it?"

"It?" he asked.

"You *membrum virile*," she said, contracting her inner muscles. "The one-eyed cyclops, the—"

"I follow you. I thought that you and Richard had been formally introduced." He stopped speaking as she contracted her muscles again.

She laughed. "I'm afraid that he always left so hurriedly that I didn't catch the name."

"Well, he's in no hurry tonight. At least, he wasn't until just a couple of minutes ago."

"But now?"

"Now I think that perhaps I had better be on top. You obviously don't have the knack of this yet. We really do fit together if you do it right."

"Rory!" But she didn't fight when he rolled her under him and wrapped his fists in her hair.

"Did you know that the female pudenda used to be called Abraham's bosom?" he asked as he rocked his hips against her, reversing the roles of torturer and victim.

"I thought you said his name was Richard."

"Will you be upset if I call you Richard's bosom?"

Chloe signed and lifted her hips. "Probably not if you whisper it in my ear, but at this point I think it would be better to just let Richard speak for himself."

"Hell, yes! I couldn't agree more. You want poetry or prose? Richard does both equally well."

"Lyrical is nice, but let's start with the short words—the four-letter kind." She spread her hands over his flank and squeezed lightly. He shivered.

"If we start there it will end there," he warned. "He doesn't mix his messages."

"Don't worry. You're young. We'll just practice until Richard gets it right."

Rory answered with his body. He slid up her belly until their loins met, proving that they did indeed fit together. He was showing off, the way he kept himself suspended above her on forearms the whole time, but she allowed it since he brought with him the fire she needed to burn off the last of her bitterness and distrust.

His body said what he had not been able to confess with words. He'd missed and wanted her. He trusted her, too—at least as much as he trusted anyone—and he had hope for their future. Surely this was what he meant. He wouldn't have come to her otherwise.

Granny Claire might have been right. It was possible that Chloe could be happy—and safe— with Rory. Love, which would come with time, could be enough.

A man must serve his time in every trade
Save censure—Critics come all ready made.
—Lord Byron

Chapter Sixteen

The morning was hot and wet, washed over with lingering rain and uneasiness. That afternoon, she and Rory were to take MacGregor to his Nancy. But first there was something else they had to do. The dead would have to wait on the living.

Chloe woke first and slipped from her bed as quietly as she was able. It didn't really matter if Rory woke up, but she wasn't ready to face him in the light of morning when some conversation would be required. She didn't want to face him with her dreams so close that they all but whispered in her ear.

Clothes were gathered before she glided into the bathroom to wash and dress. She wrote a note to leave on the bedside table telling Rory that she had to go into town for some film and wouldn't be back until three o'clock.

The note was a lie, of course. It was also a test, a way of discovering what he knew and therefore what she should do. If he didn't take the bait, then he was probably innocent. Chloe figured that if he was aware of what was in that tomb, then he needed to act now, while the river was in spate and would carry away the body. At least, that was what she would do if she wanted to get rid of a corpse—and she was fairly certain that Rory would want the body gone. He didn't have any of MacGregor's sentimentality, and he understood how the police worked.

In a way, she hoped that he wasn't ignorant of what had happened. If he didn't know what had occurred, then she would either have to leave him in darkness, with an unexploded bomb ticking away in tomb forty-six, or she would have to tell him—maybe even prove—the nightmare of what had really happened to Claude Patrick.

But if he did know, if he had in fact participated in—or, if her dream was correct, even perpetrated Claude's demise . . . Well, she still didn't know what she would do. If she could stay. That might be the one line that she could not cross.

Chloe stopped for some breakfast, eating quickly but thoroughly since she didn't know when she would be back for another meal. Then, taking a blanket from the trunk of her car, she went to the cemetery.

It was an effort to climb the gate of the necropolis, but the vines aided her both with handholds and with cushioning from the spikes. It would have been easier to steal the keys from MacGregor's desk, but she didn't want any reason for Rory to be alerted to her presence in the cemetery.

She walked slowly, strolling through the disappearing park and appreciating the monuments for a last time. She was fairly certain that Rory would not want her to finish the job of cataloging the tombs, and she could understand why. After all, once the cemetery was added to the database—assuming that the database was actually secure, something that Chloe had come to doubt—then there would be a record, an official listing of the cemetery at Riverview.

Bell was like a dog with a bone. Once Claude Patrick's manhunt wore down and there were still no clues to his whereabouts, that ambitious lawman might make the connection between one illegal burial and the other missing man. And he might start making enquires of other agencies.

It was only a slim chance that they would think to access this database—very few people knew of it—but with Isaac having been found in the slave cemetery, there was always the chance of someone looking up cemeteries and finding that Riverview had two.

And as for keeping copies of the cemetery photos with Digital Memories, that wasn't an option either. If the police obtained a search warrant or subpoenaed Roland, he would have no choice but to turn over the photos.

Of course, if Claude were to disappear—really disappear—that would take care of any criminal charges ever being leveled against MacGregor or Rory. But it would still not prevent some eager beaver like Sheriff Bell from eventually electronically prying into Riverview out of sheer nosiness and revealing its contents to the world. And there was always that pesky lingering DNA evidence to worry about. It wasn't likely that they would open up every tomb and search out every set of bones for testing, but still . . . statistical safety had been beaten out by fate more than once.

Chloe found a concealed spot on the far side of Edana and Calvin's tomb and spread her blanket over the damp oak leaves. She lay down on her back and settled in to wait.

She smiled at the tomb's decoration looming over her. It really was overbuilt by a Gothic imagination on steroids. It looked like a castle from a fairy tale—one of the darker tales, to be sure—but it was still beautiful in an otherworldly way. All of Riverview was this way. She would miss it if she had to leave.

She closed her eyes and waited. She half expected to hear from Granny Claire, but the old lady stayed away. Maybe she could only visit when there was a storm. That was one more thing that Chloe needed to know about.

It wasn't too many minutes later that she heard footsteps coming down the path. As she had half expected, she heard keys scraping in the mausoleum's lock and the door being pushed open. Someone went inside.

She waited, breath held, to hear if the shoddy brick wall was battered by a mallet, but there was nothing. Just the normal silence filled with the droning of bees.

Chloe sat up. Finally decided and unable to wait, she rose to her feet and went to meet Rory.

Rory stepped back out into the daylight and was not at all surprised to see Chloe waiting for him. He turned and locked the tomb door, giving himself another moment before speaking.

When he again faced her, she looked briefly at his empty hands and then nodded once.

"I wondered if you would have a pick or mallet." Her voice was quiet and neutral, as was her expression.

"Not in daylight. I . . . So you guessed after all," he said, feeling suddenly bleak.

"Yes."

Rory looked up at the bower overhead. Everything was so peaceful. It didn't seem possible that his nightmare had finally happened and that this place would soon be invaded by outsiders. His father would be rolling in his grave—supposing he was ever permitted to be interred in one.

"So what now?" he asked finally. It took an effort not to rub at his chest, so heavy was the ache behind his sternum.

"Nothing."

Rory lowered his gaze to his lover's face and stared, disbelieving.

"Nothing?" he asked, not persuaded that his ears had heard correctly.

"I've thought about it from every angle. Bottom line, I promised your dad that I wouldn't say anything about Claude, you, or this cemetery. In fact, his last words to me were that I should look after you and see that you didn't move Claude."

"You knew even then?" he asked, stunned and disoriented.

"No. I didn't understand what he meant. I didn't know for certain until yesterday when I came out to the tomb, but . . ." She trailed off.

"But you knew something was wrong? You've sensed it all along."

She nodded, eyes watchful.

"My Granny Claire says I have the Sight, an affinity for the dead. Maybe I do. It certainly runs in our family. I kept having these dreams."

He digested this, uncertain if he could believe this.

"I didn't know what MacGregor had done until after you found Isaac's body. He told me then." Rory shrugged, unable to explain his actions. "He was terribly sorry that you found the body—that you were upset. I . . . I am damned sorry too. We never meant for you to get messed up in this."

"I know. MacGregor said that when we were at the hospital."

"You were hoping that Isaac killed Claude and

MacGregor only killed Isaac in retaliation, weren't you?"

She shook her head.

"That was one possibility that never occurred to me. . . . I wonder why? I think MacGregor could have done something like that."

"It could have happened that way. MacGregor never said for sure."

"Yes, it could have happened like that," she said kindly. But she didn't believe that, and he knew better.

Chloe suddenly offered her hand. It was a tentative gesture, her palm turned up with fingers curved inward, as though she were uncertain that he would want to touch her and was prepared to curl up and withdraw the offer at any sign of hostility.

Rory stared at her extended hand, also uncertain of what to do. It seemed impossible that she could want to touch him, that she wasn't reviling him for being a liar and the son of a murderer. Or worse. Among the thoughts that hadn't occurred to her was that he might have committed the murders himself. In some ways, that made more sense than suspecting his father. MacGregor was old and had a bad heart. Hauling around a bunch of bodies should have been beyond him.

"I don't know what to say," he confessed. "I want you too much to know what is best to do."

Chloe took a slow breath and then said deliberately: "I think that right now we should take your father to his Nancy. It would be wisest to move Claude, but I don't think we will. In spite of what he and Isaac tried to do, MacGregor wanted him here with family. If there is never any record of it, we can just let the cemetery grow over and forget about doing anything with the photographs. In five years, there won't be a single trace of it visible, not even from the air. And by then the mortar will have aged enough that no one will ever guess it wasn't original . . . if we decide to open the cemetery back up again some day."

Her words were a gift, perhaps the most precious Rory would ever receive.

He exhaled and took her hand. His own fingers were trembling with the aftermath of emotion—with relief. He squeezed gently as he laced their fingers.

"What about Roland?"

"You'll just have to hire me to work on your catalogue if he sacks me—and he probably will when I tell him that I think I'm done with graveyards."

"It's a deal." Rory took a breath, feeling maladroit but also compelled to confess. "This is one hell of a time to tell you this, but I love you. I would have told you before, but I couldn't, not under the circumstances. I didn't let myself think about it—not when I wasn't being honest with you and didn't know what would happen."

Chloe nodded and smiled a little. "I love you, too, you know. That's still surprising."

"You must love me. No one who wasn't completely over the moon would do anything this outrageous." He laughed a little. Relief made him giddy.

"No? Not even a Patrick?"

Rory shook his head. "We weren't all that insane. MacGregor was a throwback."

It was Chloe's turn to laugh.

"Yes, you were all insane. I've been reading the diaries. Your relatives were absolutely nuts. All of them. And that's okay. I have some things to tell you about my family too. For starters, I have a grandmother who is a real, live witch. And not a nice one either." She looked dead serious as she said this.

"A witch?" He found this as hard to believe as her belief in divination through dreams. It sounded a bit mad. But perhaps only a crazy woman would be able to know the truth and to love him.

"You think I'm kidding?"

"No, but we can talk about it another day. I'm more interested in us. What do you think we should do now? About being in love, I mean," he asked, dropping an arm over her shoulders and pulling her against him. He was awed and humbled. This should never have happened. He had truly believed that he would never hold her in his arms again.

"I don't know. This happened awfully fast," she answered, wrapping her arms about his waist and laying her cheek against his shoulder. She sighed.

"Let's just take care of business as it comes, hang around for the summer, shoot pictures for your catalogue and see what happens in the fall?"

Rory nodded and then buried his face in her hair. Hr breathed deeply, loving the scent.

"Okay. We'll just wait and see what happens." But he was lying again. He knew what he wanted and would be working toward his goal. It was Chloe's fault if she ended up legally tied to him. She should know better than to trust him.

Epilogue

That night Chloe dreamed. At first she wasn't aware that she slumbered. Granny Claire's voice was as clear as the telephone as it shrilled in her ear, demanding her attention as she swayed back and forth in the old rocking chair in Rory's bedroom.

"So, you figured it out. But are you going to admit what you know? Of course not," the voice nagged. "You're *in love* and would rather trust yourself to a murderer than face up to what the Sight has shown you. How am I ever going to train you if you remain deliberately obtuse?"

"You're not training me. Now go away. It's the middle of the night," Chloe muttered. Then, annoyed: "And what do you mean I'd rather trust myself to a murderer? MacGregor's dead. It doesn't matter if I trusted him. Anyway, he would never have hurt me."

"Stupid girl. I'm not talking about MacGregor. Like all the rest, he's gone and no more important than anyone else whose name was writ on water."

Chloe's eyes opened. Angered, she rose quickly. It was only when she got up from the rocking chair and saw her body still snoozing in the bed that she realized she wasn't truly awake.

"I said *I'm not talking about MacGregor.*" The tone was louder and crueler. Chloe turned toward her angry grandmother, but before she could respond another voice answered this accusation. It offered a fair imitation of the good witch, Glinda, from *The Wizard of Oz.*

"Be gone, evil one, before someone drops a house on you too," the poisonously sweet voice ululated. "I cast you out, unclean spirit!" Something that looked like raindrops flew through the air and landed on the old lady with a fizzing hiss that made Granny Claire shriek and twirl about.

"Fool—you won't get anywhere without me," the woman swore as she spun, but the fizzing sound grew stronger and whorls of smoke began to rise from her body. Chloe watched in horrified fascination as the head began to inflate. Granny Claire's face grimaced as it stretched to twice its natural size and then popped like a balloon. The old lady was gone, leaving only a faint whiff of sulfur in the air.

"Wow. That's a neat trick. Was that holy water?" Chloe asked.

"Of a sort," she heard her own voice reply, and

she turned toward the dresser where another Chloe stood. This one was dressed in an enormous pink ball-gown and wore a gold and crystal crown, just like Glinda. She laid her scepter on the dresser and tugged at the bodice of her gown. "Hello. I thought it was time that we meet formally."

Not knowing what else to say, Chloe said hello back.

"Do you know who I am?" the second Chloe asked, and when Chloe didn't reply, her doppelganger said: "I'm the shadow you. The Other. The Knowing. The Sight. I'd like to be friends, but you'll have to be a little patient with me as I'm only just waking up. Sorry about your grandma disturbing your sleep. I'll be more diligent from now on."

"Oh." Chloe thought about this. She felt odd, unsettled but accepting of what this other Chloe said. She thought that it might be because this was a dream, but also because it was real. "That's a nice thought, but can I trust you? You've frightened me a lot, you know. Those dreams are terrible and not very long on specifics. I'm never quite certain what I'm supposed to do."

"I'm sorry. They're terrible for me too. I don't like them, you know. I'd rather we get stockmarket tips or be able to guess the sex of unborn babies. But I am what I am, a sort of harbinger of death."

"Great." But it was hard to be annoyed with anyone who dressed like Glinda.

"As to what one should do with the information . . ." The shadow Chloe sighed and looked around. "I do know that you're going to need a friend to help you out with all this—someone who understands what's happening. If not me, then who?"

Chloe smiled. "Well . . ." Both selves turned toward the bed and looked at their sleeping body cuddled in Rory's arms.

"Yes, I suppose there's Rory. If he accepts. I think he will."

"I can trust him then?" Chloe asked. "Granny was just being mean when she said that stuff?"

"Oh yes. You can trust him to keep you safe."

"You *know* this?"

"I know. That you'll be safe."

"Good. That's what I've been thinking. More or less."

Chloe thought about asking something else of her shadow, but couldn't bring herself to do it. MacGregor was dead. Claude was dead, too—and better the circumstances of his death stay buried, even in thought. Rory *hadn't* killed anyone. And if he had, it would only have been to defend his father because Isaac or Claude was doing something to him. Chloe understood and condoned that. She wasn't close to her own father, but if someone like Isaac had threatened him, she would have done the same thing.

"That's the best way to view it," the shadow Chloe agreed. "Why ruin what could be the finest thing that's ever happened to you because of that nasty old lady?" She turned her back on the bed. "You can go to sleep now if you want. And don't worry about your granny. We don't have to talk to her if we don't want to. I know how to stop her sneaking in now."

"Thanks. She still scares me a bit." Chloe added awkwardly: "I'm glad we've talked face to face. Words are easier for me than pictures. If you need me to know something, just tell me."

"I'll remember that, and do it if I can," she promised. Her image wavered for an instant and she blurred like the object of an out-of-focus lens. "I have to go now. This kind of communication is still difficult for me. I'm sure I'll see you soon— though hopefully not too soon."

"Amen to that. I've had enough excitement for a while."

"Me, too." The shadow Chloe hesitated a moment. "You might want to plan on a trip to Hawaii soon. I think Rory is going to want to go there on business. Best avoid Maui if you can. Not that anything really bad will happen. Not to you. But you'll have an easier time if you stay off the island."

"Okay. No Maui," Chloe agreed. And then she found herself back in bed, cocooned in moonlight, linen sheets and strong arms. Her double was gone.

Rory stirred. He raised a large hand and smoothed back her hair. Those couldn't be the hands of a murderer, Chloe told herself. Granny Claire was just trying to ruin her happiness.

"Bad dreams?" Rory asked. His voice was gravelly.

"Not tonight," Chloe answered, rolling over and smiling at him. Her shadow side was right. If she couldn't trust herself, who could she trust? "I may not ever have bad dreams again. I've made peace with myself."

Rory looked at her oddly, but said, "I'm glad."

"Me too," she said. And because she felt safe to: "I love you."

He blinked. "I love you, too. I always will."

"I know." Chloe sighed happily and snuggled back into his arms. Unable to help herself, she asked, "Rory, are you thinking of going to Hawaii?"

"I have been, yes. I have a new contact there who specializes in native mosses. Why do you ask?" His voice was more awake.

"No reason," Chloe assured him, twirling a finger in the hair on his chest. She stared at it raptly as she added, "I just thought maybe I would go with you."

"That would be nice," he said carefully. "Is that all? It seems a rather small thing to be keeping you awake."

"We wouldn't need to go to Maui, would we?" she asked, knowing it was a strange thing to say, but unable to help herself.

"Not if you didn't want to."

He laced his fingers in her hair and gently tilted her head back so he could study her face. His hand was large enough to cover her skull. Chloe knew that there wasn't much to see even if the moon was bright, but she was certain he was finding answers anyway. She tried not to squirm.

"I don't want to." She waited for Rory's answer, not willing to be any plainer.

"Then we won't," he promised, releasing his hold and again smoothing her hair. His voice had grown thoughtful.

"Thank you." She tucked her head back into the crook of his neck, not wanting to talk about Hawaii any more. "We can go back to sleep now, if you want."

Rory's hand skimmed down her back and then her thigh. He paused there, kneading her skin.

"I don't think that's what I want right now."

"Oh, good." Chloe laughed a little and rolled on top of him. He obligingly fell back.

"I think you've bewitched me," he said, hands settling on her waist. He smiled wryly.

"Not yet. I'm still learning how. But give me time." Chloe leaned down and kissed him.

And they *would* have plenty of time, she assured herself. They had the rest of their lives. Because they certainly wouldn't be going to Maui.

AUTHOR'S NOTE

Dear Reader,

As ever, there are people to thank since books don't happen in a vacuum. This time out, in addition to my husband, I owe a lot to my cousin, Richard Magruder. My original idea for this story did come from a piece I saw on CNN and then a story in *People* magazine back in 1996, but the feel of this particular tale is owed in large part to Richard, who shared some wonderful family photos and stories of a particular (to remain unnamed) cemetery in Louisiana.

Richard, not being a native of Southern climes, also shared with me his thoughts about who should and should not sing the Southern blues. I had always thought blues were the blues, except that in some places they played slide guitar, but that isn't the case. Chicago blues don't look quite the same as Louisiana blues. For those that are as uncertain as Chloe about who is and who is not allowed to sing the blues, I suggest you take the quiz at the front of the book. (I hated to break the news to Chloe, but by the standards of the test, neither she nor I really should be trying to sing the blues. However, she's stubborn and I expect she'll keep on doing it anyway. I will, too.)

The technology in the book is slightly outdated—a lot has happened in the last ten years. Just squint a bit and you won't notice the lack of cell phones and so forth.

If you are interested in seeing some fabulous tombs, look for the book *A Beautiful Death*. It has a fascinating foreword by the horror writer Dean Koontz.

Thank you again for joining me. It's always a pleasure to spend time with you. If you want to get in touch, I can be reached online at www.melaniejackson.com or by snail mail at: PO Box 574, Sonora, CA 95370-0574.

Best,
Melanie Jackson